PROLOGUE

WEDNESDAY, MARCH 7, 1866
WHITFIELD HALL, COWETA COUNTY, GEORGIA

The South may have ceded defeat in the recent war, but peace had yet to arrive. The struggle continued, albeit on different battlegrounds—courthouses, for one. And the weapons of choice were words and influence.

Hannah Whitfield fumed all the way home from her recent skirmish, if it even qualified for such a term. Barely aware of her surroundings as she drove the carriage over rutted country roads, she trusted Old Duke to find the way to his stall. The county clerk had refused to provide her any information at all, though he'd taken the pittance she'd scraped up to pay against the overdue taxes on her home. Like a parroting bird, he repeated the same phrase to every question she asked. "I'm not permitted to give information to anyone except an adult male connected to the estate."

Unfortunately, all the males at Whitfield Hall were bedridden, underage, or illiterate. Uncle Liam could barely communicate after his stroke, while her surviving brother, Caleb, wouldn't reach his majority for fifteen years. Hannah had attempted to help Quentin learn to read, now that his status as a free man allowed it, but his verbal skills made it difficult. How ironic that the people who'd kept Whitfield Hall from collapsing—namely Hannah, Aunt Ginny, and Quentin's parents, Thomas and Silvie—couldn't save it because of their gender or skin color.

Hannah slowed the horse as they entered the semi-circular drive that curved in front of the house. Six columns rose to the second floor from the broad porch which stretched between them at the top of a dozen steps. The white pillars contrasted with the red brick of the house and its eight windows with black trim. She had always thought of the house as an elegant lady who welcomed her occupants and visitors alike with Southern hospitality. But unless Hannah could come up with enough money to keep the predators at bay, it would become another trophy for a Union officer to gloat over.

She left the drive and guided the horse onto the path leading to the red-brick stable adjacent to the barn. Quentin, still lanky at sixteen, emerged from the open door, where he'd likely been waiting since she'd left. She surrendered the horse and carriage into his capable hands, then took the brick walkway to the wooden ramp on the western side of the porch.

When Hannah dragged herself into the house, Aunt Ginny met her in the front hallway. Before her aunt opened her mouth to ask, Hannah merely shook her head.

"They wouldn't tell you anything?"

Hannah removed her bonnet and gloves. "Not a word. Just took the few coins I had, but I watched him write the amount in his ledger."

If only Uncle Liam could bear the ride to town...or if he'd not had a stroke...or if Pa had lived...or a thousand other possibilities that had never happened.

"Liam's growing weaker by the day, and still no word from

REDEEMING RUPERT

RESCUED HEARTS OF THE CIVIL WAR ~ BOOK 5

SUSAN POPE SLOAN

ISBN: 978-1-963212-19-8

Cover design by: Carpe Librum Book Design

[Love] bears all things, believes all things, hopes all things, endures all things. Love never fails.

— I CORINTHIANS 13:7-8 (NKJV)

To Ricky, my own low-key hero, household authority on weapons, tools, and various masculine reactions, and the "author" of some of Rupert's teasing remarks.

our friend Henry McNeil. I can't credit it, except he must not have received my letters." Aunt Ginny passed a shaky hand over her eyes and sniffed. "I wonder if he remembers being named as Caleb's trustee. Since his sweet wife passed away, we've lost touch, but I knew he would come to our aid once he learned of our plight." Her gaze drifted in the direction of Uncle Liam's room, a deep sigh escaping her lips. "If we can't come up with another plan, I suppose we'll have to move out."

"I won't let that happen." Hannah squared her shoulders. "If I have to marry Captain Prescott—"

"That won't preserve Caleb's inheritance." Her aunt shook her head. Though the carpetbagger courted Hannah's favor with hints of marriage, his true interest was claiming her home for himself. "No. When you marry, your portion will go to your husband, and you can't rely on that carpetbagger to do right by your brother. If only we could talk to Henry, I'm sure he'd come and set everything to rights."

Hannah strode toward the parlor, keeping her lips pressed closed. Not the oh-so-powerful but elusive savior again. She dropped her hat and gloves on the side table and continued to the window that overlooked the front yard, where she crossed her arms and leaned against the window frame. For once, the view failed to inspire her.

A cardinal flew from the leafless white oak to the porch rail. He tweeted a few notes, darted to the dormant azalea bush, then as if he spied what he searched for, took flight.

"'Oh, that I had wings like a dove, for then would I fly away and be at rest.'" Mama's favorite Bible verse slipped from Hannah's lips. Fly away? She couldn't fly, but she could walk or ride. She whirled back to Aunt Ginny. "How far is it to Mr. Henry McNeil's farm?"

Aunt Ginny tapped her chin. "It's just beyond the Georgia-Alabama line, but I've never been good at figuring distances. What are you thinking?"

3

"What if we sent someone to talk with him? How long do you reckon that would take?"

Aunt Ginny heaved a sigh. "It took Liam and me two days to make the trip to Grandmother's, but it had rained the week before, which slowed the horses. We went to Henry and June's afterward, a couple of hours farther."

"Two days there and two days back, at least. If we add several more days for Mr. Henry to make arrangements to be away..." She paced, renewed energy quickening her steps.

"And who do you propose to make that journey?" Aunt Ginny's hands went to her hips. "I can't leave your uncle. Caleb's too young, even if he were capable, and it would be too dangerous still for Thomas. I've heard tales of people attacking former slaves for no reason."

Hannah crossed her arms. "*I* will."

"You certainly will not."

"I won't be going alone, of course. Elmer and Esther plan to head west tomorrow, looking for more work. Their circuit takes them to the Alabama line before they turn north. Maybe they could go a little ways farther and take me with them."

The former slaves had visited a few times since starting their traveling business. They'd stayed at Whitfield Hall longer than usual this visit while Esther regained her health from a bout of ague. The more Hannah talked about it, the firmer her determination to seek out Henry McNeil. "It makes sense for me to be the one to go. After I explain the problem, Mr. McNeil will bring me back."

It took a half hour to convince Aunt Ginny—not that she was convinced, but she gave up arguing, throwing up her hands. "Only because I know of nothing else we can do, not with Liam's recovery unlikely. We have to show Captain Prescott that Whitfield Hall is not available for purchase at any price."

"Will you ask Silvie to fix up a basket of food for us?" The cook and sometimes-maid would know what to pack better than Hannah would. Hannah replaced her bonnet on her way to the door. She'd figure out the travel details on her walk to the cottage—a former slave cabin—that they occupied. "I'll go tell Elmer now. Esther will be happy to have me along. I can help her with the children."

Aunt Ginny's soft words floated behind her. "Dear Lord, please protect my sweet Hannah and prepare the way. Henry's our last hope."

CHAPTER 1

SUNDAY, MARCH 11, 1866
RANDOLPH COUNTY, ALABAMA

"*A*shes to ashes, dust to dust, but the spirit returns to its Creator."

Twittering birds and droning bees provided a pleasant—if contradictory—background to the minister's words over the freshly turned earth where Rupert McNeil's Uncle Henry now lay next to his beloved June. The family burial plot lay a couple of acres from the farmhouse but only a stone's throw from Aunt June's beehives, neglected since her passing two years earlier.

Rupert clutched his handkerchief and pressed it to his brow, wishing Brother Trotter would wind up his comments. Of course, then everyone was liable to crowd into the house for another round of condolences, meaning he'd have to shake hands and accept hugs from neighbors, some of whom he barely knew.

Beside him, Millie, the wife of his younger brother, Troy, swayed in the unseasonable heat. Rupert took a half step closer to assist while Troy's arm circled Millie's waist. Into the pause of the preacher's inhale, Rupert raised his voice in a hearty, "Amen."

Troy nodded his thanks and ushered Millie toward the house, but Brother Trotter's mouth hung open at the outburst before he snapped it shut.

Ma sidled up to Rupert. "Was that you? I don't believe I've heard you raise your voice in years, especially not during a church service."

Warmth filled his face. "I didn't fancy havin' to help Troy pick Millie up off the ground if he kept going." He steered Ma toward the house but kept his pace slow.

"Ah, the poor dear." Ma's gaze followed the couple ahead of them. "The new baby is wearing his mama thin. She should've stayed in bed longer after delivering, but she loved Henry like a father. I'll go see if I can do anything to help."

No sooner had Ma left Rupert's side than his old nemesis and cousin, Wilma Thurman, maneuvered to take her place. Wilma threaded her arm through Rupert's. "I'm glad Pa left the farm to you, Rupie. I certainly wouldn't know what to do with it."

Rupert at first ignored her use of the juvenile nickname he hated. Wilma, Henry's younger daughter, didn't need the farm's income, not with her house in Jacksonville and her late husband's vast holdings. She'd put off her widow's garments last year, and according to rumor, she didn't mind flaunting her wealth. How such a selfish, conniving creature had come from Uncle Henry and Aunt June baffled him.

On second thought, he returned the age-old taunt. "Hello, Willie."

When she glowered, Rupert bit his tongue to keep from smiling. "I'm surprised you made it in time for the funeral. Thought you'd gone to Mobile."

"Oh, I left as soon as I got Uncle John's wire. Whatever you may think of me, I did love Pa, you know." She dabbed at her eyes with a lacy square of cloth.

Rupert nodded. "Like all the rest of the family. He was the one person any of us could count on for help when we needed it."

Would the family maintain the tenuous peace they'd achieved when the war ended, or would old hurts and disagreements tear them apart?

Wilma raised an eyebrow. "Your folks seem to have emerged from the war fairly intact. I heard even Simon finally came back and brought you a new sister-in-law."

Rupert's shoulders stiffened at her implication. Did she mean to stir him up or only to deflect from her own escape of hardship? Her late husband's wealth and connections proved good insulation, even after his demise. With effort, Rupert kept his voice neutral. "Yeah, we did right well. Paul lost half a leg, Simon spent nearly a year in Libby Prison, Troy got carried off to Camp Chase, and I couldn't save my best friend who died from a gut wound."

Perversely pleased to see Wilma's jaw drop, he regretted it a moment later. He had no business antagonizing someone who'd just lost her father. Besides, the cruel reminders bit at his heart. Wilma always brought out the worst in him. As children, she'd bossed and used him to her own advantage until he'd learned to avoid her. Why had she sought him out now?

∼

*F*rom her perch in the barn loft, Hannah peeked out the window to gauge the activity below. She should've expected the people to return from the gathering soon, but she'd barely hauled her knapsack up the ladder when voices alerted her to their proximity.

Aunt Ginny had insisted that Henry McNeil lived alone. Of

course, he must have workers to help with the farm and the house. Hannah scolded herself for not considering that visitors might be here when she arrived. In most circumstances, she examined all potential problems.

Earlier, she'd knocked at the front door and even walked to the back of the house when no one answered. Perhaps Mr. Henry had gone to town for supplies. She wouldn't dare go inside the house, but she could wait on the porch. The large number of wagons and carriages parked around the barn drew her eye. Too many for a small farm, but no one at the house. Surely, someone had to be nearby. She shied away from meeting Mr. Henry in front of a bunch of strangers, dusty from travel as she was. After Elmer and Esther dropped her off, the walk had been longer than she'd anticipated. She'd gotten directions from a couple of local residents and learned that some folks' estimation of distances fell shy of the truth.

She'd climbed into the barn loft where she might have a better view of the farm. Aunt Ginny would be appalled at Hannah's actions. When Hannah argued for making this journey, she hadn't counted on the sudden bout of anxiety that gripped her. Her parents would never have countenanced such an undertaking—traveling such a distance, the last few miles alone, and risking the Whitfield reputation with her appearance at a gentleman's home to beg his help. No matter that Papa's rash actions had triggered the events that pushed the family close to penury and made this journey necessary. She shoved aside the memories of hiding in her family's barn whenever Papa went into one of his rages, for the weight of her mission lingered.

Of the six barn loft windows, one overlooked the fields and a slight rise where a group of people gathered. A church service, maybe a baptizing in the nearby creek? It couldn't be a funeral—otherwise, the doors and windows would be covered.

Whatever the reason, she'd make her appearance when the others left.

As she peered out the window, two couples separated from the group, one of the women leaning into her companion as if she couldn't make the short trip on her own. Hannah ducked to the side as the second woman deserted her escort and hurried to catch up with the other two. Did an argument brew there, or did she go to lend support? None of them looked toward the barn but continued on to the house.

Relieved they hadn't come to collect a wagon, Hannah resumed her original position. Now a different woman clung to the second man, and the rest of the people followed at a distance. Maybe two dozen, plus a couple of babes in arms. It was more than she would expect to attend a simple farm service in this isolated area. Would any of them remain overnight? She'd have to watch when the visitors loaded their vehicles and figure out how many stayed.

A couple of hours later, with the sun sinking toward the horizon, it seemed everyone had left except some close family members and servants. Six adults and three children, one of them an infant with a strong wail. The sound ripped through Hannah, reminding her of Caleb's long-ago cries of pain, which still crept into her troubled dreams. Though he'd begged her not to go on this journey, at the age of six, her brother refused to cry and eventually accepted her explanation. His inheritance hinged on what she might accomplish.

Hannah riffled in the knapsack for another biscuit. There was none there, only her change of clothes and a sliver of soap wrapped in a rag. At least she didn't have to worry about attracting rodents during the night. As she replaced the items, the scrape of the barn door startled her. She slowed her breath, listening to the movements below and praying the person didn't have reason to climb into the loft.

~

*T*he quiet of the barn embraced Rupert after a day among chattering people. Inhaling the familiar blend of hay, leather, and animals, he welcomed the cool interior. Bessie's soft lowing called him to the far stall, where he set down the lantern, then situated his stool and bucket to tend to her.

"Sorry to be late, old girl. There's been a passel of folks up at the house, all wantin' to talk to me and ask questions I ain't got answers for."

The soothing rhythm of the chore and the satisfying ping of the milk hitting the bucket eased his tension. With visitors lingering past sunset, he'd missed his evening stroll. Thankfully, his parents had stayed on to help entertain the company after Millie and Troy retired to bed. As much as he loved them all, he'd be relieved when they headed home.

Though he neared his twenty-fourth birthday, had spent a year away from home and fought in a few battles before his capture, his mother worried over him living alone on the farm a dozen miles from where she and Pa lived. He grunted and spoke aloud. "I don't know why Ma thinks it would be any better if I was married. Does she think a woman can protect me or take better care of me than I can myself? Dang! All she has to do is look at Troy to witness how havin' a family has run him ragged."

With the milk foaming close to the top of the bucket, he stood and shoved the stool into the far corner. He rubbed the cow between her ears and thanked her, as he always did.

He shuffled to the aisle and started for the door, moving slowly so as not to slosh any liquid from the bucket. In the lantern's light, a long strip of fabric stuck to the bottom rung of the ladder caught his attention. He set the bucket down and bent to remove the cloth. What was it? A man's neckcloth? He didn't recall seeing anyone wearing something this color. Someone had lost this—one of the visitors who'd called, though Rupert had no idea who'd been in and out of the barn.

He folded the fabric and stashed it in his pocket. Whoever it belonged to might come asking for it later.

~

*H*annah relaxed the pose she'd held to keep from giving away her position. 'Twas a wonder she didn't faint dead away from trying to hold her breath. She pulled up the hem of her skirt to muffle her laughter. She hadn't dared lean out to try to see Henry McNeil, but she'd heard his mumbling. Only a farmer living alone would talk to his cow. From the sound of it, he didn't care for having his solitude interrupted by visitors.

His conversation revealed that Aunt Ginny had described Mr. McNeil well—gruff and cantankerous but tender-hearted toward his family. Though some of his words had been indiscernible, his tone had come through loud and clear. He preferred to be left alone, which suited Hannah just fine. Having friends and neighbors drop by without warning now could jeopardize her mission and delay her return home.

Of course, neither she nor Aunt Ginny had expected her to arrive in the middle of a church service. With Mr. Henry's preference for solitude, Hannah was surprised he agreed to host it on his farm, but such kindness testified of his helpful nature. For her sake as well as Mr. McNeil's, she prayed the last of his visitors would take their leave in the morning.

Her growling stomach added another vote to that sentiment. She wouldn't sneak into the man's kitchen to steal a quick meal, but hunger could make a person desperate. For now, she concentrated on her plan to approach Mr. McNeil, hoping to block the demands of an empty belly. She'd need all her wits about her tomorrow.

Eventually, her exhaustion overrode other fleshly considerations. Tomorrow would come soon enough and, as the Bible said, bring its own trouble.

$\sim$

*R*upert set the milk bucket on the table, leaving it to Jewel to store or use right away. "If Amy's still awake, keep out a cup for her, please."

The cook dipped a ladle into the bucket. "'Zactly what I planned to do, Mistah Rupert."

Standing on his tiptoes, Jewel's son and his niece's favorite playmate peered into the pail. "Enough there for me, too, Ma?"

Rupert patted the boy's head. "I think you better have two cups of milk, Levi. I'm dependin' on you to grow strong muscles so you can help me and Malachi out in the field."

With a hand to his brow, Levi saluted the way he'd seen soldiers at the Freedmen's Bureau do. "Yes sir, Mistah Rupert. I be the best helper you ever have."

Rupert took the cup Jewel handed him and sauntered to the front room.

Ma was reciting a familiar story, her clear voice drifting into the hallway. He slowed his pace, not wanting to interrupt the tale as it reached its conclusion.

With Amy wedged between Pa and Ma on the settee, Pa leaned his head against the high back.

As Ma's voice faded, Rupert couldn't resist joining them and teasing her. "She's not even two, Ma. Do you really think she'll understand or remember those fanciful tales?"

When Ma made as if to swat him, he held the cup aloft. "Don't make me spill Amy's milk."

The little girl beamed her bright smile on him. "T'ank you, Unca Wuper."

Rupert's heart warmed. His niece had charmed the whole family from the first time they met her, when Troy and Millie came back from Kentucky the year before.

"You're welcome, sweetie." He pulled the cloth he'd found from his pocket. "Do you know who might've lost this piece of cloth, Ma? I found it in the barn." He held the fabric where she could see it while she helped Amy with her cup.

"I don't recall seeing it before." Ma wore a speculative smile as she set the cup down. "Might belong to one of the Varner girls. Maybe Becky thought leaving it would be a clever way to get you to visit."

Rupert snorted as he sank into the chair across from them. "She can scheme until the next century. I ain't got no intentions of courtin' her." When Ma scowled, he knew what was coming.

"You mean you *don't* have *any* intentions of courting her."

"That's what I said." He couldn't hold back a teasing grin. "Her sister, Blanche, might not be so bad. She's quiet most of the time, but she's too young."

A dramatic sigh preceded Ma's reply. "It's a pity there're no more young women nearby. Perhaps this winter, you should visit Simon and Daviana. You might find someone over their way to catch your fancy."

Pa saved Rupert from giving his standard answer of not being able to leave the farm. "Why don't we all make it a matter of prayer?" He patted Ma's knee. "God saw fit to bring all our boys home and provided wives for the others. I'm sure He has someone in mind for Rupert too."

Opening the Bible in his lap, he declared the subject settled. "Listen to what the prophet Jeremiah says. 'For I know the thoughts that I think toward you, saith the Lord, thoughts of peace, and not of evil, to give you an expected end.' The people were going into captivity, but even then, God was preparing for their return to Jerusalem. He had a plan for them, and He has one for each of us."

Rupert caught a silent exchange between his parents. A private, shared memory, perhaps, or an agreement of sorts—one that excluded him.

Though it lasted only a moment, loneliness pierced his heart.

Before Henry passed, Rupert had been content. Helping his uncle around the farm had given him purpose. Now, Henry was gone, and the farm was his. Funny how he felt more alone with so much family around. With all his brothers married now, he was the odd man out, but he'd better get used to it. Marriage didn't figure into his plans. He'd lost too many people he loved and wouldn't risk losing another.

Would Ma and Pa pressure him to visit his brother in Georgia to find a prospective mate? Didn't they realize that only courted tragedy?

CHAPTER 2

A crowing rooster warned Hannah she'd overslept. Drat. Someone would be coming to milk the cow soon. If she wanted to avoid getting caught hiding in the barn, she needed to make herself presentable and approach the house. Not to mention...breakfast.

She shook the straw from her clothes, picked off the bits that refused to release, and peered out the window. From her limited perspective, the house showed no evidence of activity. Perhaps, if she hurried, she could reach the creek and freshen up before she approached Mr. Henry's home. After placing the washcloth and sliver of soap in her reticule, she found the top rung with her foot and descended the ladder.

The sudden cackling of chickens made her pause, then she remembered the coop sat between the barn and the house. If she kept to the far side of the barn, maybe no one would see her, and the hens' noise would cover the squeak of the rusted barn door hinges. She pushed the door only far enough to squeeze through and closed it, taking a quick glance around the yard. Breathing more easily after her successful escape, she hurried to the creek.

While she cleaned up as much as possible, Hannah practiced how to announce herself to Mr. McNeil. "Hello, I'm Hannah Whitfield, the niece of Virginia and Liam Murphy." She made a quick curtsy. "I believe Aunt Ginny wrote to you about me."

Since they'd never received a reply to any of the letters, she'd have to gauge his reaction. A simple apology might be in order. "So sorry to appear at your doorstep unexpectedly, but we're in desperate straits. I know it's a good deal to ask from an old friend, but we had no other alternatives, and Aunt Ginny assured me you'd do your best to assist."

There, that sounded sufficiently humble and yet confident of his goodwill.

Hannah picked up her reticule, took a deep breath, and marched off to meet her fate. If Mr. McNeil was as honorable as Aunt Ginny said, she had no reason to be nervous about meeting him.

She passed the path to the barn and took the longer route to the road so it would appear she'd just arrived. Regardless of other family members still being in the house, she must present herself today so she could get home in time to keep her property off the auction block. Their presence might even help her cause.

Shoring up her courage with a deep breath and a quick prayer, she veered off the road onto the quarter-mile approach to the McNeil house. She counted her steps to distract her thoughts from what lay ahead. Two hundred. Four hundred. On six hundred and twenty-two, she gained the porch. Five more and she lifted her hand to knock.

"Hold on there!"

Hannah's hand fell, and she whirled to find the speaker behind her. A tall, bearded young man stood a few yards away, his hands propped on slim hips. His shirt clung to his muscular chest in places and was only half tucked into his trousers, which appeared to be damp. What had he been doing to work up such a sweat already? Though the clear sky foretold another warm day, the morning air cooled Hannah's face as she stared. She forced herself to glance away.

"Who're you looking for?" His voice commanded respect but didn't seem hostile. Probably this was one of Mr. McNeil's family, someone who lived nearby and helped with the farm chores.

Hannah's lips trembled, and she lifted her chin to conceal her unease. "I'm here to see Mr. Henry McNeil. This is his home, is it not?"

The man slicked back his hair and shook off water droplets. He must've been bathing. Or swimming. Alarm streaked through her, warming her face. She prayed he hadn't come from the same creek where she'd just been. The intense curiosity in his eyes as he assessed her made Hannah drop her gaze.

He shifted from one foot to the other before he answered her question. "I'm afraid you've missed him by a few days."

He was gone? Then who'd been in the barn the night before? Her shoulders drooped as she considered what to do. She bit her bottom lip to keep from crying. "Do you know where I might find him? It's a matter of some importance."

He gestured behind him. "He's up on the hill there. I'm sorry to tell you, we buried him yesterday."

Buried him? Henry McNeil was dead? Hannah only realized she'd swayed when the man darted forward and caught her by the arms.

"Easy, now. Maybe you'd better come in the house and rest a bit."

*K*eeping his arm around the woman, Rupert pushed open the door and strode to the front room. Surprised to find it empty with so many folks in the house, he called, "Ma, can you come to the parlor?"

He shuttled the stranger to the nearest chair and released his hold. It wouldn't do for Ma to see them so close and jump to conclusions. He squatted next to the chair. "Can I get you anything? Maybe a drink of water?"

Her fingers shook as she reached for her bonnet ribbons, and her pink lips twitched as if trying to smile. "A cup of water would be good."

When he stepped into the hallway, he nearly collided with his mother's apron-wrapped figure. "Rupert? Is something wrong?"

He picked up the smell of bacon she'd brought with her. "You're cooking breakfast?"

"Just helping. Jewel burned her hand yesterday. Now, what do you need?" She peered past him into the parlor. "Oh, we have a visitor?"

Rupert lowered his voice. "She said she's here to see Henry. When I told her he was gone, she went all limp, like she was gonna pass out. I'm getting her a drink of water."

He made his escape to the kitchen to avoid more questions. Seeing the young woman on the other side of the creek had rattled his brain. A line of bushes had served as a barrier between them, and the noise of birds and tumbling water kept him from discerning the words she spoke. At first, he thought she must have a companion, but no one had gone with her when she walked away. Curious, he'd rushed into his clothes before drying off and followed her to the road. He'd expected her to go past his house, but she'd marched right onto his porch.

What business did she have with Henry? To the best of his memory, he'd never seen her before, although her heart-shaped face and green eyes reminded him of someone. Who was she? Had she given her name? No, and he hadn't asked.

"Dunderhead."

"I hope you not startin' to mumble like Mistah Henry now." Jewel turned from the stove with a platter of biscuits. "Just 'cause you got the whole farm to worry about don't mean you gotta take on his habits." The sparkle in her brown eyes belied her scold.

He pulled the black armband from his pocket and slipped it over his shirtsleeve. "I'm afraid you're late to the race, Jewel. I've been talking to myself for years, just not usually where anyone else can hear."

He found a cup and dipped it in the water bucket. When he headed toward the hallway again, Jewel blocked his way. "Now I know you got sumpin on your mind. You didn't even grab a biscuit off'n the table. What's wrong?"

"We have a visitor in the parlor."

"Afore breakfast?" Her eyes widened. "What kind o' manners is 'at?"

"She came asking to see Henry."

Jewel frowned and wagged her head. "She can't be from 'round here if she ain't heard o' Mistah Henry's passin'."

"Yeah, well, I expect we'll find out. You might want to set another plate on the table."

Though he'd never met the young woman before, something about her seemed familiar. When he'd told her about Henry, the turmoil in her green eyes stirred his sympathy, made him want to shield her from further pain. But questions surrounded her. How did she know Henry, and even more puzzling, why had she come?

∾

*H*annah had only a moment to observe the room's furnishings after the young man left. Several chairs, a settee, and a horsehair sofa provided ample seating. Lamps graced each occasional table, and a clock in a mahogany cabinet claimed center place on the mantel over the fireplace. Her gaze swung back to the parlor door as a woman entered.

From the moment Connie McNeil introduced herself as Henry's sister by marriage, she'd set Hannah at ease, despite the strange circumstances. Though an apron covered the woman's dress, her demeanor marked her as someone used to taking charge.

"Let me see if I've understood you correctly." Mrs. McNeil leaned forward from the parlor settee and touched Hannah's hand. "Henry's wife, June, was a beloved cousin of your Aunt Virginia, who met Henry at a family wedding several years ago."

"Yes, ma'am. Aunt Ginny corresponded with Miss June until she passed. With the war goin' on and Uncle Liam not in good health, she regretted she couldn't send her condolences. From their meeting and Miss June's letters, Aunt Ginny developed a great admiration for Mr. Henry and learned about his willing-ness to help out anyone in trouble."

Mrs. McNeil smiled. "That was Henry, all right. Gruff and grumpy on the outside, soft as butter inside." She raised the tail of her apron to dab at her eyes. "Everybody loved him. The world just won't be the same without him."

"I'm sorry I never got to meet him." Nausea roiled in her stomach. What would she do now? Where could she turn? Knowing all her family's hopes rested on her, Hannah had to think of something—and fast.

"Pardon my interruption." The young man who'd brought her into the house stood at the parlor threshold. "Here's your water, miss."

No sooner had she taken the cup than a toddler with a mop of golden curls attacked the man's legs. "I got you, Unca!"

The child's squeals commanded everyone's attention as the man detached her from his leg and swung her up to his shoulder. "And now I got you, Amy." He emitted a fake roar and dipped his head to nuzzle her belly, bringing on peals of laughter.

Taken aback by the demonstration, Hannah paused with the cup on her lips. A glance at Mrs. McNeil revealed a broad smile as she observed the play. Such behavior must be a common occurrence, then. She couldn't remember Papa or Uncle Liam ever acting in such a way.

The man's clothes still appeared damp in spots, and Hannah's face warmed. She took a gulp of water.

Rapid steps in the hallway warned her other family members might be joining them. Hannah drained the cup and set it atop a doily on the side table.

Two men passed by the first, their grins wide and approving the young man's antics with the child until they entered the parlor and met Hannah's curious gaze.

Mrs. McNeil rose. "Troy, John, come meet our visitor. This is Miss Whitfield, who's come from Georgia, hoping to see Henry." She drew the older man to her side. "This is my husband, John. And that's Troy, our youngest son and the father of our little scamp, Amy. You've already met Rupert, of course."

That would be the man who'd assisted her. She glanced his way and found his blue eyes staring at her. How was it fair for a man to have such beautiful eyes? Her gaze drifted lower, over his straight nose, and encountered well-formed lips framed by his short beard.

"We didn't exchange names, Ma." An interesting shade of pink dusted his cheeks. "I just followed, er, come up from, uh, the barn as she was about to knock." His gaze fell to the floor.

The poor fellow acted as if he'd done something wrong by assisting her. Did he fear a reprimand, or was he that shy?

~

*N*ever would Rupert admit he'd followed Miss Whitfield from the creek, although anyone with two good eyes could tell he'd thrown on his clothes before he dried off. He'd caught the speculation in Miss Whitfield's green gaze when they met outside, not unlike the way she regarded him now. She'd removed her bonnet, and wisps of blond hair framed her heart-shaped face. Her stiff posture told of genteel training, but the rapid pulse at her throat gave away her nervousness.

Millie's entrance saved Rupert from saying more. Bouncing the baby in her arms, she brushed by Rupert and peeked inside the parlor. "Hey, y'all, Jewel says breakfast is ready. Oh, sorry, I didn't know we had a guest."

Her gaze swung from Miss Whitfield to Rupert, whose face was still uncomfortably warm.

Ma spoke to the stranger. "Miss Whitfield, this is Troy's wife, Millie, and my newest grandson." She crossed the room and held out her arms toward the infant. "Let me hold him while you eat, dear, and Miss Whitfield can finish telling us what's brought her here. Come along, now."

Like a mother duck leading her offspring, Ma swept down the hallway. Pa followed and caught Amy as she reached for him. He tilted his head toward their guest as he passed Rupert. "See to our guest, son."

Though Pa's quiet command was meant for Rupert's ears alone, the whisper set his face aflame again. Even worse, Troy shot him a teasing grin, and Millie's eyebrows rose to her hairline. But she took pity on him and held out her hand to Miss Whitfield. "We don't stand on ceremony around here, Miss

Whitfield. Please join us, if only to have a cup of tea or coffee."

The visitor accepted Millie's invitation, and the women linked arms as they left the parlor.

Rupert had only taken two steps before Troy pulled him back. "Where did you find that woman? I must say, I'm impressed at your courage in bringing her right in—"

"I *found* her on the doorstep, just as I said, looking for Henry."

Rupert got as far as the hallway before Troy jerked his arm. "What's she want with Henry?"

"Maybe we'll find out during breakfast, if you'll stop yankin' me back. C'mon. I'm hungry, and the gravy will be gettin' cold."

Troy gave him a gentle push toward the kitchen. "Yeah, I hear your stomach roarin' at me. Whatcha bet Ma puts you right beside the girl?"

While Rupert groaned inwardly, he frowned at Troy. "Watch it, little brother. I can still take you down if I've a mind to."

A hearty guffaw and slap on the back announced Troy's disagreement. "That'll be the day. Maybe we can test your strength before Miss—"

"Shh. Save it." Rupert's elbow made contact with Troy's side a moment before they faced the others already seated at the table. With a grin, Troy slapped his back again and nudged him forward to the empty spot beside Miss Whitfield.

Ma sent them a smile much too innocent for Rupert's liking.

Pa's fingers drummed the table as he waited for them to sit. "Glad you boys decided to join us. Let's pray."

After Pa blessed the food, he passed bowls of grits, gravy, and biscuits. Rupert took a generous helping of grits, then offered the dish to Miss Whitfield. She eyed his plate before spooning out a smaller amount and passing it to Ma. When Rupert selected two biscuits and she reached for the bread platter, her fingers brushed his.

A jolt ran the length of his arm, and his face burned.

Her hand jerked, and three biscuits tumbled onto her plate.

"Oh, sorry, I didn't mean to be so greedy." Using her fork, she returned two of them and set the platter in front of Ma.

Rupert dared not turn to Miss Whitfield. To prevent a recurrence of that accidental touch, he set the bowl of gravy on the table between them, dipped his helping, then turned the spoon handle her way. He concentrated on eating his meal and tried to ignore the woman beside him.

"Miss Whitfield was telling me about her connections to Henry," Ma said. "Her aunt is Ginny Murphy, June's cousin. Do I have that right?"

After swallowing a sip of her tea, Miss Whitfield nodded. "Yes, ma'am." She glanced at the others seated at the table. "That's how Aunt Ginny knew to contact Mr. Henry when we found ourselves in need of a friend. Knowing Mr. Henry's kind nature, she hoped he'd help us."

"Her aunt wrote letters to Henry earlier this year." Ma poured gravy over her biscuit and glanced at Miss Whitfield again. "But she never received any reply to those letters?"

The younger woman set aside a half-eaten biscuit. "That's right. I believe she sent four or maybe five. In each, she explained everything that had happened and why we were seeking Mr. Henry's assistance." Her voice lowered to nearly a whisper. "I can't imagine why he never replied unless something happened to those letters."

Rupert swallowed his spoonful of grits and cleared his throat. "Henry always picked up the mail in town. He never said anything to me about your letters."

"What about these last few weeks," Pa asked, "when his health started failing so quickly? Did you get the mail for him?"

"It never occurred to me." Guilt poked at Rupert. "Maybe Byron Harris or Mr. Varner did, but I don't recall them mentioning it." He faced Miss Whitfield. "Seems I'm the one to blame, Miss Whitfield, if anyone is. I'm awful sorry I didn't think to check Henry's mail. I might've saved you a trip."

At the utter despair on her face, his guilt doubled, and he added, "Guess I got to learn that being a homesteader means more than just runnin' the farm." He should remember to visit the post office, as well as ask the bank about a loan, on his next trip to town.

Pa grasped his shoulder. "You'll learn, son." He turned to their guest. "Tell us what you need. Maybe we can help in Henry's absence."

Miss Whitfield laid her utensils across the plate. "I'm grateful for the thought, Mr. McNeil, but I guess all is lost. I don't have much time to find another man like Henry McNeil, someone who might agree to marry me and save my home."

CHAPTER 3

*H*ad Rupert heard right? Did she say she'd planned to ask Uncle Henry to marry her? Didn't she realize he'd been old enough to be her grandfather? And what made her so sure Henry would've gone along with such an idea?

A glance around the table revealed he wasn't alone in his thinking. Pa's mouth hung open, and Ma's eyes widened as if she choked on the bite she'd taken. Millie's hands shielded her mouth while Troy shifted in his seat and dipped his head. Even little Amy stared at the rest of the family until she broke the spell by banging on her highchair tray. "Mo' gra-vee, pease."

While Millie tended to the little one's demand, Pa collected himself, sitting straight in his chair to address Miss Whitfield's strange statement. "I suppose you must have a particular reason why you'd expected to marry Henry?"

Her doe-eyed innocence called for sympathy. "He's the person named in my father's will as the trustee of my brother's inheritance. He's the only one who can convince the carpetbaggers that Whitfield Hall is solvent and not for sale." She dropped her gaze to the table. "And the will stipulates I must marry someone chosen by the trustee. Since he's a widower, I figured he might as well be the one."

"You do realize, Henry was just shy of sixty when he died?" Troy asked.

Miss Whitfield's hand flew to her mouth. "That old?" Her cheeks flushed pink. "I'm sorry, I mean...I thought he was probably my father's age since he was still running his own farm and all."

Pa nodded in Rupert's direction. "Rupert's been livin' here and helpin' him the last couple of years, and Troy spent some time here, too, before he was sent north. The workers and neighbors here are good folks. They all watch out for each other."

"The place belongs to Rupert now," Troy added. "Seems neither of Henry's daughters wanted it or needed it, since their husbands were well-heeled. Rupert worked here for years and earned the right to be named Henry's heir."

Feeling that he ought to say something, Rupert uttered the first thing that came to mind. "I reckon I could search Henry's office, see if he left any instructions regarding your brother. We can also hunt for those letters you said your aunt sent." He had his doubts that he'd find anything, though. Wasn't it too coincidental that she'd arrived *after* his uncle's burial? Not that he could figure why she'd make such a claim. Surely, Henry would have mentioned it....

By the look on Ma's face, he'd said something wrong. Judging from the mirth dancing in her eyes, he must have sounded really stupid. Or did she think he'd taken a fancy to Miss Whitfield and wanted time with her to become acquainted?

Before he could amend his offer, Miss Whitfield latched onto it. "Oh, that would be so kind. Would you mind if I aided in your search?"

"N-not at all." His breathing sped up. Was it wise for them

to tackle the job together—alone? His gaze ran around the room. Why did no one else volunteer to help—and get him out of this awkward situation? "I can spare a little time, but farm chores are waitin' too."

Troy rose from his seat, a suppressed grin twitching his lips. "Pa and I can help Malachi with those. You go ahead and help Miss Whitfield."

Rupert shot him a glare, then braved a look at Miss Whitfield again. "Uh, are you done eatin'? I guess...we can look now before I go outside to work."

"Oh, yes." She smiled and reached for her cup. "But would it be all right to take my tea with me to the office?"

"Certainly, dear," Ma said. "Millie, I think this little one needs a fresh nappy." She rose at the same time as their guest, and the men hurried to stand also.

Miss Whitfield directed a hopeful expression to Rupert. "Shall we begin our search?"

"Uh, for sure." He swept his hand toward the hallway. "This way." At the door, he called over his shoulder, "Anyone else want to help?"

Only the clatter of dishes being stacked answered him.

~

*H*annah grasped at the one straw of hope offered in this dismal day of discovery. Perhaps Mr. Henry had left instructions that would help to secure Caleb's inheritance. A small sum of money wouldn't go amiss, either, to satisfy the back taxes. She wouldn't mention that, lest these good people think she'd come begging for more than she needed.

Finding her aunt's letters would prove the truth of her words and hopefully assure their help. Anything more would be a blessing.

Rupert McNeil slowed and allowed her to come beside him in the hallway, flicking a quick glance her way. "How far did you travel to get here?"

"It took three days on my friend's wagon with all the stops he made along the way." When he stared at her with raised eyebrows, she rushed to explain. "Elmer does odd work, so he never passes a homestead without asking if the folks need something fixed. And his mule gets onery going uphill."

Rupert gaped. "You traveled three days with a man? Without a chaperone?"

"Of course not. His wife and children were with us. I've known Elmer and Esther all my life, so I knew I could trust them to get me as close to the Alabama line as possible."

"Not *into* Alabama? Which left you with at least eight miles, dependin' on where they left you." He stopped at a closed door, his hand on the knob.

"It wasn't far. Only took me half a day on foot." Hopefully, that would redirect his attention.

Frowning, he pushed the door open and allowed her to precede him into the room. She immediately halted, causing Rupert to brush against her before he shifted to the left.

Could anyone find anything in this disaster? Books filled a case as tall as she was, and more books had been stacked around a desk. A lamp sat at one corner of the surface, and papers littered the rest of it. A curved-back chair was pushed beneath it, and another sat in front of the window. The two chairs were the only furniture not suffocated with books and papers.

Hannah faced her host, certain her horror showed on her face.

He had the grace to blush. "Um, it needs a bit of tidying up."

How long had it been since this room had seen a broom or duster? No wonder no one else had volunteered to help them.

"Your barn is cleaner than this." She clamped a hand over her mouth. Best keep her observations to herself.

"Where do you think we should start?" From Rupert's voice, he was as overwhelmed as she was at the prospect of tackling this task.

"Why don't we take all the books into the hall? Then we'll clear off the desk and see what we can find."

Rupert picked up a stack from the floor, and Hannah did the same. He shifted his load and faced her. "Put those on top here."

Hannah eyed the two loads. He already held eight or ten thick volumes. Was he trying to demonstrate his strength? She added her six books. Without blinking an eye, he pivoted, carried the books to the hallway, and lowered them to the floor.

Spinning back to the room before he could witness her watching him, Hannah grabbed another pile of books and set it in the hall beside the first load. Together, they cleared the office floor and desk of books. At least they had a clear path to the desk.

"Now we can go through the papers," Rupert said.

"Would you mind finding a dust rag first, so we can wipe off the chairs?" She had no intention of getting dust all over her dress since she'd only brought one more.

Rupert mumbled something as he left, though she didn't pick up the words. Did he regret his offer to search for evidence to support her story? That he harbored doubts about her was clear. Besides the need to prove the truth, Hannah wanted him to believe her, to see her as worthy of his trust.

She grasped a pile of papers and started creating neat piles. She wouldn't take more of Rupert's time than necessary to accomplish the task.

A sudden thought arrested her movements. What if Mr. Henry hadn't received the letters or, in the fog of illness, had destroyed them? Would his family turn her away?

~

*J*t took some searching before Rupert found the rags. He usually left the cleaning to Jewel. He grabbed a handful and made his way back to the office.

The view that met him there brought him up short. Standing in front of the bookcase, Miss Whitfield ran a finger along the spines of the books. The papers were stacked in orderly piles, and the curtain at the window had been pushed aside to let in more light. In a matter of minutes, she'd made the room more livable.

He cleared his throat, and she spun around and smiled.

"Oh, good, you're back." She crossed the room and held out her hand.

Stunned by the way her smile lit her face, Rupert stammered. "Oh, uh, here." He thrust the cloths into her hand and moved to the desk. "Sorry it took so long."

"I did what I could while you were gone." She waved toward the desk, then bent to wipe down the chair behind the desk. Wow, she was a pretty thing.

She spun around and caught him ogling her. Warmth spread from his neck to his hairline.

"Here you go." She pushed the chair toward him. "You sit here, and I'll take the other." She took a step in that direction at the same moment Rupert moved forward. Both stopped when only inches separated them. They blocked each other's way.

"Oh, pardon me." He stepped sideways to allow her to pass. As he rounded the desk, he stared at the chair. Henry's chair. How many times during the past year before his uncle got too sick had Rupert poked his head into this room to ask his uncle a question, never noticing the papers or the books—the mess— in here? Having Miss Whitfield see it in such disarray—what must she think of the McNeils?

He should have cleaned the room during Henry's illness.

Then he might have found the letters she mentioned and helped Henry send a response. That would have saved her a trip and Rupert a good deal of embarrassment.

He eased into the chair, unable to keep his gaze off the appealing woman on the other side of the desk. A few tendrils of hair dangled near her ears, and she pushed at a hairpin that had come loose from the bun at her nape. He banished the images of pulling out the pins and running his fingers through those blond tresses. He should be outside, marking off his fields instead of acting as host to a beautiful stranger who claimed a connection to his uncle.

It seemed his legacy involved more than eighty-five acres of Alabama soil.

In a few days, he'd start planting his crops and building his future. How blessed could one man be? His gaze roved over the desk and landed on the woman dusting off the other chair. The only thing he lacked was a family to share his life with.

The one thing he couldn't risk having.

CHAPTER 4

*H*annah dragged a pile of papers toward her and tried to keep her attention from straying to the man across the desk. The top page showed a list of supplies with figures beside each and *Mercantile* in bold letters at the top. From the prices and the feminine handwriting, she'd guess the list dated back a couple of years or more.

Should she offer a suggestion? She pushed past her hesitation. "As long as we're going through these, why don't we put them in categories to make it easier for you to file them later?"

As he stared at the paper in his hands, his lips pinched, but he said nothing.

Perhaps she should call him by name. "Mr. McNeil, how do you want to divide these so you can find them more easily later?"

He raised his head. "Excuse me. I'm confused by the writing on this paper. It appears to be a receipt for some purchases."

"May I see it?"

"Of course." He held it out to her.

Like the one she first reviewed, it contained a column of items with numbers she assumed to be prices. "You're right.

And here's a date at the bottom. February tenth, 1862. Is this Mr. Henry's signature?" She passed it back to him.

He pulled it close. "No, Henry's signature slanted backwards. This appears to be signed by someone named Norman, but I'm not sure who that is. What do you think we should do with it?"

Exactly the question she'd asked him. "I think we should break them into categories first. How about we put anything related to farm supplies here"—she laid her sheet on a clear spot in the middle of the desk—"correspondences here, and miscellaneous here." Leaning over the desk to plant her hands on each side of the first sheet, she raised her eyes to Rupert's.

"Good idea." He looked flushed, and his voice had gone husky. "Maybe later I can figure out what needs to be kept and what I can throw away."

Puzzled by his strange response, Hannah sat back and resumed her task. Perhaps he didn't read very well or felt uncomfortable in his new role as a farm owner. Hopefully, he wasn't becoming ill. What would she do if no one else would help her?

For the next couple of hours, they spoke little, working through each sheet of paper. Voices carried from the rest of the house, but Hannah worked to keep from getting distracted. She was stretching when Millie peeked inside the office.

"Miss Whitfield, I should've offered to refresh your tea earlier. I've put water on to heat. Why don't you two stop for a bit and have a light meal? I believe we have some corn muffins."

Rupert pushed back his chair and stood. "I wouldn't turn down food. This is a bigger job than I thought it would be."

Glad for the promise of tea, Hannah rose. "That does sound lovely. Thank you, Mrs. McNeil."

"Now, none of that. I'm just Millie to my friends."

"Thank you, Millie. And I wish you'd all call me Hannah."

She joined Millie, and they walked toward the dining room, leaving Rupert to follow.

"I suppose you haven't found your aunt's letters or any helpful papers as yet?"

Hannah sighed. "Not yet. I can understand why the letters might have gone astray, though, if someone put them in the office. We've found correspondence dated five years ago."

"And plenty that had no date and no explanation as to what they are," Rupert added. "It seems Uncle Henry just tossed everything on the desk and never looked at it again."

Rupert's mother must have heard him as they entered the kitchen. She spoke as she helped Amy sip a cup of milk at the table. "June took care of the book work for the farm. She often joked that Henry married her for her ciphering skills."

Rupert waited until the women had tea and were seated at the table before he got his own. "Where'd Pa and Troy get off to?"

Miss Connie's eyes lit up with her smile. "John went to visit Thaddeus Varner"—she nodded to Hannah—"one of the neighbors. Troy's napping with the baby." She pulled a purple cloth from her pocket and wiped Amy's mouth, then groaned. "Oh, dear, I forgot this was in my pocket with my hankie. Now I'll have to wash it before we find out who it belongs to."

With a gasp, Hannah patted her waistband. She'd thought she put the sash back in her knapsack, but it must have slipped to the barn floor when she riffled through the contents searching for food. "I believe it's mine. I didn't realize I'd lost it. Where did you find it?"

The other women exchanged glances, then switched their focus from Hannah to Rupert.

Rupert shifted in his chair and faced Hannah. "I found it in the barn last night."

Uh-oh. Her face warmed under his scrutiny. "So that's where I lost it."

~

*T*he details of Miss Whitfield's arrival were starting to make sense to Rupert. She must have stayed in the barn the night before. Maybe she arrived while they were all up on the hill. Why didn't she announce her presence then? Was she afraid to meet new people?

Ah, yes, she'd traveled the last however-many miles alone. It wouldn't be wise to let that be widely known, perhaps. Did it never occur to her that Henry was the one they were burying? Her shock at that revelation had appeared genuine. And she'd been prepared to marry a man decades older than she was, which spoke to her desperation. But why would marrying Henry be the answer to her problems? They'd all been so caught up in the mystery of the missing letters, they hadn't gotten to the heart of her motivations.

A glance in Ma's direction, however, meant he had a problem of his own. Her smirk meant she was plotting something—or else she thought Rupert had encountered Miss Whitfield in the barn and hidden it from them. How was he going to explain the situation without bringing on more questions?

Although he hated to cast Miss Whitfield in a bad light, he wouldn't encourage the speculation about meeting her before today. "Then you must have been in the barn yesterday. Why did you wait until this morning to come to the house?"

She fiddled with her cup handle. "When I arrived, no one answered my knock at the house. I noticed several wagons parked near the barn, so I climbed up in the loft to see more of the property." Long lashes hid her eyes as her cheeks darkened to a rosy hue. "When I looked out the window, I saw all the people on the hill." With a shrug, she glanced up. "I thought y'all were having a church service, maybe a baptizing. A funeral never occurred to me since none of the doors were covered."

"Henry didn't abide by such customs," Rupert said. "He

called it superstitious nonsense, wouldn't permit it when Aunt June died, so we carried out his wishes."

Hannah nodded. "I see. I'm sorry to have intruded in such a manner."

Ma reached across the table to pat Hannah's arm. "Don't give it another thought. I can imagine how intimidating it might be to face so many strangers at once, with such a personal errand as you were on. I just hate that you spent the night in the barn when you could've stayed in the house."

The more Rupert thought on the matter, the stranger it seemed. "How did you know how to get here? What if you'd come to the wrong place?"

"An elderly man I met at the edge of town gave me directions." Her hands turned palm up. "Then I saw a young boy on that rise to the east, and he pointed out the house for me."

Rupert narrowed his eyes. "And neither of them mentioned that Uncle Henry had died?"

"No." She dragged out the word and tilted her head. "I suppose they thought I was going to the funeral."

"I reckon that makes sense." Although Rupert's nature was to accept what people said without question, his exposure to a larger world, courtesy of the Confederate Army, had taught him to be more discerning. He couldn't detect any purposeful shamming in Miss Whitfield's demeanor, but it bothered him that she'd been willing to travel so far alone with intentions of tying herself to an old man she'd never met.

An infant's cry from the hallway preceded Troy's entrance with Little John in his arms.

Millie gave a rueful smile. "Guess my time of leisure is ended." She stood to take the baby.

Aware of their habitual kiss whenever they passed the infant from one to the other, Rupert directed his attention the other way. His gaze collided with that of Miss Whitfield, who also glanced away from the couple, sipping her tea.

Without a hint of embarrassment, Troy plopped in the chair Millie had vacated. "How's the search going?"

"Slowly." Rupert shook his head. "From all the papers we've found, Henry never threw away anything."

Troy's gaze bounced from Rupert to Miss Whitfield. "I guess that's good, then. If he ever received those letters, they should be buried in the mess somewhere." Did Rupert detect a note of skepticism in Troy's voice?

Miss Whitfield rose from her seat, prompting Rupert and Troy to do the same. "I should get back to work now. Thank you for the repast, Mrs. McNeil." She stopped at the door. "Please, take your time and enjoy your meal, Mr. McNeil. I'll be fine now that I know the way."

Which only served to make him hurry behind her. He didn't *think* she was after anything other than what she'd told them, but he wasn't ready to turn over the search to her. "I've eaten plenty. Thanks, Ma. Troy, would you find out how Malachi's coming along with repairing the harness? And tell him I'll be out later to discuss which fields we should plant first."

His family would leave soon to tend to their own farms. Hopefully, he and Miss Whitfield could solve her problem right away so Ma wouldn't feel obligated to stay and act as the woman's chaperone.

Back in the office, Miss Whitfield hurried to sort papers, giving each page she picked up a quick perusal before slapping it in the appropriate place. Perhaps she was just as eager to leave as he was to have her gone. Having Miss Whitfield in the house threw everything off track, not the least of which was his peace of mind. Such a woman could make him forget his decision to remain unattached.

∽

*W*hy did she care whether the papers were organized? If the other McNeil men were as untidy as the recently departed Henry—God rest his soul—then it would do little good.

Hannah's compulsion for tidiness wouldn't allow her to leave it as it had been. Better to touch something one time and put it in its proper place than to repeatedly consult the same page by accident.

Mr. McNeil took his place on the other side of the desk. Neither of them spoke until Hannah placed the last paper in a pile. She set a heavy object—a pair of scissors, a pocketknife, and a letter opener—on each stack to keep them from getting scattered again. "The letters are not here." The words sounded like a judge's pronouncement on her task. The death knell for Whitfield Hall as her family's inheritance. If she couldn't prove her case to these good folks, why should they help her?

"Maybe Henry stuck them in one of the books." Rupert's suggestion delivered a breath of life into her deflated hopes.

Hannah pointed to the top shelf. "If you can get those down and put them on the desk, we can leaf through each one and then replace them." She grabbed the dust rag and advanced on the bookcase. "But only after I wipe off the dust."

Soon they developed an efficient process of removing, dusting, leafing through, and returning each book. They worked their way down to the bottom shelf. Still no letters.

Propping his hands on his hips, Rupert surveyed the area. "At least it's cleaner."

Through the door, she spotted the stacks in the hallway. Heading that direction, she called across her shoulder, "Do you think we can fit all those books in the bookcase?"

Bracing himself on the doorframe, Rupert hovered close. Hannah shifted to the side to give him room.

"If we lay 'em flat, we should be able to put most of them in there."

She lifted her face the same moment he looked down—and forgot what she'd wanted to say. His blue eyes captured her. With warmth climbing into her cheeks, she jerked and ducked under his outstretched arm.

"I'll start on those already on the shelves." Hannah scampered to the case and flipped four books onto their backs, careful to keep the spines outward for easier identification.

"Here you go." The voice so near to her ear startled her.

Keeping her focus forward, Hannah motioned to a clear spot on the top shelf. "Did you flip through those pages?"

"Yes, ma'am, I did. Even ran the dust rag over them." The grin he offered set off a fluttering in her belly. When did he go from resistant to accommodating? Maybe he figured he'd be rid of her more quickly if he helped move the process along.

Hannah forced a sugary smile. "Why don't you bring the rest of them in and set them on the desk now that there's room? Then we can both search through the pages as we replace them."

As soon as he returned from the hallway, she grabbed the rag and started on the new stack. When she opened the second book, a loose page flew out and drifted to the desk. Hannah caught it before it landed, her heart thumping. Could this be one of the letters? Bringing it closer, she sagged against the desk. The multiple lines of typeset print on how to treat a snake bite proved it wasn't what she'd hoped. With a sigh, she opened the animal husbandry book and replaced page twelve.

She was almost out of options. Would the McNeils help her if she couldn't convince them of her need?

CHAPTER 5

*A*fter four more trips between the hallway and the office, Rupert stood beside Miss Whitfield to continue their search for the elusive—perhaps nonexistent—letters. He hadn't squatted and lifted so much since Bessie birthed her last calf. He'd grown soft over the winter, staying inside more than usual while Henry was sick. He could consider this preparation for planting season, but moving books around seemed pointless and less likely to yield any fruit for their labor.

At least, the exercise afforded him the opportunity to observe Miss Whitfield with discreet glances. Like a flower sprouting in the middle of a dormant field, she drew the eye, her movements as graceful as a dancer's. Her single-minded dedication to the task earned his respect and persuaded him of her honesty.

With every book they dusted, the woman beside him became quieter and more withdrawn. As the bookcase filled with volumes, the room resembled its original purpose as an office rather than a depository for books and forgotten papers. At least the hours spent searching had produced this visible benefit.

What this house needed was a library. A ridiculous notion, perhaps, for a simple farmer, but Henry certainly had accumulated enough books to warrant it. Maybe next winter, Rupert would take an inventory of them and decide which ones to keep. That would give him something to fill the lonely hours now that Henry was gone. Byron, who maintained the local office for the Freedmen's Bureau, was the only person close enough to come and visit for a game of checkers or dinner. Of course, Rupert could always—

"That's the last one." Miss Whitfield ran the dust rag over the surface of the desk and sank onto the chair.

Her despondence tugged at his heart. Searching for any ounce of encouragement to offer, Rupert rounded the desk and sat in the other chair. The aroma of greens and cornbread drifted from the kitchen. "I should've sent Troy or Pa to town to ask if there's any mail. I reckon one of us can go tomorrow."

Only a nod from Miss Whitfield.

Rupert tipped his weight so the chair's front legs lifted off the floor. His head touched the wall behind him.

Had her aunt truly written to Henry? Letters could go astray, but according to Miss Whitfield, there'd been four or five, and it was hard to imagine so many not getting delivered. When was the last time Henry had collected the mail? At least a month ago. January's rain and February's cold had kept them inside most days. Despite that, pneumonia had settled in Henry's lungs and overtaxed his weak heart.

"Do you have any pictures of Mr. Henry and Miss June?"

He jerked, the question catching him off guard, and his chair teetered on the back legs. He grasped the desk to counterbalance, and a drawer slid open, sending him sprawling. His chair crashed to the floor, along with the drawer and all its contents.

Miss Whitfield rushed to his side. "Oh, my goodness! Are you all right?"

Unless a person could die of embarrassment. "I'm fine. Ma always scolded us boys for sittin' like that. I should've listened." He scrambled to his knees to pick up the items that'd come from the renegade drawer. Buttons, nails, and coins surely could fly everywhere, besides making a lot of noise.

Ma appeared in the doorway. "What happened?"

Rupert glanced up to find her, Millie, and Amy gaping at the new mess.

Miss Whitfield caught a rolling button, then rose. "Mr. McNeil pulled the desk drawer out when his chair slipped."

Amy's giggle invited more, and soon all the women joined in.

Warmth seeped into Rupert's face, but he grinned.

"Well, since you have everything under control here," Ma said, although her smirk indicated she wasn't convinced, "I'll go see how Jewel's coming with supper. I expect it will soon be ready." Muffled laughter followed as she walked away, and Millie followed with Amy in tow.

Rupert dusted his trousers. "I think a broom might be the next step in this cleanup."

Miss Whitfield averted her gaze. "Right after we pick up all these buttons and coins." Her skirt billowed around her as she knelt to collect the scattered objects. "Why, this is Union money." She held up a coin. "You'll want to put it somewhere safe."

A folded paper had lodged beneath a leg of the desk, and Rupert tugged it free. The flowery handwriting ended with a short line at the bottom. He brought it closer. "Miss Whitfield, what did you say your aunt's name was?"

She dumped a handful of coins on the desk and faced him. "We call her Aunt Ginny, but it's Virginia Murphy. Why?"

Rupert held up the paper. "If this is her signature, we've found one of those letters."

~

*H*annah reached for the letter, but Rupert didn't hand it over.

She crossed to his side and stood on tiptoe to peer over his arm. He shifted the paper higher, tilting it to catch the light streaming in the window. Was he trying to prevent her from reading it?

With a huff, Hannah folded her arms. "I only wanted to see the date on it."

Behind them, Troy rapped on the doorframe. "Hey, y'all, Ma says to wrap up your search and—" His eyes went wide. "Hey, is that one of the letters?"

He strode to Rupert's other side and leaned in. Rupert folded the paper into a square and stuck it in his pocket. "I believe I'll let Pa read it first and ask what he thinks we should do."

Why was Rupert being so evasive? Would the paper give John McNeil guidance on solving Hannah's problems? She could only pray so.

Troy stalked away. "Suit yourself. He just got back from visiting the neighbors, but Ma says we're about ready to eat, so he might be headed to the kitchen."

Was it that late? A glance at the window confirmed the day had advanced more than she'd suspected. Hannah's gaze fell on the dislodged drawer, which still lay on the floor. The desk had two more drawers on one side and a cabinet door on the other, none of which had been searched yet.

"You comin'?" Rupert was leaning against the doorframe, waiting for her.

She ignored his question and pulled on the top drawer, tugging until it broke free as if it hadn't been opened in a long time. Inside, a bottle of ink, a penknife, and a box of matches lay nestled beside a stack of folded papers. A burst of success swelled at the sight of her aunt's name on the top page. She lifted them out, only to have a larger hand clamp over hers as Rupert reached her side.

"What's this?"

Hannah's elation transformed into possessiveness. With a tighter grip on the pack, she pulled them to her chest. "My aunt's letters, right there in that drawer. Did you know they were there all this time?"

His chin firmed, and his brows lowered over his eyes, now a stormy blue. "Of course not. I've been in here all day, helpin' you search and clean this place when I should've been out gettin' ready for spring plantin'. Why would I care whether the letters were here or not?"

When Hannah opened her mouth to respond, Mr. John spoke from behind them. "If you children are through with your tug o' war, why don't we postpone this discussion until after supper?"

Hannah ducked her head.

Mr. John held out his hand. "Why don't I hold onto those until later?" When Hannah released her grip on the letters, surrendering them to her host, he smiled, then gestured to the hallway.

Hannah swept toward the door, batting back the sting of tears. How disappointed Aunt Ginny would be in her. Heavens, she was a guest in this home, which now belonged to Rupert McNeil, according to what the family had shared earlier. She owed him an apology.

Would he be able to forgive her foolish accusation, borne out of desperation?

*H*ow humiliating to endure a scold from Pa as if he were a misbehaving youth. The real problem was knowing Pa was right. As the host, Rupert should give preference to his guest—uninvited though she was. He couldn't account for why he'd blurted out his irritation, except he didn't like the way Miss Whitfield could manipulate him into doing her bidding. She'd dominated his time all day with her casual suggestions. Why, she was as bad as his cousin Wilma, just in a more pleasant manner. Which was surely more dangerous.

On a spur-of-the-moment decision, Rupert took the turn to his bedroom to collect himself. He hadn't moved into Henry's bedroom yet, leaving it for Ma and Pa while they visited. Whether he'd ever be emotionally able to move into Henry's larger bedroom was a question for the future. Pretty much the same way he doubted whether he could possibly become the kind of man Henry and Pa had exemplified all their lives.

He crossed the room and pushed aside the window curtains. With the glass cool against his forehead, he stared across the yard, where Aunt June's dogwood tree had put forth tentative blooms the day before. It was too early, not spring yet, and a cold snap could cut short the tree's flowering season.

What was he going to do about Miss Whitfield? As Henry's heir, he felt obligated to help her, but heck if he knew what to do. He had little money and a whole pile of expenses and hard work coming up.

"I sure would appreciate it if you'd send me some wisdom from up there," he said aloud. Speaking to Henry came easier than praying. Although he went through all the motions his family expected—attending church, saying grace, generally living right—Rupert had little confidence in his own prayers being heard. Either his faith was weak, or he didn't say them right. The few times he'd prayed for someone close to him, the results had been disappointing.

But Henry had had the Lord's ear, so he figured his uncle could intervene for him.

CHAPTER 6

fter struggling through an uncomfortable start to the meal, Hannah took advantage of the cook refilling everyone's glasses and leaned toward Rupert. "Please forgive me for—"

"I'm sorry I spoke so carelessly," he said at the same time. His mouth quirked up on one side, and Hannah felt her face warming. "I reckon both of us were tired and irritable after a long day of disappointments. Let's put it behind us."

"Agreed." She picked up a spoonful of black-eyed peas, then put it down. Keeping her voice low, she asked, "What did your pa do with the letters?"

"I dunno," Rupert whispered. "Should I ask?" He laid his fork on his plate.

"No." Hannah set a hand to his arm. His gaze went from his arm to her face, and she snatched her hand back. "It can wait."

No sooner had she resumed her meal than Miss Connie called her name. "Miss Whitfield—Hannah," she corrected, "did you leave any baggage in the barn? If so, we should have one of the men retrieve it for you before it grows too dark."

"Oh, yes." Hannah's hands went to her warm cheeks. What

else would she do to cast herself in a poor light with these folks? "How foolish of me to forget about that."

"I believe you had your mind occupied with other matters." With a smile, Miss Connie shifted her gaze to Rupert. "I'm sure Rupert will be glad to bring it in for you after he milks the cow."

On the bench beside her, Rupert nodded. Did he resent the extra work she caused? She would happily relieve him of that burden. "If you don't mind, I can go along and bring it down from the loft while you take care of your chores."

His ma's eyes widened, but she nodded. "I believe that would be acceptable."

"No need for that." Rupert shot a disgruntled glance his mother's way. "I can get Levi to go with me so he can practice milking. He's been asking to do more on the farm, and that's a good place to start."

Perhaps Rupert had had enough of her company today. Hannah directed her question to his mother. "Who is Levi?"

"He's Jewel's son. He helps her in the kitchen sometimes, but lately, he's become Malachi's shadow."

"Malachi is his grandpa," Rupert added, "and my main farmhand."

Across the table, Troy addressed his father. "How soon do you plan to head back to your place?"

"Well, now, your ma and I haven't decided for sure. Paul can manage just fine without me looking over his shoulder, and we figured Millie could use the rest, so we can stay a while yet." He slanted a look at Rupert. "As long as Rupert can put up with all of us, we're in no hurry."

Content to let the conversation drift around her, Hannah concentrated on finishing her meal while the men talked. They didn't mention it, but did they consider her presence another reason to prolong their visit here?

"You know you're welcome to stay for as long as necessary," Rupert said.

"That's good." Troy pushed his plate away. "I ought to make a run over to the Georgia office and check on Preacher Dan Holt. There might be a shipment to pick up too."

Hannah's confusion must have shown on her face. Miss Connie patted her hand. "Troy's finishing out his military commitment with the Freedmen's Bureau. He serves from this area north of Roanoke to his and Millie's home over in Campbell County."

Hannah sucked in a quick breath as her fork clattered to the table. "How can that be? I thought everyone around here supported the Confederacy." Did Troy McNeil work with carpetbaggers like those near her home? Had she come all this way only to find herself in the middle of folks who would help those trying to seize Whitfield Hall and her family's legacy?

∾

*D*id Miss Whitfield's tense posture when she learned about Troy's job with the Freedmen's Bureau indicate fear or anger? Either way, an explanation might help.

Rupert half turned to her. "Our family is a mixed lot. My older brother, Paul, served in the Confederate Army, but our middle brother, Simon, was already up north and joined the Federal forces. Troy was bent on evading because he didn't want to shoot at anyone."

"Did a pretty fair job of avoiding both armies." Troy picked up Millie's hand and kissed her knuckles. "Until the summer of '64 when I went tryin' to find this woman and got myself arrested on the road to Marietta. The Union Army sent me to Camp Chase with other prisoners, but then they let me join and serve as a guard there."

Millie added more. "When General Lee surrendered, Troy

still had a year and a half left in the army. His commander worked it out so he could come to this area with the Bureau to finish out his time."

Hannah stared at Troy as if she could see through him. "You confiscate the houses of Southerners who sided with the Confederacy?"

Troy's eyes grew round. "No, ma'am. I help farmers hire former slaves to work their land. Which benefits everyone."

"And he helped to start a school for the freed people so they can learn to read and write," Miss Connie added. "Then they can get jobs other than farming, if they like, and support themselves."

"Ma teaches at the Freedmen's school." Rupert directed the attention away from Miss Whitfield. "Who is teaching while you're away this week?"

As the talk centered around Ma's involvement with schooling the former slaves, Hannah seemed to withdraw. She ate a few bites of her food but mostly moved it around on her plate.

Pa had followed the conversation in his quiet way, observing their guest's reaction. "Miss Whitfield, I believe you said Henry was named as the trustee for your home. Exactly where is it located?"

"It's southwest of Atlanta, in Coweta County, Georgia."

"Out of my jurisdiction." Troy shook his head. "And I collect you're having trouble with someone there disputin' your right to the land?"

"A former Union officer is trying to find a way to take it— even suggested I should marry him or lose it because Papa aided the Confederate cause." Her gaze drifted to the window. "My brother Colin was killed at Bentonville, so only Caleb and I are left. He's just six, so it's up to me to secure Whitfield Hall until he reaches his majority."

Rupert's esteem for their visitor increased, along with his

sympathy. What a heavy burden for a young woman. Uncle Henry surely would have come to her aid. Would he expect no less of his nephew?

~

*H*ad she come on a fool's errand? Aunt Ginny had been sure Henry was their best hope, that he would do everything in his power to save them. But was their trust misplaced? With Henry gone, should she seek help elsewhere?

Hannah's resolve firmed. She'd do whatever she must to secure their home and heritage. Though Papa wasn't alive to see it, she would prove herself worthy of the Whitfield name by preserving the family legacy. A daughter could be as useful as a son.

Mr. John stood. "Why don't we move this discussion to the parlor so Jewel can clean the kitchen and retire for the night? Miss Whitfield, I trust you won't object to sharing the contents of these letters with all of us. Perhaps it will clarify how we can help you."

"Of course, you're welcome to read them aloud." Hannah followed the family, her mind spinning. Perhaps they would finally find out what Aunt Ginny had written—and whether Rupert's uncle had suggested any remedy.

In the parlor, Troy and Millie took the settee, the sleeping baby nestled in Millie's arms, while Amy settled in Miss Connie's lap. To Hannah's surprise, Rupert offered her one upholstered chair near the empty fireplace while he took the other.

Perching a pair of reading glasses on his nose, Mr. John sifted through the papers in his hands. "I suppose we should start with the earliest letter, which seems to be this one." He laid the others on the occasional table and took his seat beside the doily-covered table.

"It's dated January tenth of this year. This first paragraph appears to be belated condolences on June's passing and a reminder of how they met. Ah, here's where she explains the problem. 'I know not where else to turn for help and pray you will be able to advise me. My own dear Liam suffered a stroke and is unable to take charge. In fact, it is impossible for me to leave him as he requires constant assistance.'"

Mr. John skimmed the page. "She goes into some detail about Mr. Murphy's disability and her responsibilities in caring for the household. 'The local government has been overtaken by men who served in the Union Army and others who descended upon us last autumn. There is one in particular who has set his sights on Whitfield Hall, and I fear, has plans to persuade my niece that she must wed him in order for us to remain here. I have told him that you are named trustee for my nephew, Caleb, who is the heir to the property. You will probably know how to secure that better than I, but it may be necessary for you to marry my niece to convince those carpetbaggers to give up their efforts. Please reply quickly, as I grow concerned they will not be put off long. Your friend, Virginia Murphy.'"

Mr. John peered over his glasses at Hannah. "Just as Miss Whitfield has said." He refolded the first letter and picked up another. He gave it a quick scan. "This one reiterates the problem as described in the first. It was dated late January. This one"—he selected another and opened it—"is dated February eleventh. She seems to be getting rather desperate and anxious to get a response. There's a second page here."

With a quick intake of breath, he blinked at the new sheet. "It seems Henry started a reply on March first. I don't...." He paused to choke back his emotions.

Hannah leaned forward, holding her breath. What had Mr.

Henry written? Did he have a solution? Did he indicate his willingness to help? "Please, Mr. John. What does it say?"

"Rupert should see this before I read it aloud." He held out the letter to his son.

With obvious reluctance, Rupert accepted the single page and read silently. When he didn't seem inclined to share the contents, Hannah stretched out her hand, but Troy plucked the paper from his brother's grasp.

"He wrote," Troy said, "'Since I greatly doubt that I will recover this side of heaven, I recommend to you my nephew, who happens to share my name and would make an excellent mate for your niece...'" He lowered the sheet and glanced between Hannah and Rupert. "Huh. That's an easy solution. Miss Whitfield, I present to you Henry Rupert McNeil. He's quite eligible and should make a most exemplary husband."

A surge of astonishment coursed through her veins. Was Troy serious? Hannah stared at the man who had spent all day in her company. "Your name is Henry?"

His slow nod affirmed it, though his gaze darted away. "I never use it." With his hands in his lap, Rupert tapped his fingertips together. Was that a sign of nervousness or annoyance?

"He was named for my brother, who never had a son," Mr. John explained. "We've always called Rupert by his middle name to avoid confusion since all the McNeils live in the same general area."

Troy passed the paper to Hannah. "See for yourself. I think that's why Henry left the farm to Rupert, plus the fact both his daughters moved away after they married. Neither of their husbands had any interest in farming."

With trembling fingers, Hannah smoothed the paper over her skirt. The writing showed a shaky hand had penned the words. Henry had ended abruptly without finishing the last sentence. From what she'd gathered, he'd sickened, grown steadily worse, and died within a matter of weeks. Tears pricked her eyes as it became clear he'd tried to reply to his old friend while he was so ill. How many people would spend their last days trying to help someone else? His generosity overwhelmed her.

The only rub was whether his nephew would accept this solution. Although she was prepared to dedicate her life to ensuring her brother's legacy, how could she expect the same of Rupert—a man who'd never heard of Whitfield Hall until a few days ago?

⁓

*M*iss Whitfield's sniffling indicated tears, which confounded Rupert. Why did she cry now, when they had found proof of her claims and Henry's concern for her family? Did she consider Rupert such a poor choice? Hadn't he forgone his normal chores all day to help? And her ordering him about like a schoolboy, telling him to tote books and organize papers to her liking. He'd even wiped dust from the furniture.

Then again, she might have interpreted his silence as displeasure with Henry's proposed solution. Throughout the day, they'd worked well together, but they'd also argued. Did that provide an insight into what a future together could be like?

Rupert tried to work up some sympathy. "Miss Whitfield, it was only what Henry thought might help. It's certainly not the only solution to your dilemma."

Her chin jerked up, revealing wide green eyes and quivering lips. The sight sent a surge of longing in Rupert's chest. Pushing it down, he focused on the paper she clutched.

"Do you have another, Mr. McNeil? I would very much like to hear it."

"I... No. I wish I could help, but...." He turned to his brother. "With Troy's knowledge of the government's new regulations, he's the one to figure out what can be done."

Troy held up his hands, palms out. "Most of my experience has been setting up agreements between farmers and workers, plus providin' for refugees and settlin' small disputes. With the reports I have to file every month, I've yet to hear of anyone tryin' to take another's land. That would be more in line with Simon's work as a lawyer."

"Well, Simon ain't here." Rupert cringed at the note of belligerence in his voice.

"Boys," Pa chided. "We're not here to argue but to help Miss Whitfield, if we can, to find a way to keep her home. Right now, I think we should all do like Amy there"—he nodded at the sleeping child—"and get some rest. It's been a long day for everyone. Maybe an answer will come to us in the morning."

Troy stood and helped Millie to her feet. "Good thinking, Pa. I'll take Amy, Ma."

While she transferred the child to Troy's arms, Ma spoke to Miss Whitfield. "Hannah, I'll show you to the room we've prepared for you. Rupert, don't forget to bring her bag from the barn after you milk the cow."

Eager to make his escape, he headed for the kitchen. "I'll do that right now."

After he grabbed the milk bucket, he stepped into the yard and gazed at the night sky. Thousands of lights dotted the inky expanse, reminding him again of how small a part he played in this great universe. A Scripture he'd memorized as a youngster came to mind. From one of the Psalms, if his memory was right.

What is man that Thou are mindful of him? Indeed. Why would God care about their troubles? They were so insignificant compared to everything out there. "You've got planets and stars, maybe even people on other worlds to take care of." He heaved a deep sigh. "It sure would be nice, though, if You could show us a way to clear this up."

The whine of the door behind him warned he wasn't alone. He swung around.

Miss Whitfield held out a lantern. "Your ma thought you might need this."

Abashed that he'd left without the light, he scrambled for an excuse. "Just wanted to enjoy a moment out here with nothin' but the stars."

She raised her face to the view. "It is quite a wonder, isn't it? To think God made all this creation in only a week."

"I've read some people of science have different ideas about how everything developed."

In the glow of the light she held, her incredulity amused him. What an expressive face she had. Eyes wide and eyebrows raised to wrinkle her forehead. Her cheeks puffed up like a chipmunk's whenever she smiled, those lips the color of a wild rose. He jerked his gaze back to her eyes. Hopefully, she couldn't discern his thoughts.

"Well," she said, "whatever method God used, only He could produce such beauty and perfection."

"I have to agree with you." With an example of the earth's beauty standing next to him, he shook his head. "I'd better get on to the barn."

He held out his hand for the lantern, which she surrendered. "I think I'll wait here until you get back. Maybe the light from inside will keep the wild animals away while I keep watch."

"Afraid for my safety?"

Her laughter floated softly on the night air.

Yeah, he'd be safer alone in the barn.

CHAPTER 7

*W*aking up in a comfortable bed surely beat a hayloft, although that had been a sight better than sleeping under Elmer's wagon. At least the hay was dry and gave way when a body turned over, unlike the hard ground. Hannah stretched her arms and legs as far as she could, then left her warm cocoon to dress for the day.

She wandered to the window and peered across the field that extended beyond the barn to the hill, where pink clouds streaked across the sky. A crowing rooster startled her, and she laughed. "Ha, you're a little late, old boy. I guess you were busy elsewhere."

Feeling more optimistic about her future, she smoothed the covers on the bed and pulled on her shoes. Aunt Ginny's letters had validated her reason for showing up at the McNeils' door unannounced. Assured of the family's willingness to help, she looked forward to returning home.

Beyond the bedroom, the sounds of voices and footsteps indicated the others had begun their day. Would there be any awkwardness when she joined them, since everyone knew the contents of Aunt Ginny's letters and Mr. Henry's proposed solution? Rupert's reaction hadn't been promising, but then, he must've been surprised too. Now that he'd had time to consider the matter, how would he act?

Their work together yesterday had shown him to be mostly agreeable. Memories flashed in her mind—their first meeting at the front door, their efforts to organize books and papers, Rupert sprawled on the floor when his chair toppled. His relaxed nature appealed, as did his handsome face and physique, though she would never say so aloud. His mischievous smile and those striking blue eyes created quite a picture.

Hannah fanned her face and waited for her heart to resume its regular rhythm.

None of that mattered, though, unless he agreed to his uncle's proposal. How could she approach the topic without giving the impression she expected them to lay aside their own concerns to focus on hers?

She pulled the door open to find Miss Connie poised to knock. "Thank goodness, you're up and dressed," the older woman said. "We have a minor crisis on our hands, and I wonder if you'd watch the baby while the rest of us search outside for Amy and Levi?"

Hannah was already nodding before she finished. "Oh, my! I hope they're nearby. Of course, I'm glad to help. Where is the little one?"

"In the parlor," Miss Connie called over her shoulder as she led the way. Hannah caught up with her as they reached the room. "I remember you saying you have a young brother, so I felt you'd be able to care for Little John if he wakes up before we get back." She pointed out the crib beside the sofa, then hurried to the front door. "Hopefully, we'll find them soon."

What a welcome chore to start her day, watching over the baby. She whispered a prayer for the missing children. At least her presence allowed the others to search without worrying about the youngest one.

Hannah perched on the sofa and peered at the tiny person in the old-fashioned crib made from a hollowed-out log. It must have been in the family for decades. She'd forgotten how small new babies were. With Caleb having celebrated his sixth birthday back in November, he hated others referring to him as the baby of the family. As the second oldest, Hannah had loved to help Mama with the younger ones—and mourned their loss when they died so young. Now, with her older sister, Rachel, far away in Savannah and Colin killed in the war, she was all Caleb had. He'd endured so much loss, more than any child should have to. The weight of her responsibility to him grew heavy when circumstances pushed her beyond her abilities.

While she admired the smallest McNeil, outside, the other adults called for Levi and Amy. How frightened they must be, not knowing where the children had gone or if one of them might be injured.

"The Bible says children are a heritage, and they are a joy, for sure." Hannah spoke her thoughts to the sleeping infant. "But you little'uns can bring on some heartache." It was almost better not to have children than to risk the pain of losing them. Her mother's sorrow at losing four to various illnesses had taken a heavy toll. At least Mama had passed before the war stole her first son. Papa, on the other hand—

The infant gave a weak cry, and she patted his back, urging him back to sleep. "Shh, little one. You're just fine."

That worked for half a minute, then he started crying again, more insistently this time. With great care, she lifted him from the cradle and put him to her shoulder, crooning softly. In moments, the crying subsided, his breath evened out, and she relished the closeness.

If she and Rupert married, perhaps...

Better not travel that line of thinking. He hadn't exactly jumped at the opportunity last night.

From the sound of water splashing in the kitchen, someone

had come in the back door. Maybe that meant they'd found the children. The thump of boots on the floor drew closer, and she turned to warn the person to quiet down.

Rupert stopped at the threshold and peeked in. Coatless, with sleeves pushed up to his elbows and his black armband, his shirt showed damp spots, much the same as when she'd met him yesterday. The lines on his forehead smoothed out when his gaze went from the crib to the fireplace where Hannah stood. Had he expected to find the little one left on his own?

She closed the distance between them so she wouldn't risk waking the baby and spoke softly. "Have y'all found the children? Are they all right? What happened?"

"Uh, yeah, we found 'em. Amy slipped out when Troy left to go check on his place this morning and went runnin' after him. Fortunately, Levi saw her and followed her. She got as far as the road, then somehow tumbled into the ravine on the other side of the lane. Levi tried to pull her out, but she wouldn't listen." He chuckled. "She wanted to stay there and play." He motioned toward the kitchen. "I came ahead to fill the tubs with water to clean them up."

That explained the splotches on his shirt. At least the rest of him appeared dry.

He stroked the baby's head. "Did you have any trouble with Little John?"

"Not at all. So he's named after your father?"

"Yeah. Millie wanted to name him Henry, but Troy overrode that, said she'd named Amy so he would name this 'un."

Mention of the name he shared with his uncle brought warmth to Hannah's face. While the missing children were in focus, her problem had been shoved aside. Now the question loomed between them. Would Rupert agree to honor his uncle's plan?

And what would she do if he refused?

~

*A*ll through breakfast, Rupert replayed the parlor scene in his mind. Hannah holding Little John, turning to greet him as he stood at the door. Here in his parlor, in his house, she looked as if she belonged. A desire to keep her here surged, but—there were too many "buts" to consider. Her home was in Georgia, under threat from a carpetbagger, and she seemed to think only she could save it. By marrying one Henry McNeil. How in heck did Uncle Henry get named as her brother's trustee? He'd never mentioned the Murphy family in Georgia, let alone being listed as guardian for the heir to Whitfield Hall.

The biggest reason, though, was that Rupert couldn't risk losing anyone else close to him—and feeling he was the cause and helpless to save them. His real mother died before his first birthday after never recovering from his birth. Then his favorite horse when he was five, due to his own neglect, and then his best friend, Lloyd Dennis, who took a bullet during the war trying to get Rupert to safety. Now Henry. No, he wouldn't take such a risk.

Besides, what did he truly know about Miss Hannah Whitfield?

Pa interrupted his musing as they finished the meal. "Let's you and I go to the office so I can help you figure out Henry's books."

When Rupert started to object, Pa peered down his nose, his message clear. He must want to discuss more than Henry's bookkeeping, such as what Rupert ought to do about Miss Whitfield.

The clatter of a carriage outside drew them to the front door and onto the porch.

Seeing the visitor, he wished he'd had a loud, clear warning.

The stylish surrey stopped close to the porch steps. Why had Wilma Thurman returned to the farm?

Rupert must have groaned because Pa said, voice low, "Be nice."

They left the porch while Levi ran from the barn to grasp the horses' bridle. He held them still while Pa offered his hand for Wilma to step down. "Mornin', Wilma. What brings you out so early in the day?"

"Good morning, Uncle John, Rupert. I thought I'd drop by before I go back to Mobile."

As the three of them mounted the steps, Ma swept out the front door. "Why, look who's here. Wilma, I didn't think we'd get to see you again for a month or more. Have you already been to Jacksonville and back?" She looped her arm through Wilma's and led her toward the rocking chairs.

Wilma released Ma's hold and aimed for the front door. "Can't we go inside? I thought to visit a little while."

If Rupert hadn't been so wary of his cousin's motives, he might have found some humor in the gentle tug of war between the women. He surely wouldn't lay any money against either one. Wilma knew how to get her way, but Ma could be a formidable opponent.

"Of course, we can. I believe Millie just got the baby back to sleep, so we'll have to speak quietly."

"That's fine. Oh, Rupert, tell that boy to bring my satchel inside. I'll need some papers from it." Wilma reached for Pa's arm and pulled him toward the door. "Now, Uncle John, I need to know what you think about the new laws...."

Her voice faded as Rupert turned to make his escape, but Ma grabbed his arm. "Don't tarry now. I know Wilma can be a pain, but it's your house. Don't let her take over."

His history with Wilma had taught him the best way to deal with her was to avoid her. When they were youngsters, she'd pushed him around, declaring he had to obey because she was older. As an adult, she conducted herself more discreetly, but she still expected to get her way. Old habits often reappeared, but he wouldn't let that happen anymore.

He sighed as he turned toward the barn. Just when he thought things could not get more complicated, he now had another woman to deal with.

~

*H*annah stared at the elegant woman standing at the parlor door who leaned against Mr. John possessively, demanding his full attention as she nattered on about estate laws. She wore one of those stylish new hats that covered only part of one's hair and did nothing to shade the face. Her dress of deep burgundy was topped with a white collar that dripped lace to her elbows and matched her shawl.

Who was she to Rupert? And the rest of the family?

Minutes earlier, Millie had taken Amy and the baby to the bedroom for some "quiet time"—a clever name for Amy's mild punishment after her early escapade.

The woman halted mid-sentence when her narrowed gaze landed on Hannah. Her mouth dropped open, then snapped back. "Who is *she*? I thought everyone but family had gone home."

Before Hannah could speak, Miss Connie stepped to the woman's other side and pulled her forward. "Wilma, allow me to introduce Miss Hannah Whitfield from Georgia. Miss Whitfield, this is Wilma Thurman, Henry's younger daughter." Miss Connie urged the visitor to the settee and took the place beside her, speaking to her husband. "Would you let Jewel know we have company and need tea for everyone? Thank you, dear." To the woman, she said, "Now, Wilma, what brings you back to the farm so soon?"

The lady huffed. "Well, I only went as far as Martha's, rather than to Jacksonville, since I plan to return to Mobile. In fact, I was thinking of selling the house in Jacksonville and staying in Mobile year-round. Of course, I need to discuss this with Uncle John, since the law requires his approval as the trustee named in Mr. Thurman's will."

Hannah followed the conversation out of curiosity. From what she gathered, Mrs. Thurman's situation might be similar to her own, requiring the consent of a male relative to sell or secure her home.

Rupert's entrance redirected the women's attention. He carried a travel satchel, which he gave to Wilma before choosing the chair closer to Hannah, the one he'd occupied the night before. When his gaze met Hannah's, he offered a slight smile and hitched one shoulder as if to apologize for the sudden disruption.

Mrs. Thurman abandoned her explanation to focus on Hannah. "Aunt Connie said you're from Georgia, Miss Whitfield? What brings you to this little place in Alabama?"

Dismayed to find the attention on her, Hannah caught her breath. "Why, I came to see your father—"

"To pay her respects and offer condolences on behalf of her aunt and uncle," Miss Connie said quickly. "Do you recall your mother corresponding with her cousin, Virginia Murphy?"

"Hmm. The name does sound familiar." She tilted her head and eyed Hannah as one might consider a strange specimen. "I wonder why no one from your family came when Ma passed?" Her voice rose at the end, clearly inviting Hannah to answer.

Before she came up with one, Rupert said, "You might remember there was a war goin' on then, Wilma. I couldn't make it for Aunt June's funeral either."

Determined to speak for herself, Hannah leaned forward to address the woman. "Also, my uncle suffered a stroke about the same time. With only Aunt Ginny and me there to care for him and my young brother, we couldn't leave home."

All conversation stopped when Mr. John and Jewel arrived with an antique tea service on a tray. Hannah accepted a cup and retreated to her chair.

While the others busied themselves with the tea, Rupert caught Hannah's eye. "Well done," he whispered under the clatter of cups and spoons.

His unexpected praise created a flutter in Hannah's middle. Why did he and his parents tread on tenterhooks around this woman? Did she wield an unspoken power over them, or did her aura of self-importance intimidate them? No, *intimidate* was the wrong word. It was more like their natural congeniality demanded they tolerate her when they'd rather not.

Hannah had witnessed—indeed, participated in—the same reaction at home on more than one occasion. When she was younger, the former minister's wife had been pushy and demanding. Lately, the person who provoked such conduct flaunted his uniform and depended on it to gain him prestige and a foothold in local society. Captain Prescott's persistent visits had incited her desperate flight to Alabama in search of a champion.

Peeping from lowered lashes as she sipped her tea, Hannah considered the proposed substitute for the man she'd come to plead her cause with. Would Henry Rupert McNeil risk his future to help secure hers? She didn't dare hope for such an outcome, but what other choice did she have?

CHAPTER 8

*I*t was rare enough for Rupert to have one female
visitor in his house—who wasn't a close relative—
and he couldn't remember a time he and Henry had enter-
tained two. Rupert took advantage of the opportunity to study
and compare his cousin with Miss Whitfield.

Each had come for a specific reason. Miss Whitfield had
explained hers outright, but Wilma's usual method was to circle
about the subject on her mind until she decided to spring it.
Did that make Miss Whitfield more trustworthy? Possibly, but
caution would be wise in either case.

They looked different, of course. Where Wilma had inherited her dark hair and blue eyes from Henry, Hannah's dark
blond hair and green eyes reminded him of Aunt June, though
the two could be only distant relatives.

Until Rupert hit a growth spurt in his youth, Wilma had
been taller, and being eight years older than Rupert, had
enjoyed bossing him around whenever their families got
together. The top of Hannah's head barely grazed his chin, but
after her initial reticence to approach the family, she'd exhib-

ited a similar take-charge nature to Wilma. In fact, every female he could think of acted that way to some degree. Maybe it was God's way of preparing them for motherhood.

He'd let his mind drift from the conversation while Wilma talked about her visit to Mobile on the Gulf of Mexico. Then she raved about new fashion plates from Paris. Her sudden mention of buying farmland drew his attention.

"Maybe just a small parcel," she was saying, "near the creek on the west side of the farm." She batted her eyes, and Rupert stiffened. What did she want?

Pa sent Rupert a pointed stare. "I don't know what Rupert's planning to do with that section. He's just beginnin' to prepare the ground for plantin'. What do you think, son? You willing to sell off a couple of acres?"

"The western strip where Pa used to grow wheat." Wilma smiled at him. "While I'm here, we can walk out there, and I'll mark it off for you."

She wanted some of his land? "What're you wantin' it for?"

Wilma's tinkling laugh sounded like a warning to him. "Why, to build a house on, of course."

He wasn't falling for her innocent act. "Now, why would you want to have another house? You got one in Mobile and one in Jacksonville. Ain't that enough for you?"

"If you'd been listening instead of ogling Miss Whitfield, you'd know I plan to sell the house in Jacksonville. I've got no ties there since Mr. Thurman died and no need for such a big place."

Rupert's face flushed with warmth. He didn't ogle. He didn't need to since he'd seen plenty of the woman yesterday. Wilma smirked, and he chastised himself for not recognizing her ploy. She expected him to refuse to sell, maybe even hoped he would so she could haggle over it. Unlike most of the family, she had the funds to spare...funds he could use...and maybe he wouldn't have to ask the bank for a loan. Besides, saying no to her would be virtually impossible, seeing as how she was Henry's daughter.

Forcing back his ire, he nodded. "All right, let's go take a look at it." He stood up.

"Oh, not today, Rupie." Her protest reminded him of the rusty wheels on an old wheelbarrow. "I'm not dressed to go tramping about the grounds."

Frustration ate at his patience. He'd already missed one day in the field. He couldn't afford to miss another. "Look, Wilma. I've got work to do and no time to waste. You can change clothes now or give up your opportunity to convince me to sell."

Ma's eyes widened, but she didn't chastise him for his lack of hospitality. Maybe she gave him credit for managing his own house, or maybe she was ready to send Wilma on her way.

Pa set down his cup. "Best do it today and soon. I noticed dark clouds buildin' to the west. Tomorrow's liable to be a wet one."

With a mighty huff, Wilma grasped her carpetbag and stood. "Where shall I change? My old bedroom?"

"Millie's staying in there with the children." Ma rose and steered her toward the hallway. "Use Henry's bedroom. I'll just move our things out of the way."

When the women were out of hearing, Rupert moved to Hannah's side. "I'm sorry my cousin showed up like this. As you can see, she has a way of takin' over when she comes around." He turned to Pa. "Why do you think she really wants the land?"

"I have no idea. I'm surprised she wants to sell the house up north, but she's right about not needin' such a big place. I'll have to go with her to set up the sale."

"I hope you're gonna walk out with us to view the property she wants. I'd rather not have to deal with her alone." Because she always seemed to convince him she was right, even when his gut said she'd duped him. *And I can't handle more than one bossy female at a time.*

≈

Though Mrs. Thurman's arrival posed a delay to solving Hannah's problem, it gave her an opportunity to witness how Rupert handled the troublesome woman. Was there a history of contention between the cousins? Mr. John and Miss Connie tended to step in when needed to keep the peace. Perhaps Hannah could learn more from Miss Connie after the men took Mrs. Thurman to view the land in question.

Hannah set her empty cup on the tray and shifted toward Rupert. "How many acres do you have here, Mr. McNeil?"

He blinked. Maybe he had trouble remembering his Uncle Henry was no longer the *Mr. McNeil* in residence. "Eighty-five, which really is too much for one man to work alone. That's why Troy and I would visit Henry for weeks at a time. He didn't keep slaves, and sometimes he had trouble finding good workers to make the most use of the land."

"So you wouldn't be hurt any by selling a small portion to Mrs. Thurman?"

He lowered his voice. "If it was anyone else, I'd be glad to carve off a couple of acres."

"But you'd rather not sell it to her?"

His frown returned. "What you saw here today was just a taste of how demanding she can be. She's been like that all her life, and it didn't help when she married a man who had more money than all of Randolph County. She thinks—"

"That's enough," Pa said. "No need to spoil the water with more oil. It's not our place to judge." He headed for the door. "I'll go ask Malachi to hitch up the wagon."

Hannah pressed her lips to keep from laughing at Rupert's mulish frown. She'd heard enough to convince her to stay out of Mrs. Thurman's way while she was here. And to be glad that Mr. Henry's demise had prevented Hannah from being closely related to such a creature.

After Mrs. Thurman emerged from the bedroom in more suitable shoes and clothing, she turned her full attention to Rupert. "All right, Rupie, I'm ready now. Your ma said we should hurry, so we can take my carriage out to the field." She took his arm.

"Pa's gettin' the wagon ready." By the simple act of turning to speak to Hannah, he freed himself from Wilma's hold. "Would you like to accompany us on this outing, Miss Whitfield?"

"Oh, no, thank you." The invitation surprised her, but she should offer an excuse. "I believe I'll write a letter to let my aunt know I've arrived." There. Let Mrs. Thurman think whatever she wanted about Hannah's visit.

Rupert answered with a smirk. "You do that. I'm sure she'll be interested to learn about your journey."

Mrs. Thurman followed their exchange with obvious impatience. "Come on, now. We can *all* visit with your guest later."

As she dragged Rupert out the door, Hannah's humor transformed into dread. Did the woman expect to stay a while? If so, how long would it be before Hannah could get back home?

~

*T*he ride didn't take long, and except for Wilma's constant chatter, Rupert enjoyed it, admiring the view along the way. Gentle hills gave way to large fields bordered by trees in the distance. While the ground's present condition showed little signs of life now, in a few weeks, crops would spring up and decorate it with a myriad of colors and textures.

Rupert slowed the horse to a walk. "Whereabouts do you want to stop?"

Wilma pointed to a group of pines off the road. "Right there will be fine."

He drove the wagon to the place she indicated, stopped, and set the brake. Pa leaped from his seat and offered his hand to help Wilma down. Rupert followed them to the slight rise that allowed a better view.

The section of land Wilma wanted to buy backed up to his closest neighbor's farm, which suited Rupert fine. The farther away Wilma was, the better. He weighed whether he should hold out for a while just to make her work for it. Unfortunately, that would mean dealing with her longer, and though he wasn't above it to try her patience, he would suffer too.

He kicked a stone into the woods. "The only potential problem would be getting Mr. Callahan to approve the sale. The creek flows on both properties, and I'm not sure how he uses it. Give me a day or two to check with him, and I'll let you know."

Like lightning, her surprised expression changed to a smile of victory. "Well, I'm sure that won't be a problem. We can talk to him together tomorrow." She consulted her lapel watch. "I must leave now. I have a fitting appointment in an hour."

Rupert didn't hide his surprise. "You're not leaving for Mobile? I thought you were eager to get back there."

"I want to finish this business before I leave." She gave him a pat on the shoulder. "Plus, Uncle John has to go with me to set up the sale of the Jacksonville house."

Pa twisted from his survey of the area and glanced from Rupert to Wilma. "We can go after you and Rupert talk to Mr. Callahan. So long as we leave before midday, we should reach Jacksonville before the bank closes."

Giving up on a few days of peace, Rupert scratched his head. "All right, then. Can you be here about nine in the morning?" he asked Wilma. "How long does it take you to drive from Martha's house?"

Wilma turned wide eyes his way. "Why can't I stay here?"

Exasperated, he spread his arms. "Because all the bedrooms are taken."

Wrinkles creased her forehead. "Who's in Martha's old room?"

Pa walked away to inspect a dormant tree—no doubt a guise to stay out of the discussion. Which left Rupert alone to deal with Wilma's questions. He glared at Pa's back as he answered. "Miss Whitfield, of course, since Millie has yours."

Wilma's voice rose. "Why isn't she staying with whoever brought her here? I'd think that would be a better choice than a bachelor's home."

Matching his cousin's indignation, Rupert leveled his glare on her. "The person who brought her had other obligations. Naturally, we offered her a place to stay. You might have noticed, two other women are currently in residence, in addition to the cook and three small children. If their presence doesn't make it acceptable, I don't know what would."

Wilma glared at him and pinched her lips.

Finished with his perambulation, Pa returned to Wilma's side. "We'd best leave now so you can make it to Martha's in time for the noon meal. Maybe the rain will hold off till you get there."

Wilma cast a glance at the sky. "All right. Let's be on our way. I'm ready to get this business done so I can get back to civilized company."

For once, Rupert agreed with her. The lure of exchanging the small parcel of land for ready cash was too tempting to disregard. If he agreed to help Miss Whitfield secure her home, he'd likely need even more capital than he'd figured. And he'd have to get a quick start on spring planting. Maybe Pa would lend a hand—or some plowing equipment. As soon as Wilma was gone, he'd ask.

$\sim$

*A*t the threat of a rainstorm delaying her journey, Mrs. Thurman remained at the house only long enough to gather her belongings while Rupert hooked up her carriage. The woman refused to sit and stayed near the parlor door to exchange a brief word with Miss Connie before she left. Her rudeness baffled Hannah.

"Is she so afraid of driving in the rain?" Hannah asked Millie. The visitor had offered Millie the barest of nods and hadn't acknowledged Hannah or the children at all.

Working on mending, Millie placed a stitch in her fabric. "I couldn't say since I'd never met her until Henry's funeral. Troy didn't know her well because she'd already married and left home before his first memories of coming here. We had a family reunion back in the fall, but Wilma didn't attend it."

The idea of a large family gathering stirred Hannah's longing. With most of her family gone and her older sister so far away in Savannah, she couldn't count on attending such events. She folded one of Little John's nappies. "How many people came to the reunion?"

Millie's hands stilled as she counted silently. "I reckon two dozen or more, but that includes several friends and farm workers. There was Henry's and John's younger brother, Ellis, and his three children—who aren't really children but not quite adults either. Their sister, Lydia, and her husband. Troy's and Rupert's brothers, Paul and Simon, with their families. Our friend Byron Harris, who has a law office and used to work with Troy. Of course, all of us you've met here."

"How wonderful to have such a large family and so many

friends you can depend on." Though Hannah meant her words as a compliment to their unity, her wistfulness slipped through.

Speculation lit Millie's eyes. "From what we learned last night, you might become part of it. I hope you do, for I quite like you, and Rupert needs a good woman. I believe Henry offered the perfect solution. Has Rupert given any indication of what he'll do?"

Unwilling to share her feelings on the subject, Hannah shook her head. "We haven't spoken of it."

Before Millie could respond, Rupert spoke from the doorway. "I've hardly had time to consider all the ramifications that could result from my decision, thanks to my overbearing cousin who thinks everyone should bow to her wishes."

Frowning, he strode into the room and marched to Hannah. "Did you write to your aunt?"

Goodness, his cousin had certainly soured his mood. But why did he need to be short with Hannah? "Yes, I did." She paused her mending—she'd persuaded Millie to let her help— and pointed to the envelope on the side table. "There lies the letter, ready to be posted whenever someone can take it to the post office." Though she hoped to have returned home by the time the letter arrived, she'd written it, anyway. And Miss Connie had assured Hannah she could stay as long as she needed.

"Yes, ma'am." With stiff posture, he swiped it up.

Hannah grimaced at the note of petulance in her voice. "Pray forgive my short tone, Mr. McNeil." She'd let his mood affect hers. Why would he want to help her when she spoke so? As Aunt Ginny often chided, she needed to exercise patience.

"Forgiven." He sighed. "And you might as well call me Rupert like everyone else does. Whenever I hear 'Mr. McNeil,' I think you're talking to Pa."

"Rupert," Millie said, "I know you just learned of this last night, but Hannah must be eager to return home. When do you think you'll be ready to share your decision with us?"

He sat on the chair beside the fireplace, facing them. "It's not so much the decision that takes time. It's trying to figure out how to keep everything working here while I escort Miss Whitfield back to Georgia and consider what needs to be done there. It calls for careful deliberation and planning."

Hannah caught her breath. So he wasn't turning her away without hope. He must be one of those people who had to plan every detail before committing to something. "It's kind of you to consider helping me. I'm truly grateful. If I can be of assistance, please let me know, Mr. McNeil."

"Rupert." He corrected her.

She nodded. "Rupert."

"I'm sure I'll have questions for you. We can start making notes after the noon meal. That is, if you're finished with your other chores." A lopsided grin chased the frown from his face. With those blue eyes sparkling, he was quite handsome.

The thought warmed her face. "I believe I can manage that. Thank you."

He stood and started toward the hallway, then turned back at the door. "And if the folks making trouble in Georgia are to believe that our relationship is real, I probably should call you Hannah. Would you agree?"

Hearing him say her name set her heart to beating faster. How could a single word have such an effect?

When she simply stared at him, his brow puckered. "Hannah? Is that all right with you?"

"Yes, that's fine. Rupert."

After he left, Millie snickered, then burst into laughter. "Oh, I can't wait to discover how this turns out. Troy made me promise not to interfere, but I'll be happy to watch you two figure out how to get along."

Hannah sighed. "I dare say we'll give everyone fits before it's over. We're so different. He may drive me mad with his careful deliberations."

"You may not believe this," Millie said, "but I think you're already driving him mad for a different reason. I've never known Rupert to become flustered like he is around you. He's good at avoiding the young women around here, but he acts different with you."

Hannah shook her head. "I doubt that's much of a recommendation. He'd have to leave the house to avoid me."

CHAPTER 9

What had just happened? Had he really promised to help Hannah Whitfield? For heaven's sake, he'd as good as said he would marry her. Of course, they'd have to be married if they traveled together without a chaperone, and with planting season at hand, no one here could serve in that role. Millie couldn't make the trip so soon, and she needed Ma close by to help her. It was unlikely they could make the trip in one day with the carriage, and no telling how long he'd be away. He should consult a map to get a better idea of how far it was to Hannah's home.

His steps took him to Henry's office—no, his office now. Although it was hard to retrain himself, he had to stop thinking of everything here as Henry's. "My office, my books, my bills to pay." With a groan, he accepted the truth. His legacy was a blessing that included many advantages, but it also brought its share of troubles and challenges. Four years of war had been hard on everyone in the South, and nature hadn't been kind, either, as if the whole earth groaned at the notion of brothers turning against each other. Many areas that escaped the armies' destruction had suffered drought, resulting in slim crops. The South desperately needed a good harvest this year.

Rupert's memories of military service sickened him. Conflict was contrary to his nature, and he'd planned to stay home while Paul represented the family in the Confederacy. Simon had gone north years earlier and ended up joining the Union forces. When the conscription started, both Rupert and Troy tried to avoid it. Only Troy had succeeded until the Federals caught him and sent him to Camp Chase. Rupert never knew whether some neighbor had tipped off the army to his location, but the Confederacy was desperate for men. He'd survived nearly a year of war before being captured, then exchanged, and then wounded. Some would call him a deserter, but the South was already defeated. When he left the hospital tent, he left the war.

Rummaging through the books on the shelf, he found an atlas with a map of the South. Hannah was right—they needed to arrange these books by subject so it wouldn't be so hard to find what he wanted. He found the town of Wedowee and the Tallapoosa River, the closest landmarks on the Alabama side. He made a pencil mark where he thought the farm would be in relation to those. Then he searched on the Georgia side for Coweta County and measured against the legend. Depending on where Whitfield Hall might be, he estimated the distance somewhere between forty and sixty-five miles.

Would Hannah be able to guide them back to her farm? Pa might have some advice. Rupert would speak to both of them during the meal.

A knock at the office door interrupted his thoughts. "Excuse me, Mistah Rupert. I heard you wanted to see me."

"Malachi, come in. Take a seat, and tell me what you found when you scouted the farm."

The lanky black man eased into the chair opposite Rupert's.

"Well, suh, if we gonna plant same as last year, we be needin' more seed and more folks to work it."

"That's what I thought." Rupert's chair squeaked as he leaned back. Not wanting a repeat of yesterday's embarrassing spill, he straightened it. "I have an offer for a couple acres at the western end. We can use the money from the sale to purchase seed if it's available. How about if we let two more acres rest this year? You think we can work the rest with two more workers?"

Malachi rubbed his bearded chin as he considered. "Yassuh, I reckon we can, long as the Lord gives us good weather."

"You might've heard we have an unexpected visitor, someone who hoped to get Uncle Henry to help her with her home over in Georgia. I may have to take his place and leave for a while, so I'd like to get an early start on our work."

Malachi's eyes widened. "'Zactly what you thinkin'?"

Rupert passed a hand over his jaw. "We'll see if we can borrow plows and mules or horses from our neighbors to turn up the soil and plant our first crops this week. I know..." When Malachi shook his head in protest, Rupert raised his hands. "We risk a late frost spoilin' things, but it's a risk I'm willin' to take. If we can get crops in at least a quarter of the land, it will take a burden off both our shoulders."

On a clean sheet of paper, Rupert drew lines to represent the areas of the farm as they discussed which crops to plant. He used pictures to represent the areas for cotton and different edible plants since Malachi still struggled with written words. What he lacked in education, though, was offset by the man's wisdom.

"All right, then." With his hand outstretched, Rupert stood, signaling an end to the meeting. "I've asked Pa to let us borrow his plow and animals for a few days. If we can work out loans from Mr. Callahan and Mr. Varner, maybe we can start day after tomorrow. Ask around and try to find two more workers and explain what we have. Byron might know of new folks in the area. When I leave, you'll be in charge, and I trust you to finish workin' the land as you think best."

A hint of tears shone in Malachi's eyes as he gripped Rupert's hand. "I 'preciate it a heap, Mistah Rupert. I won't let you down."

"I know you won't, Malachi. Henry trusted you, and so do I. And tell Levi he can help as long as he obeys you. I don't want your grandson tryin' to do too much and gettin' hurt. Now, let's go find something to eat."

He rose to follow Malachi and stepped past the shaft of light from the window. Dust particles danced in the beam that fractured as it hit the desk, tinting the neat stacks of paper in gold. Rupert grimaced and shook his head. Hannah's dusting would have to be done all over again.

A vision of her in this room yesterday lit his imagination. If they married, he'd have to guard his heart, for both their sakes. To manage that, he'd need to keep his distance as much as possible. In fact, maybe he should take a quick walk now to get his mind on something besides Hannah Whitfield.

~

While Millie fed and cared for the baby, Hannah kept Amy occupied with her doll to give Miss Connie time to pen a letter to her son and daughter-in-law in North Georgia. Mr. John had promised to take her letter and Hannah's letter when he and Mrs. Thurman left for Jacksonville the next day.

When Miss Connie set her missive aside, Hannah took advantage of the moment. "I'm sorry if my presence is keeping you from returning to your own home."

"My dear Hannah, I'm more than happy to be here. And I think Millie would rather stay here also. Although she gets along well with Jane and Paul, having other children around the baby can cause some issues. Of course, I'd much rather have her stay here, only a dozen miles from my house, instead of a full day's ride to their place in Georgia."

Hannah sighed. "Thank you. That does relieve my mind."

The older woman studied her. "You miss your family, don't you?"

"Yes, and I worry about how they're getting along. Caleb wasn't happy to see me leave, and Aunt Ginny has her hands full caring for Uncle Liam." Hannah twisted the ties hanging from her waistband. Her nervous movement had loosened the bow she'd fashioned this morning. She smoothed the fabric and retied the bow. "I'd hoped to be on my way back by the end of the week."

"Well, from what John told me, Rupert is already setting things in motion for work to be done here while he's gone." Miss Connie stuffed the letter in an envelope and sealed it. "Malachi will be in charge of any workers they hire, and John will be available if he should need any help or advice."

"So he's really going along with Mr. Henry's suggestion?"

"I'll tell you this about Rupert. He considers decisions carefully and doesn't broadcast his reasons until he's made a choice. But once he's set a course, he sticks with it. You can rest assured, he will do everything within his power to set things right for your family."

With a shaky laugh, Hannah asked, "Even if it means marrying someone he hardly knows?"

Miss Connie's smile added weight to her answer. "Even then." She shifted her attention to Amy as the child toddled to her chair. "What do you want, sweet girl? Should I take your doll?"

Amy patted the doll. "Hannah."

"Yes, Hannah helped you fix your doll," her grandmother said.

The child shook her head. She pointed to Hannah, then patted the doll again. "Dolly Hannah."

Miss Connie grinned and met Hannah's gaze. "I think she's named her doll after you."

Tears sprang to Hannah's eyes at the sweet gesture. "Why, thank you, Amy. I'm honored to share my name with your doll."

"I suppose that's only right," Millie said from the parlor threshold, "seeing as you're likely to be sharing our family name soon."

When Hannah started to protest, Millie laughed. "Hey, I didn't come to start a debate, but we can discuss it over the midday meal."

"Mama!" With arms lifted, Amy ran to Millie, and Millie squatted to give her a hug. "Mama can't pick you up, sweetie. The doctor said I have to wait another week before I lift anything heavy. Go with Granma."

The child pouted and rubbed a fist against her eye.

On impulse, Hannah stepped forward. "How about I carry you, Amy?" Gratified to see the child's tears stop, Hannah bent to pick her up. "Maybe Dolly Hannah will take a nap while we go eat. Is that good?"

"Yes. Hannah sleep." Amy handed the doll to Millie, who tucked it into the corner of the nearest chair.

Miss Connie snickered as she came beside them. "Well done, Hannah. You've won over the most important person in the family."

Hannah chuckled. "Not Rupert, then?"

On her other side, Millie agreed. "If you've won Amy, you've won Rupert."

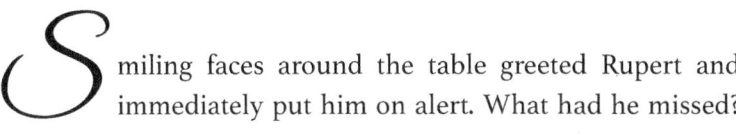

Smiling faces around the table greeted Rupert and immediately put him on alert. What had he missed?

If the mirror in his room showed a true reflection, his face was clean, and he'd tamed his hair, despite its tendency to curl. He'd even remembered to use his tooth powder this morning. Should he have splashed on some of the smell-good Troy had given him for Christmas?

"For someone who's known to be the fastest runner in the county," Pa said, "you keep bein' the last one to the table nowadays."

Ma tittered.

Rupert flinched. He'd never known Ma to titter.

Fighting to squelch the warmth creeping up his neck, he slipped into the seat next to Hannah. "Just tryin' to get everything laid out for Malachi before I leave." Next to him, Hannah avoided his gaze, but her cheek wore a rosy glow above the curve of her mouth. He whipped his head forward as Pa prayed over the food.

When the bowls came around, Rupert took a spoonful of each offering without paying attention to what it was. Intensely aware of the woman beside him, he concentrated on how to bring up the subject of their trip. He scooped up the food next to his fork and lifted it to his mouth. The smell repelled him.

"Rutabagas?" He zeroed in on Ma's face.

Her wide eyes and hand covering her mouth told him she'd expected him to bypass that bowl. "Jewel found them in the cellar behind a crock of honey. She thought they'd be a treat."

After years of lean provisions and eating whatever was available, Rupert understood his parents' long-standing edict to finish everything on his plate. He hesitated, glanced around the table to find the others watching him, and put the fork in his mouth. At least the rutabagas were soft, so he didn't have to chew much before he forced himself to swallow. A bite of cornbread helped to cover the lingering taste.

Pa's cough sounded suspiciously like a chuckle. He pointed

his spoon at Rupert. "I reckon you'll be ready to leave the day after I get back from Jacksonville?"

"Yes, sir. Have you ever been to that part of Georgia? I'm not too clear on the best route or how long it might take to get there."

Pa's gaze shifted to Hannah. "Miss Whitfield should be able to help with directions."

"Well, as to that, Mr. McNeil—"

"She traveled with a family who made several side trips before they reached Alabama," Rupert said. Without forethought, he had covered her hand with his. The warmth radiated through his arm, and a glance revealed her watching him, her brow furrowed.

He removed his hand and turned back to Pa. "I found a map in the office. Perhaps we can study it together and plot a likely route. If Millie was up to travelin', she might could help us."

"Oh, no." Millie put up her hands in protest. "Troy says I have no sense of direction, so don't count on me."

"John could tell you how to get to Millie's house, but that might not help." Ma touched a napkin to her lips and studied him. "Did you see Georgia when you were in the army?"

Rupert shook his head. "They kept us in Virginia. Probably figured we'd quit if we got too close to home."

With a touch to his arm, Hannah turned her pale face his way. "You fought for the Confederate States?"

He scowled. "Not by choice, but yeah. I was conscripted and attached to the Fourteenth Alabama Infantry."

Hannah removed her hand and bit her lower lip. Why did his answer bother her?

When she didn't comment, he probed. "Is something the matter?"

"I'm afraid your service in the CSA might pose a problem." Her gaze circled the table and came back to Rupert. "Not that it matters to me, but one reason Aunt Ginny chose Henry McNeil was his stand against secession and the war. She won't be pleased."

Was she afraid her aunt would spurn his help or forbid them to marry? If they were in such dire straits, he couldn't imagine that would happen. Besides, they'd already be married when they reached Whitfield Hall.

"We'll explain the situation when we get there. Surely, she's reasonable enough not to hold it against me."

"Maybe. But that's not the only thing. We need someone who didn't have a connection to the Confederacy to save Whitfield Hall." She lifted her watery green eyes to his and swallowed. "Because both my brother and father died wearing Roswell gray and defying the Union to their last breaths."

Rupert stared at her, unable to form a response. So all of this planning had been for naught? He couldn't help her?

CHAPTER 10

*H*ow could she have failed to ask about Rupert's activities during the war? According to Aunt Ginny, Henry McNeil's nephews were Union supporters. Had Mrs. June's letters said as much, or did Aunt Ginny assume it was so? Regardless of the cause, all was lost. A whole week gone, including traveling to get here, and now she'd have to go home and figure out what to do next.

Rupert shifted in his seat. Was he relieved to be free of her?

His brow puckered over those blue eyes as he faced her. "I believe we'll be all right if everyone assumes I'm my uncle Henry."

Jerked out of her misery, Hannah opened her mouth to remind him about Aunt Ginny, but he continued speaking. "Only your aunt would know the truth, right?"

She nodded. "With Papa and Mama gone, no one else ever met him. Except Uncle Liam, and he's unable to leave the house."

"Now, Rupert." Mr. John set his fork down. "You don't want to compound the situation by lying." His warning wasn't harsh, but placating, as if he didn't want to mention it.

Rupert straightened. "I won't be lying, Pa. All I have to do is answer to my first name and sign it like Henry always signed his—Henry R. McNeil."

In a voice soft as a sigh, Miss Connie said, "John."

He looked her way, and some private message seemed to pass between them, creating a curl of longing in Hannah. Would she ever enjoy such a relationship? Someone who knew her so well that they could communicate without words? Reality intruded. If their plan succeeded, she'd spend the rest of her life with the man sitting beside her. There'd be no finding another in the murky future.

What about Rupert? Did he yearn for another girl somewhere? Would he be giving up his hopes and dreams to come to her aid? Hannah cast a sideways look at him as she sipped her tea. Nothing indicated he held back. Perhaps it was as Miss Connie said—when he set his mind on a course, he'd see it through.

At last, Mr. John gave a curt nod, and Rupert heaved a hearty sigh. He scooped up more rutabagas from his plate. "Then, soon as everyone's done eatin', we'll take a gander at the map." He peered at Hannah. "I guess you'll be ready to leave early the day after Pa returns?"

Warmed by his gentle persistence, Hannah swallowed the lump in her throat. "Of course. If you're sure you want to go through with this."

But his gaze had gone to the window, and his brow wrinkled. "It might be a good idea to consult with Bryon before we leave. And I could send a wire to Simon if we need advice on the law in Georgia."

Hannah didn't follow his rambling. "Simon?"

Rupert grinned. "Simon is my brother who went north and fought on the Union side. Before that, he studied law. When the war ended, he married a girl up in North Georgia, where they have a farm, but he also has a law office."

Clued by the mention of North Georgia, Hannah glanced at Miss Connie. "That's the one you wrote the letter to?"

"Yes." Miss Connie picked up her teacup and tilted her head toward Rupert. "You could write him tonight and let John post it with mine. A lot more can be said in a letter than a wire."

"Good idea, Ma. And I'll ride over to visit Bryon after we finish dealing with Wilma tomorrow."

Mr. John groaned. "Just be glad you're not the one ridin' with her all day."

A big grin spread across Rupert's face. "Oh, I am, Pa. And let me say thank you for not naming me after you. I wouldn't want to have to deal with her in your place in the future."

"No, but when you sell her that land, she's gonna be your neighbor for at least part of the year," Mr. John folded his napkin. "You ought to consider puttin' up a fence to mark the boundary."

"I might do that." Rupert polished off the last of his cornbread. "What Wilma needs is a husband to keep her at home. At least, that's what *I* need for her, so she won't be comin' over here all the time, talkin' my ear off."

Hannah joined in the laughter, but his comment pricked her conscience. In her naivete, she'd assumed her husband— Henry or Rupert—would live at Whitfield Hall. Aunt Ginny had talked as if the matter were settled. But Rupert clearly planned to keep his inheritance here in Alabama. How would he ever manage two properties so many miles apart?

~

*W*ith Pa on one side and Hannah on the other, Rupert spread the map on the desk. "There's the Tallapoosa, so I figure my farm is about here." He pointed to the place he'd marked earlier, then slid his finger to the right and circled the faint lines on the map. "Here's Coweta County."

Turning his head brought his nose close to Hannah's, and he swung back to the front. "Where would you say Whitfield Hall is? Can you guess from its proximity to these towns?"

Hannah brushed his hand as she pointed. "About here."

Rupert pushed the pencil beneath her finger to mark the spot, trying to ignore the warmth spreading up his arm from the contact. A delicate scent teased his nose, enticing him to press closer, but Pa's voice urged him back.

"If you take the road to Franklin and continue northeast, that should put you in the vicinity. Hopefully, Miss Whitfield will recognize some landmarks on the way. If not, you should be able to ask folks who live in the area." Pa straightened. "I'd offer to go with you, but I need to stay here with the women till Troy returns."

"That's all right, Pa. We'll figure out how to get there. If we can make it to Franklin the first day, we can find a place to stay for the night." He cut his eyes to Hannah, and she nodded.

"To keep everything as it ought to be"—Pa pursed his lips as he considered both Hannah and Rupert—"do you want me to ask if Brother Trotter can come over tomorrow evening?"

"Brother Trotter? Oh." Rupert clamped his mouth shut and shot a glance at the woman beside him. In all his thinking and planning, the need for a preacher never crossed his mind. "Uh, yeah, if he can come. But you're a deacon. Couldn't you do it?"

Pa shook his head. "We need to do this right. With you two traveling together without a chaperone, there must be no question of things bein' done properly."

As Pa headed for the door, Rupert fell in line behind him, but Hannah tugged at his arm.

"Could you wait a minute? I, um, need to ask you something."

"Sure." A tingle of apprehension shot through his chest. He turned and gave her his full attention. "Is there a problem?"

A springy curl bounced at her temple when she shook her head. "No. At least, I don't believe so." She lowered her gaze to her fingers, which twisted in the bow at her waist. "I just wanted to ask...to say I know my coming here wasn't expected, and I appreciate y'all taking me right in and helping." Her voice went raspy, and she stopped to clear it. "But I should've asked.... Is there someone you'd planned to court or maybe were already courting—"

"No." He laid a hand on her shoulder, now accustomed to the sensation touching her produced. Her concern roused his protectiveness. "There's no one. You can stop worryin' about that right now."

Would she understand if he told her he'd determined never to marry? And yet, he'd abandoned that plan to implement his uncle's final proposal. Would she still think he sacrificed his own wishes to assist her? Women seemed to think marriage was the whole purpose of life—and maybe it was for them. For him, marriage represented the risk of losing someone close to him again, but he wouldn't have to worry about that if his was nothing more than a marriage of convenience. And now his family could stop trying to push women his way. All things considered, it might work out best for everyone.

But maybe Hannah was having second thoughts now that things were moving forward. She'd come here willingly enough, hadn't she? Or did her aunt hold some power over her?

"What about you? Is there someone you'd hoped to marry? Someone your aunt insisted you shouldn't accept?"

Her wide-eyed surprise gave him the answer before she spoke. "The only one I ever would have considered was killed early in the war, and it wasn't as if we had an understanding."

She stepped away, and his hand dropped to his side. "But do you remember what Aunt Ginny's letter said about the carpet-bagger? He's been trying to court me as a means of getting his hands on Whitfield Hall. Marrying me would be the easiest way, but he has friends in the local government who might help him find a way to take it if I don't secure it soon."

She sought Rupert's gaze again. "So you understand why I had to come here—to protect my brother's legacy and mine. I can't let my home go to that man."

~

The rain Pa predicted had blown in and out within minutes, leaving the sweet smell of spring and puddles in some low-lying places. When the sun came out of hiding to warm the air, Rupert couldn't ignore his restlessness. He needed to be outside. Besides, he had equipment loans to arrange. It was too muddy to walk the fields or go for a run, but he could ride.

He strode into the parlor, where the women had gathered with their needlework. "Ma, I'm going to ride over to speak to Mr. Callahan, then into town to see Byron, so I'll take those letters to the mercantile for you."

Three pairs of eyes focused on him.

He resisted the urge to squirm as he asked the obligatory question. "Would anyone want to go along? If so, I'll hitch up the carriage or buckboard."

Ma laid aside her knitting and picked up the letters. "I've no reason to go this late in the day, not enough time to do any real shopping. What about you, Millie? Hannah?"

Millie peered at the watch on her bodice. "I'd love to go, but Little John will be awake soon. Hannah, do you need anything?"

With the slightest of smiles, Hannah regarded him with raised eyebrows as he fingered his hat. Did she detect his impatience to get away?

"I have everything I need for now, thank you. Enjoy your outing."

Ma brought the letters to him and dusted some invisible substance from his shoulder. "You should ask if Jewel needs anything. And why don't you invite Byron for supper? That way, you won't have to rush your discussion."

"Good suggestion, Ma. I'll check with Jewel, then be on my way."

Armed with Jewel's list, he left by way of the back door.

The meeting with Mr. Callahan went as well as he expected and provided the added bonus of earning his neighbor's goodwill for considering whether he had any objections to the proposed sale. They arranged for the use of Mr. Callahan's plow and mule in exchange for Jewel's help with a special celebration meal in June. He made similar arrangements with the Varner family.

Twilight was still a couple of hours away, so he should have plenty of time to speak with Byron in private. He didn't push the mare but let her set the pace while he enjoyed the countryside, with its new leaves sparkling in the afternoon sun. A few dogwoods put out their snowy blooms, and azalea bushes blossomed in varied hues of pink along the road. Maybe winter was truly gone and more plants would soon join the parade of green. He always looked forward to the honeysuckle for its perfume and delicate flowers.

When he passed the turnoff for the road to Pa's farm, Rupert's thoughts went to his oldest brother. If Paul had been present when Hannah arrived, things might have gone differently, and not in a good way. Though Paul and Simon had mended their relationship during the family gathering last year, Paul still held onto some bitterness over the war. That was understandable since he'd lost part of a leg fighting for the Confederacy, but it colored his perspective on changes happening in the South, so the family never knew how he'd react to new developments.

The mare picked up speed as they neared town as if she knew their destination was close. Rupert tied her in front of the mercantile and dropped off Jewel's list with the shopkeeper.

"Here's some letters to go out too. How long before they'll get picked up?"

The shopkeeper checked the calendar. "That'll be tomorrow. Say, I was mighty sad to hear about Mr. Henry's passin'. I reckon you'll be the one comin' to town for supplies now, huh?"

"Either me or Malachi. I trust you'll treat him the same as you would me." If the former slave suffered any ill treatment when Rupert wasn't around, he'd hear about it.

Joshua blinked. "For sure. I know Henry always said the same."

"Good. I'll be back in half an hour to get our order and settle the bill." He left and crossed the street. Situated between Duffy's boardinghouse and the bakery, Byron's office doubled as the school for former slaves, supported by the Freedmen's Bureau with a proper classroom in the more spacious back area.

Rupert opened the door to find the front office empty. "Byron? You around?"

From the back room, the familiar voice called, "Be right with you."

Unable to sit still with thoughts of all that had happened in the last few days crowding his mind, Rupert roamed the space. Stacks of papers near the lamp and an open book with a pencil resting in the seam littered the desk. The bookcase held a limp plant, a dozen books, and a second lamp. Rupert wandered to the wall and peered at the framed certificate that proclaimed Byron Harris had completed his studies of United States law at the University of Pennsylvania in 1857.

Remembering how Byron had appeared at their doorstep

last year made Rupert smile. Millie had wanted to send the cocky Union corporal away, but he'd come to help Troy with setting up the Freedmen's Bureau office. Before long, Byron had become like family.

Byron dusted his vest as he entered the front room. "What can I do for you?"

With a gesture toward Byron's coatless attire, he said, "Have I interrupted your work?"

"Just putting out some books for the next class tomorrow. I'll be glad when your ma gets back to teaching it. Having her here in the weeks before Henry died spoiled me."

"She enjoys it, and before I forget, she said to invite you to supper tonight. Are you free to join us?"

"I'm always free to eat Jewel's cooking." He propped a hip against the corner of the desk. "Now, what brings you to town? Henry's will was the most straightforward one I've ever seen, so I doubt there's a problem there."

Mention of the will gave Rupert pause. Would Wilma think about having their agreement drawn up? Maybe she planned to bring a lawyer from Jacksonville. "It happens that Wilma, his younger daughter, wants to buy a couple of acres from me. I hope you'll be able to handle the paperwork for the agreement."

"I'll be glad to. Is she the wealthy widow?"

"Yep." Rupert rolled his eyes. "I reckon you met her at the funeral."

"Your pa introduced us, but she barely acknowledged me. Guess I didn't strike her as important enough for her attention."

"Wilma doesn't bother with anyone she can't manipulate. She must have figured you're too smart for that, even though you're near her age and might be considered a good catch." He poked Byron's arm in a playful punch. "I have another matter I'd like to discuss with you, too, but we can talk on the way to the farm if you can leave in the next ten minutes or so."

"Sure. I'll just put a note on the door in case anyone needs to find me."

"Meet me in front of the mercantile, then." Rupert opened the door and pointed to the bookcase as Byron took his coat from the chair. "And water that plant before it withers away, or Ma will have a fit when she comes back to the school."

CHAPTER 11

*A*lthough Hannah had volunteered to help in the kitchen, Jewel soon evicted her and Miss Connie, assuring them having an additional visitor presented no problem. They joined the rest of the family in the parlor. Hannah helped Miss Connie sort her sewing basket while Mr. John read pieces from the newspaper aloud.

Later, at the sound of hoof beats in the yard, Mr. John rose to peek out the window. "There they are. I'll let Jewel know she can put the food on the table while Levi and I help with the horses."

While Hannah tied off the yarn she'd been winding, Millie laid the baby in the cradle at her feet and stretched her back. "I believe he's already up to ten pounds." She chuckled. "Amy, let's go wash up before we eat."

As Miss Connie, Millie, and Amy headed to their rooms, Hannah stayed to watch over the sleeping infant. Gazing at the tiny bundle evoked memories of home. Her mother had finally produced a son with her third full-term pregnancy, and several of Papa's friends had come to celebrate with him after Colin's christening.

"Glad you finally got the boy you been wantin', Whitfield." One inebriated man slapped her father on the back. "Too bad the previous ones were all girls."

A third man had chimed in. "Oh, I don't know, Senator. Girls are plenty useful at times, just not as daughters."

At that, all the men roared with laughter, and Hannah slinked away in tears. Since then, she'd tried her best to prove her worth to Papa, but he rarely acknowledged her efforts, and he'd certainly never praised her.

The baby snuffled in his sleep, and Hannah set the cradle to a soothing sway as she banished the hurtful memories and hummed an old lullaby. Her song faded at the sound of stamping boots and men's voices in the hallway. Then Miss Connie's warm welcome greeted their visitor and ushered him to the parlor door.

"Let me introduce you to Miss Whitfield. I believe Rupert might have mentioned her to you. Byron Harris, Miss Hannah Whitfield. Hannah, Byron is our resident lawyer and substitute teacher when I can't fulfill my duties."

The man doffed his hat and gave her a slight bow. His polite smile softened the sharp angles of his jaw and warmed his hazel eyes. The noticeable mole near his left eyebrow didn't detract from his pleasing appearance. Something about him tugged at her memory, but she knew no one by that name. No sign of recognition sparked in his eyes, so maybe he merely resembled someone she'd met before.

By habit, she rose and offered a quick curtsy with her "pleased to meet you," then searched for Rupert beyond the visitor. He stood beside his pa as they waited for the ladies to lead the way to the dining room. Hannah drifted his way while the others exchanged pleasantries.

Millie approached Mr. Harris, leading Amy by the hand. "Byron, good to see you again. I don't suppose you've heard anything from Troy?"

"No ma'am, but he's only been gone a day."

With a playful swat, she grinned. "Then I suppose you'll have to escort me and Amy to supper."

"I'll be happy to do so." He bent to pick up the little girl, who went willingly. He then offered his arm to Millie.

Mr. John took his wife's hand and followed them, leaving Hannah and Rupert to bring up the rear.

Surprised at Millie's behavior, Hannah said, "They must have known each other for a long time." 'Twas the only excuse she could fathom for such familiarity.

Rupert followed them with his gaze. "They have an interesting history. You should get Millie to tell you the story." He placed her hand on his arm and grinned. "Shall we?"

At the touch of his hand, her thoughts veered away from Millie and Mr. Harris. His smile set her insides to fluttering. In days to come, would people make similar comments about her relationship with Rupert? They'd certainly had an interesting beginning. Would the future bring even more surprises?

∼

*A*s the meal progressed, Rupert's mood went from confused to downright irritated. He couldn't credit it, but Byron was flirting with Hannah as surely as he sat there. Why would he do that?

Rupert had expected the two of them to be curious about each other, especially after he'd told Byron about Hannah's unusual situation and how she'd become part of Rupert's future. A mild interest would be normal, but Byron showed signs of more than a casual curiosity, his gaze going to her often, even when someone else was speaking.

And now Hannah knew Byron was a former Union officer. Rupert scoffed. Byron's political standing should be plain to anyone who knew he worked for the Freedmen's Bureau.

Because of Troy, all the McNeils had accepted Byron and developed a mutual friendship—so much so that Rupert never expected Byron would try to move in on his woman.

His woman?

Where had that come from? Hannah didn't belong to him, at least not yet.

Once Hannah had repeated the reason for appealing to the McNeils for help, she directed a question to Byron. "I suppose you visited many places during your time in the army, Mr. Harris. Did you stay primarily in Virginia?"

"My company was in West Virginia, but mostly we stayed in Tennessee, Alabama, and Georgia."

"Were you part of the troops who followed Sherman across Georgia?" Her tone might've warned Byron to tread carefully, had he known her better. But Hannah sweetened it with a polite smile.

Some cruel part of Rupert was glad to watch Byron squirm. Why would that tickle him? He couldn't be jealous of Hannah's attention to Byron, could he?

Byron stirred a dollop of honey into his tea, taking his time to answer. "Only partly. Our company's orders were to control the river, destroy the mills, and send the workers to Marietta." He sent a sidelong glance at Millie. "That's where I met Millie's fist."

Familiar with the story, Rupert and his family laughed.

Hannah gaped. "I beg your pardon?"

Millie shook her head. "He wasn't exactly behavin' like a gentleman, and I'd already been attacked once a few months before. So I punched him in the nose. Turns out he was trying to protect me from his licentious companions."

With a dramatic sigh, Byron went on. "After that, we tore up the railroads east of Atlanta, then we went back close to the Alabama line while General Sherman continued to the Carolinas."

Hannah poked at her potatoes. "What about last spring? We had a small unit come to our property in Coweta County and threaten to burn us out. Thankfully, when the leader saw it was just the four of us left—my aunt and uncle, Caleb and me—he ordered the soldiers to leave us in peace."

In the momentary silence, Rupert held his breath. Hannah's gaze held steady across the table.

Byron's head tilted as if daring her to accuse him—or did he search her face, looking for recognition? "That was your place?"

Her nod was so slight that Rupert would've missed it if he hadn't been sitting beside her. In a wavering voice, she explained. "The first arrivals had already gunned down Papa after he stormed at 'em like a crazy man. We'd just buried Colin the week before, and Papa...."

Rupert covered her hand with his. She glanced at it, then raised her eyes with a nod to Byron. "You were one of the men who stayed behind to bury him. For that, I thank you."

When she flexed her hand under Rupert's, he loosened his hold, but she threaded her fingers through his and squeezed. His heart echoed the action, then picked up speed.

Ma spoke gently, tears in her eyes. "May I add my own appreciation, Byron, for your kindness to a family who had suffered so much? The war tore apart families as well as our nation. I pray we never witness such destruction again. For all the heartache suffered these recent years, I am unspeakably grateful for all my family and for each of you. Praise God for peace in the land again."

"Amen," Pa said, and a chorus of agreements followed.

Amy added her enthusiastic endorsement, and Rupert's breath expelled in a relieved chuckle. For a moment, he'd feared Hannah might lash out at Byron for his part in the war. To see a family member die in such a way... Rupert could only imagine the grief.

Hannah flashed him a shaky smile as she released his hand and picked up her teacup.

"Tell me how things are at school, Byron." Ma eased the conversation back to safer topics.

Keenly aware of the woman beside him, Rupert struggled to follow each comment and act unconcerned.

Hannah seemed to focus her attention on Byron as he shared stories from the classroom. Her sincere appreciation for his thoughtfulness a year before was understandable. Such gratitude could grow into a deeper emotion.

Rupert gulped his water.

Did she think Bryon would be a better person to represent her interests in Georgia?

The truth was, he might be. And where would that leave Rupert? As much as he'd resisted the pressure to pursue marriage, he suddenly found himself looking forward to a future with Hannah, despite the challenges it brought. Would he end up single, after all?

~

*R*eliving the events of that horrible day had drained Hannah's strength, but Rupert's touch fortified her. At last, she'd had the opportunity to thank one of those men for his thoughtfulness, for saving her and Aunt Ginny from the painful chore of burying another family member.

Afraid but unable to tear herself away as the soldiers dug the grave, she'd sat nearby and tried to memorize their faces. When one discarded his coat, Byron had ordered him to don it again, jolting Hannah to the impropriety of her presence, even though she watched from a distance.

To allow the men to be more comfortable in their task, she'd left, returning an hour later to find the soldiers gone and a crude cross at the head of the fresh mound. She'd placed a bundle of wildflowers on each grave, then refused to visit the cemetery again. The decision had not relieved the pain.

After supper, Mr. John led the group into the hallway, but Rupert waited at Hannah's side. "Do you feel like staying up and visiting, or would you like to rest a while?"

His thoughtfulness stirred her close to tears. How had this man remained single? Maybe no marriageable women lived in the area. With so few men left in the South, women her age had little prospect for marriage. That was one reason she'd not balked at the idea of marrying an older man. Having acted as mother to her younger siblings—burying several of them—she harbored no idealistic dreams about her own mate and children. It would be enough to dedicate herself to Caleb, who would still need her for years, and to preserving their home.

How ironic a man her own age had agreed to wed her. Mama always said you could tell a lot about a man by the way he interacted with his parents and with children. If such actions predicted how he would treat a wife and children of his own, then Hannah could trust Rupert to do right by her.

CHAPTER 12

*A*fter joining his family in the parlor, Rupert and Hannah took the last remaining seats on the settee. Without thinking, he rested his arm on the back of the padded upholstery behind her. He caught Ma's gaze as he realized how close he and Hannah sat. He balled his fist to avoid touching her shoulder.

The conversation ranged from farming topics to students at the freedmen's school and new stores in town. It eventually circled back to Hannah's reason for visiting.

Pa cleared his throat. "It seems to me that Byron might be able to give you decent directions to Whitfield Hall, seein' as he's been there before. What d'you think?"

Rupert turned to Byron. "Do you think you could? I have a map of those parts in my office."

Byron leaned forward and propped one foot on the other knee. "I believe so. I'll take a look at it before I leave." He patted the settee's scrolled arm next to Hannah. "Too bad I can't accompany you myself. I'm sure I'd recognize the house."

Rupert frowned. Was the man trying to finagle an invitation to join them?

Hannah didn't respond to Byron's suggestive smile. She tugged a small cushion from beneath her arm and held it in her lap. "Mr. Harris, are you familiar with a Captain Oscar Prescott? I don't think he's with the Freedmen's Bureau, but he has friends in the new county government."

Byron tapped his chin as he pondered. "I don't recall anyone by that name. I assume he was a Union officer?"

"Yes." Hannah glanced up once, then kept her gaze on the pillow as she plucked at its decorative threads. "From what I hear, he's from one of the big cities up north. During the war, I reckon he decided he liked Georgia's climate better."

"I gather this is the man Rupert mentioned." He reached forward and flicked a tassel on the pillow. He grinned when that caught her attention. "The one who's been trying to persuade you to marry him and take over your home? Not that I can fault his taste. I prefer the gracious women of the South myself."

Rupert squeezed his fists. A quick look at Millie and his parents revealed varying degrees of surprise. Was Byron trying to turn Hannah's head?

Hannah mirrored Rupert's actions, her eyes wide. "That's the one." She continued in a shaky voice. "I've managed to put him off, but the last time he visited, I could tell his patience was wearing thin. He threatened to get our property declared insolvent or abandoned if I didn't agree to wed him."

"I hope you won't judge all Union men by that bad example." He leaned back in his chair. "As much as it pained me to see the destruction heaped on the South, I learned that the women here are fierce and resourceful, ready to fight in their own way for their homes."

Millie huffed as she bounced the whimpering baby in her arms. "I just can't understand a man havin' that kind of greed. To think someone would turn out an old couple and a child who had nothing to do with the choices of other family members."

"We're not gonna let that happen." Rupert hadn't meant his words to come out so low or angry, but they sure reflected how he felt. "Soon as Hannah and I get there, we'll go straight to the courthouse and settle the matter."

"Speaking of going, I reckon I ought to get on home myself, soon as I consult that map of yours, Rupert." Byron stood, and Rupert did the same, more than ready to bid his friend good-night. "Thank you for the fine supper, Miss Connie, and tell Jewel she outdid herself."

With Amy asleep on his shoulder, Pa rose and extended one hand to Byron. "Glad you could join us. I'll put this little one to bed for you, Millie."

Rupert followed Pa into the hallway and waited for Byron, who bowed to Ma and then to Millie. "Good night, ladies." He moved to stand in front of Hannah, blocking Rupert's view. "Nice to meet you properly this time, Miss Whitfield. I wish you well on your journey."

Corralling his irritation, Rupert led the way to the office and spread out the map. After a moment's perusal, Byron pointed to the mark Rupert had made earlier, the spot Hannah had indicated for Whitfield Hall. "I think it's a little bit west of here, so you should make it in a couple of days without any trouble."

"Good to know." Rupert clapped Byron's shoulder. "I'm grateful for your help, and I count you a friend." He might've squeezed a little too hard when he added, "But since Hannah and I will be married soon, you can leave off the flirting."

Byron chuckled and slapped him on the back. "Just trying to make sure she'll stick with you after the crisis is over. I wouldn't want to have you jilted by a heartless woman. My experiences during the war taught me that not all women are as steadfast as those we grew up with." Byron headed out but turned at the front door. "We'll need to record the dimensions of the land you're selling and file them for a new deed. Do you want me to meet you back here in the morning, to get those specifics?"

"That'd be great. Come early enough, and you can join us for breakfast." Now that Rupert knew Byron wasn't angling for his girl, and she didn't respond to his attempts to charm her, Byron could eat all the flapjacks he wanted.

∼

On her third morning at the McNeil farm, Hannah woke with a new perspective. Soon, she'd be heading home as a married woman, and she ought to start acting the part.

If she had to marry someone—and circumstances had made it clear she did—then Hannah wouldn't fuss that it turned out to be Rupert McNeil. Knowing they shared the same values made it easier. He hadn't wanted to raise a weapon against his fellow man, but he'd not backed down from the fight to defend the South against invasion. He treated the former slaves who labored for him with respect and friendship, so she didn't fear that he would mistreat her family's workers.

All things considered, she doubted she could find anyone better suited than Rupert. The Bible made it clear wives ought to help their husbands, so she vowed to do her best to alleviate his distress when Wilma Thurman came to finalize her purchase.

As Hannah left her room, someone knocked on the front door. That would be his cousin and, with no one else close by, Hannah's chance to assist. With a practiced smile, she opened the door, then stepped back in surprise. "Mr. Harris. Good morning. Is Miss Connie expecting you?"

The gentleman doffed his hat and offered a slight smile. His eyes darted away from her as if unsure of his welcome. "Good morning, Miss Whitfield. Rupert promised me breakfast before we draw up the purchase agreement for the land he's going to sell."

With no trace of the playful suggestions from last evening, his manner was reserved. Perhaps Rupert had advised him to temper his solicitousness. Hannah opened the door wider.

"Oh, well, come in. I was on my way to the dining room myself."

He entered as Rupert came down the hallway. "Ah, Byron, you're right on time. Come in." His long strides covered the distance between them in seconds.

Hannah shut the door, turned, and collided with Rupert's chest. Her hands created a barrier between them, but he grasped them and drew her gaze upward.

"Good morning, Hannah. I trust you slept well?"

Though a common question, his words wrapped around her like an intimate embrace. His eyes darkened to indigo as they roamed her face. A shiver trickled down her spine when they reached her lips and one side of his mouth quirked in a rakish smile.

Before she could utter an answer, Mr. Harris cleared his throat. "Um, I'll just wander on back to the dining area...." He continued down the hallway and left them to follow.

Heat raced up Hannah's face. She tugged her hands from Rupert's. What must the man think of them?

"We're coming." With a chuckle, Rupert turned her in the right direction and kept one hand at her back.

"Why'd you do that?" she asked in a breathless whisper.

"Do what? I merely wished you a good morning."

"But the *way* you did it, and in front of your friend."

"Just a reminder to Byron that you're promised to me."

So he *had* noticed Byron's behavior last night—and given him some kind of warning. A pleasant warmth spread from her heart to her face. Did that mean he was a little jealous, or at least protective of her? She tilted her head to try to read his expression, but they'd reached the table where the rest of the family was taking their places.

~

*H*e shouldn't have made a scene, but finding Hannah in the hall with Byron had ruffled Rupert's feathers. And like a banty rooster, he'd raised a crow.

Now, having Byron across from him served as a reminder of Wilma's impending visit. Perhaps it wouldn't be so bad. They'd mark off the new boundaries, and the sum Wilma would pay him would keep the farm going without asking the bank for a loan. Byron would put the details in a document and file a record of the sale. Afterward, Wilma would leave for Mobile.

When the object of his ire walked into the room, Rupert jerked and splashed coffee on his vest. He dabbed at it with a napkin. Blast the woman! Didn't she have the courtesy to knock? This wasn't her house, hadn't been in fifteen years. In addition to putting up a fence, he might have to install locks on all the doors.

"You're still at the table? I thought you'd be ready to get this done." She stood next to Rupert, her cloying perfume assaulting his nose. Belatedly, she acknowledged the others. "G'morning, y'all."

Always the welcoming hostess, Ma greeted Wilma with a smile. "Hello, Wilma. I'd ask you to join us, but I know you're eager to get going."

Rupert stood and gestured to Byron. "Wilma, I believe you've met Byron Harris. He's going with us to view the land and record the details of our transaction to file for the new deed."

Wilma reminded him of an owl as she blinked her eyes. Since when had she started applying that black stuff around them? What other new habits had she brough back from Mobile?

Her laugh seemed forced. "Oh, is that really necessary? We are family, after all."

Pa pushed away from the table. "With all the regulations from the new government, it's best to have everything on paper. That way, nobody will get in trouble."

Biting his tongue to keep from speaking his thoughts and starting an argument with his cousin, Rupert tipped his head toward Byron. "Are you ready, or do you need to gather your papers?"

Byron patted his coat pocket. "I have all I need right here."

Hannah grasped Rupert's hand. "Could I come with you?"

Rupert stared at Hannah, the warmth from her small hand spreading into his chest. Why would she put herself in Wilma's path? Did she simply want to get out of the house? He was still formulating an answer when Wilma spoke, his cousin's voice taking on a haughty tone he'd heard often in his childhood. "This is private family business, not an outing for entertainment."

Did Wilma think she could come in here and boss everyone around? He drew Hannah to his side. "Of course, you may join us, darlin'."

Wilma stared, mouth agape.

Ma stood. "You'll need a warm shawl, Hannah, dear. I'll get you one."

"That will make the carriage rather crowded." Wilma's weak protest went unanswered as they headed toward the front door.

Rupert grinned. His cousin had finally been overruled.

*W*ith Miss Connie's shawl over her shoulders, Hannah squeezed between Rupert and Byron while Mr. John took the landau's front seat beside Mrs. Thurman. His arm around her shoulders, Rupert pulled her closer to his side. For a man who'd been hesitant about helping her yesterday, he'd become rather possessive all of a sudden.

Mrs. Thurman gave the reins to Mr. John. "Do we need to go by the neighbor's house first, or did Rupert remember to consult him?" Although directed at her uncle, the woman's barb was aimed at Rupert, as if she'd expected him to forget.

"I spoke to Mr. Callahan yesterday." Rupert raised his voice to carry over the clip-clop of the horses' hooves and the crunch of wheels over the rock-strewn road. "He didn't have any problems with our plan, so long as you don't mess up the creek when you dig your well."

A delicate wave of Mrs. Thurman's hand dismissed his concern. "I leave all that up to the man I'm hiring to build the house. I'll write down his name so you can go to him with any problems. He should be here next week."

"Next week?" Rupert leaned forward. "You already hired someone to build the house? Is he from around here?"

"Oh, no. I wouldn't trust some country bumpkin to build *this* house. Mr. Kent's business is up north. He's highly recommended."

"Which means you hired him before you knew I would sell it." Rupert gripped the side of the buggy as they rode over the bumpy field.

"Oh, pooh, Rupie. I hired him in January, before Pa died. Of course, at the time I didn't expect to have to *buy* the land from *you*. Pa would've given it to me. But the sale of the house in Jacksonville will take care of that." She half turned in her seat. "Unless you're reneging on our deal?"

Hannah's heart went out to Rupert as he glowered at his cousin. "I'm not going back on the deal."

Mr. John reined the horse to a stop, and the carriage lurched. "Well, here we are."

He got out and offered his hand to Mrs. Thurman. The pinched set of his mouth told Hannah he didn't like the woman's words and actions any more than Rupert did.

Byron and Rupert exited on different sides, and Hannah turned to her betrothed for his assistance.

Her betrothed! How strange it seemed to apply that term to Rupert, and to accept the term for herself. But that was the very reason she'd asked to come along on this jaunt. She wanted to support him now, to show she was fully prepared to do her part in the upcoming marriage. Although she'd appealed to his family for help, she didn't expect him to pull the full load alone. Surely, there were skills she could bring to the marriage to make it beneficial for him.

As they walked the land to mark off the section Wilma wanted as Byron carefully recorded the boundaries, Hannah breathed in the promise of spring. Squirrels and chipmunks darted away from the heavy boots while robins and blue jays whistled from the limbs of oak and pine and tupelo trees adjacent to the field. She paused to admire the blooms on a redbud tree at the woods' edge while Rupert and Byron conferred on boundary markers.

Footsteps crunched behind her, and Hannah turned as Mrs. Thurman eyed her with thinly veiled cynicism. "Uncle John tells me you and Rupert have recently decided to marry. I wonder why I never heard him speak of you before."

"You know how Rupert is. He doesn't have much to say until he makes his decision. Then there's no holding him back."

The other woman's eyes narrowed to slits. "Hmm. And do I understand you're a distant relative of my mother?"

Hannah clenched her fists, disliking the way Mrs. Thurman

questioned her, but forced a pleasant tone. "Your mother was my grandmother's cousin."

"That would make us second cousins, I believe." Mrs. Thurman sniffed. "Pity we never met before."

"Yes, isn't it?" *Then I might better know what you're about.* It was natural for the woman to be curious about her, but the way she treated Rupert raised Hannah's hackles. Did she act that way with everyone, or did she prey on Rupert because of his easy-going nature? What would it be like to have Wilma as a neighbor?

The men strolled back to them, and Rupert presented Hannah with a sprig of blooms from a jacaranda tree. "This is nearly the same shade as your dress, maybe a lighter blue."

Touched by the simple gesture, she took the bloom and tucked the stem through a buttonhole. "Thank you, Rupert. I'd love to have a bouquet of them, but I wouldn't want to rob the tree of its beauty."

Perhaps she could gather enough for a bouquet for the wedding. Not that they'd be able to have a proper ceremony with all the fancy food and decorations like her sister's years ago, but flowers would add a festive touch.

"Don't worry," Rupert said. "There are several on our side of the property putting out flowers already." He grasped her hand as they fell in line behind Mrs. Thurman and the other men. "Those tend to bloom all through the summer, so you'll be able to enjoy them for several months."

From his comment, he must intend for them to be here, then. What did he plan to do with Whitfield Hall?

CHAPTER 13

*R*upert could have kicked himself. Though Hannah didn't say anything, she stiffened at his reference to being here for the summer. How quickly he'd grown used to having her here, sitting beside her at the table, finding her in the parlor. Somehow, she belonged here, but the problems of Whitfield Hall awaited them. How was he going to save her home and maintain his?

They hadn't discussed how they would move forward, with two properties to manage. Rupert would have to view the land at Whitfield Hall and find reliable workers before they could determine the best course of action. Probably they would divide their time between the two—somehow. Though he might not grasp the particulars yet, he needed to address her uncertainty sooner rather than later.

The offer Wilma had made—fourteen dollars an acre!—was too good to turn down. With the farm, Rupert was rich in land but poor in other resources—namely, money to buy seed and pay workers. He and Malachi took care of all the maintenance but sometimes had to buy supplies to make the repairs. He expected he'd also have to lay out some cash for the Georgia property too. The sum Wilma offered was like an answer to prayer.

The one resource he needed most was time, and now he'd need twice as much. Uncle Henry's legacy turned out to be more than Rupert ever dreamed—this farm and now a wife, another home to oversee, and a child to go with it. All he had to do was figure out how to juggle them and keep Wilma as far away as possible.

They'd reached the final boundary marker, and Byron pocketed his notepad and pencil. "I'll get these figures written up and file for the new deed as soon as I get back to town." He turned to Wilma. "Do you want to make the payment here or meet me in town with it?"

Wilma scoffed. "Surely, you don't think I brought that much money with me. I can get it today or after Uncle John and I return from Jacksonville."

Byron raised his eyebrows, leaving the decision to Rupert.

Rupert scratched his chin. "Do I have to sign the papers, or can you do it for me, as my representative?"

"I can do it on your behalf." Byron retrieved his pencil and paper. "Shall I put it in the bank, or do you need to keep out some for your tra—er, trade at the mercantile?"

Relieved that Byron caught his slight head shake, Rupert clapped his friend on the shoulder. "Take out your fee and an equal amount for me. Put the rest in the bank. I'll settle up with Josh at the store next time I go in."

Pa shooed them back the way they'd come. "With that settled, let's head to the house. I expect Jewel will have a basket ready for Wilma and me to take on our journey, then we can get on our way."

Rupert slowed his steps to stay behind the others while he sorted through what to say to Hannah, to assure her he still intended to take care of her home. Keeping his eyes fixed ahead, he asked, "What can you tell me about the condition of Whitfield Hall?"

Her wide-eyed gaze met his and held, as if trying to decipher his meaning. "If you mean the physical condition, all the buildings are sound, though they might need some minor repair or whitewashing. The garden should be fine if we can get some plants in and weed it. I don't hold out much hope for planting a big crop like cotton on account of not enough workers."

"What about the finances?"

"Ah, well, that's another issue altogether. I have papers in my knapsack that will explain it better than I can."

No surprise there. Running a farm required constant upkeep. "All right. I'll study those when we get back to the house, though I'll have a better idea how to manage both farms once I see the place in person."

"Of course. Then you can study Papa's records too. Maybe you can make more sense of them than I could."

With the others several yards ahead, Rupert took Hannah's hand. He enjoyed having her beside him as he viewed nature's new cycle of life. As soon as the extra workers and equipment arrived, they'd till the ground and add the seed for crops. In a matter of weeks, those plants would contribute their own special beauty to the land.

"Tell me something." Hannah's voice was soft. "Why didn't you want Byron to mention our travels?"

He smiled. "I don't trust Wilma. I'd rather she didn't know I'll be away from the farm for a few days"—he glanced at Hannah's upturned face— "or however long it takes to settle things there."

Ahead, the others had reached the carriage.

He stopped, tugging her to face him. "We can use some of the money from this sale to apply to Whitfield Hall. However, I'd like you to consider whether we could sell a small portion of the land connected to your home. I have some ideas for how to make both farms more profitable, but everything requires an outlay of money in the beginning."

Hannah's head bobbed. "I understand. At this point, I'm happy to let you take over, and I'll do whatever I can to help."

Her trust bolstered his confidence and firmed his commitment. They'd make this work. When they reached the carriage, Rupert handed Hannah onto the bench.

Pa shot him a knowing grin. "I don't know what's got into you lately, son, but I wouldn't advise entering any races this summer."

Byron chuckled, and Hannah turned a questioning gaze to Rupert as he settled onto the seat and tapped Pa on the shoulder as a signal to drive on. He kept his voice low as an excuse to lean closer to her. "Every summer, we have a big picnic—or at least, we used to, before the war. Anyway, we always had races, and I usually won. Though it's been years, some folks still remember it."

"Don't let him fool you, Miss Whitfield," Byron said. "He ran fast enough last year to help Troy round up a couple of fellows who kidnapped Millie."

Warmth crept up Rupert's neck as Hannah considered him with raised eyebrows. With a wink, he turned the teasing on her. "You might remember that if you ever decide to run away."

❧

If Oscar Prescott had made such a remark about her running away, Hannah would have taken it as a threat. Coming from Rupert, it only demonstrated a degree of insecurity. She found his lack of arrogance comforting. The same could be said for Mr. John.

On the other hand, Wilma Thurman exhibited an abundance of haughtiness. Yesterday, Hannah had admired the woman's stylish appearance, but her air of supreme confidence soon revealed her true nature. Having Wilma build a house so close to the farm posed a concern because of the way she treated Rupert. Perhaps they could plan to be at Whitfield Hall whenever Wilma was in residence here.

Mr. John and Wilma left soon after they arrived back at the house, with Byron following a few minutes later.

Hannah gave Rupert the papers she'd brought detailing the finances at Whitfield.

He spread them on his desk, and she hovered at his side. "I doubt if I could answer your questions fully, but I can try. Papa never showed me the books he kept, so Aunt Ginny and I have been figuring it out on our own. It doesn't help that no one at the courthouse will give me an accounting. I suspect that's Captain Prescott's doing."

"I believe I can figure out what we need, but you're welcome to stay."

"I have nothing else to do." She surveyed the office. "Will it disturb you if I do a little rearranging, maybe put the books in some kind of order?"

"Not at all." He looked up from the papers. "As you can tell, no one did much to this room after Aunt June passed. I'm not sure if Henry wouldn't let Jewel touch it or if she counted it a lost cause. She only came to be with us last year while Millie and Troy were staying here. Maybe Millie told her she only needed to cook, not clean. I reckon you and Jewel can work out the house chores later."

"I'm happy to do what I can." Hannah soon devised a sensible grouping that worked—a section each for animals, plants, and general farming principles, plus one for the sizable collection of fiction books. She kept to the other side of the room, wiping down anything that had been missed earlier. The windows could use a good washing, but that would require the aid of a chair or ladder—or someone taller.

Rupert bent over the papers, a pencil in one hand poised to write while he tugged at his hair with the other. He set the pencil in motion, and she crept closer. He had filled a sheet of paper with calculations. Another page contained a long list with numbers to the side.

He paused and tapped the pencil on the desk. Her heart lurched at the action, regret building to have put him in such a predicament. But she'd seen no other way to solve her family's problems. Even if she had bags of gold to pay for workers, repairs, and upkeep, they still needed a man to protect their interests and to guide Caleb into becoming a responsible landowner. Would she have felt the same if it was Henry instead of Rupert? Henry would've had experience on his side, but Rupert had youth and the vitality to take on the physical work of the farm. Would the responsibility of two properties be too much? Would he end up resenting her?

When he caught her peeking at the papers, he smiled. "You finished already?"

A laugh bubbled up. "Hardly. If I could get a ladder and a pan of soapy water in here, it would help."

"A ladder?" He tossed the pencil aside and stood. "I bet your walls at Whitfield Hall are higher than these."

She blushed at the truth, though his tone was teasing. "Yes, but I never had to clean them, at least not by myself."

"And you don't have to clean these." He gathered the papers and tucked them into a desk drawer. "I'll see if Byron knows anyone I can hire to do the cleaning, perhaps while we're gone to Georgia. Or Jewel will, if the family decides to go back home. With all of us gone, she won't have as much cookin' to do." Rupert rounded the desk to stand before her, then he swiped a thumb across her cheek, giving her a lopsided grin. "Dust."

His touch waylaid her thoughts. What was she going to say? Something about Jewel? "So Jewel came here after the war ended? Did Troy's work at the Freedmen's Bureau help with that?"

"Not in the typical way. Malachi met Troy while searching for Jewel. She's his daughter, you know. Years earlier, they'd been separated. He learned where she'd gone, but she'd left the first place when the war ended. After searchin' about six months, he met Troy and found out she was here."

"How wonderful." Hannah's eyes misted. "Who can doubt that God directs our lives with a story such as that?" When Rupert tugged on a loose curl at her ear, her heart stuttered.

He leaned closer. "You believe God brought them here? What about us? Did He plan for you and me to meet too? Bringing you all the way from Whitfield Hall…"

Unable to move under his compelling gaze, Hannah held her breath. Did he intend to kiss her? Was kissing allowed when they weren't married yet? Shouldn't they wait?

His face hovered over hers, and she could only stare. His warm breath drifted across the place where his thumb had been.

The slam of the back door startled her, and she swayed toward the hallway. Millie's voice scolding Amy followed, and Rupert heaved a sigh as he took a step backward. Suddenly, he turned and strode into the hallway. A moment later, the front door opened and closed.

Hannah gripped the edge of the desk to keep herself upright. What had she done wrong?

~

*R*upert didn't stop until he was long past the barn. Tempted to continue on to the creek, he groaned. That was no good, the place where he'd first caught sight of her.

What had he been thinking back there? Nothing, that's

what. Not thinking, only feeling. Drawn by her innocent, wide-eyed beauty and the knowledge she'd soon be his. But she'd come for help, not for matters of the heart. Though his plan to remain single had fallen by the wayside, he couldn't let himself get too close. Theirs would be a marriage of convenience to save her family home, not a typical marriage. Of course, no one but his folks and hers would know that, so he and Hannah must give the appearance of a happy couple.

But he didn't need to play with Hannah's feelings in the process. Almost letting physical desire take over had been bad enough. Walking out without a word was like a kick in the shin. How was he to face her again after such cowardice?

In the distance, Malachi headed toward the house. Perhaps he'd found some workers who could start right away. They might need sleeping quarters if they were new to the area. So many chores to accomplish before he and Hannah left for Georgia.

Rupert sighed. More importantly, perhaps the older man could share some wisdom on how to treat his bride-to-be and still keep his heart in check.

CHAPTER 14

$\mathscr{H}$ ow fortunate that Rupert had run into Malachi, who reported good news on finding workers.

"They been stayin' west of the Callahan place, so they be here directly," he said.

"Good. Pa said he'd stop at the home place on his way to Jacksonville, so Paul should arrive with their equipment today or tomorrow." Rupert raised his face to the sky. "I'm hopeful this good weather will last a few more days. March can be unpredictable."

Malachi chuckled. "Yas, suh. Weather be just like a woman. I reckon you find out 'bout dat soon."

Rupert stopped in his tracks and stared. What made him say that?

Malachi grinned. "Heard yestidy you an' dat young lady plan to wed. Today, you's out wanderin' around like you's lost. Figgered it had to be on account of her."

Chagrined, Rupert shook his head and started walking again. "I'm the one acting like the weather. She seems content to do whatever it takes to save her home in Georgia. I'm ready to help, but what happens afterward? What if we don't get along, or her family hates me, or we get tired of running back and forth between our houses? Somebody's bound to get hurt."

When Malachi said nothing, Rupert sighed. "Sorry. I just hoped you might have some advice..."

Malachi pulled him to a stop. "Sounds to me like you afraid to take a risk on somethin' good comin' of your marriage. All of life is a risk, you know." He waved his arm toward the field. "Ever' time we put seed in the ground, we risk losin' it to storms or drought. Too little rain or too much sun, an' we lose. All dat hard work and time gone. But we don' let dat stop us 'cause we hope to get a crop."

He laid his hand on Rupert's shoulder. "You can't let fear of loss keep you from goin' forward. You got to feed your soul with hope and trust God to give you a good harvest." He cocked his head and grinned. "Marryin' dis gal might be de best gift you ever got."

Rupert nodded, drinking in the deep wisdom in this man's simple message—a man who knew about hope against all odds. Rupert lifted his arms to Malachi's shoulders in a loose hug. "Thank you, friend. I guess I needed that sermon. Now we'd best talk about getting seed in the ground soon as we can."

Taking the lead, Rupert showed Malachi the new boundary line that marked Wilma's two acres. "Let's start with this section that borders hers, so we won't have to contend with the construction work when it starts."

"That suits me fine." Malachi pointed to figures emerging from the neighbor's direction. "That looks like our workers comin' now. I got the cabin ready for 'em."

After Rupert met the newcomers, the men parted ways, and Rupert headed toward the house, his thoughts tracking like jackrabbits from one responsibility to another.

Selling off the two acres that Wilma wanted meant planting a smaller wheat crop, but he might find good ground around Whitfield Hall to make up the difference. The land and conditions there should be similar to his own, so he'd plan accordingly. Double properties meant double the labor and care, but also the opportunity for greater harvests. He might even get to start the small herd of cattle he'd been itching to buy. If he and Hannah could wind up their visit within a few days, he might be back in Alabama to help with the next round of sowing.

A glance at the sky confirmed what his grumbling stomach told him. It was past time for the noon meal. Maybe Ma and the others would be finished by the time he got inside. Good thing Pa wasn't here to tease him about being slow again.

He was still several acres from the house. After a glance around, he spotted the twisted oak with the knots that formed a face, the same starting spot where he'd practiced running for the last community race. How long it would take him to get there at a run? A little exertion might blow away his moodiness.

He checked his pocket watch, waited for the minute hand to sweep around once more, and took a running stance. Soon as the indicator reached twelve, he sprinted forward. The first few yards testified to his recent inactivity and reminded him of all the squatting he'd done while he and Hannah cleaned up the office.

Halfway to the house, the familiar surge hit, and it was as if his feet grew wings. Laughter bubbled up as he passed the barn and forced his legs to slow. He hit the porch and raised his hand to check the watch. Not bad. Not his best time, but not bad.

Bending over, he waited for his breath to catch up and reveled in the euphoria. At the sound of hurried footsteps, he raised his head and nearly lost his breath again when Hannah's wide-eyed gaze met his. One hand framed the O of her mouth, and the other pressed against her middle.

So entranced was he by the vision before him, he only noticed the others behind her when Amy giggled and ran to his side. "Unca run?"

Rupert hugged the child to him and wheezed. "Yes, Uncle

ran from the tree line. And pretty fast too." He couldn't resist the slight boast.

"Levi saw you from the window and told us." Ma patted Levi on his shoulder. "Next time, you might like some competition."

The boy's eyes gleamed, and Rupert grinned at him. "Only if you promise not to show me up too badly, Levi."

He glanced at Hannah again. Could that gleam in her eyes be admiration?

$\sim$

Sweat glistened on Rupert's brow from his dash across the fields, drawing Hannah's gaze to his eyes. Their color reflected the sky behind him. His flush remained, not from exertion now since his breathing had returned to normal, but from the pleasure he derived. Did she imagine that he directed his smile at her? Perhaps his sudden departure earlier hadn't been because of something she'd done.

"Well. Now you're here, we should all return to our meal." Miss Connie held the door open. "C'mon, children. Let's see how quickly you can get back to your seats *without* running."

Millie and Jewel followed her with the two youngsters. "After Amy's escape yesterday, I'm not sure I ever want to encourage her to run," Millie said.

When Hannah turned to join them, Rupert sprang to her side and stretched his arm across the doorframe. "I just want to apologize for leaving so quickly a while ago." His gaze drifted to one side as if he couldn't make direct eye contact. If not for his recent exertion, she might attribute his flushed face to embarrassment.

"Why did you?" Her breath quickened when his lashes swept up to capture her gaze.

Eyebrows raised, he shook his head. "Why did I—what?"

Hannah shook her head. Hadn't he just apologized for leaving so abruptly?

His gaze dipped to her lips, then slowly rose again. Oh. Did he think she referred to that?

This time, she looked away. "Why did you leave without letting me know?"

Air from his ragged sigh warmed her forehead. "I thought it was best, since we're...you know..." He cleared his throat. "Not married yet."

So he *had* wanted to kiss her. And almost did. If not for Amy letting the back door slam as she ran away from Millie, he would have. A surge of pleasure warmed her face. She dared to peek at him again.

From farther down the hallway, Millie called, "Y'all coming in?"

Rupert shifted as Hannah stepped over the threshold. When she passed by, he touched her back, then pulled his hand away as if he thought better of it. Hannah's chest squeezed with doubt. Did the man like her...or not?

❧

A strange awareness created a barrier between them. As Rupert followed Hannah back into the dining room and they found their places at the table, Ma turned her attention to Hannah. "I'm sure you're eager to return home, though I wish we had more time together. Is there anything you need for your journey?"

"Thank you, ma'am, but I believe I have everything I need."

Hannah's arm brushed Rupert's as she cradled her cup in both hands. Her plate held only small amounts of food, the same as Ma's and Millie's. He offered each of them more fried potatoes from the bowl before he placed a generous portion on his plate. His gaze snagged on Hannah as she pushed her fork sideways to collect a few beans and slid them into her mouth. Those pink lips... He jerked his attention away from that temptation.

Across the table, Millie exchanged an unspoken message with Ma, who gave a little nod. What was that about? Probably women stuff.

Rupert scooped some greens onto his plate. "I've decided to get a head start on planting while we wait for Pa to return from Jacksonville. By borrowing plows from Pa and a couple of neighbors, we should get several acres done. Thanks to the showers we've had in the last few weeks, the ground should till well."

At the sound of a cry from the other room, Millie pushed back in her chair. "That's Little John."

Ma wiped Amy's face and hands. "And just as one wakes up, the other one looks ready to fall asleep. Come on, Amy, let's go find a story to read for your afternoon nap."

The departure of Ma, Millie, and Amy left an awkward silence. Rupert would be a poor host to leave Hannah alone. "What do you plan to do the rest of the day?" He sliced off a piece of potato and popped it in his mouth.

Hannah dabbed her mouth with a napkin. "I have no plans beyond packing. Is there something you need me to do?"

Her willingness to help gratified but also prodded him. In a few days, they would bind their lives together—legally, at least. Filling his mouth with beans and cornbread gave him a few moments to come up with suggestions. He should spend some time with her. As long as he kept his emotional distance, he'd be fine.

He drained the contents of his cup to wash the food down. "No, but we could do whatever you like this afternoon. By tomorrow morning, we should have three or four plows ready to start tilling the land, and I'll be in the field for most of the day." He picked at the potatoes left on his plate. "Um, I thought you might want to work on organizing the papers in the office."

Hannah sat straighter and drew a breath to speak.

But remembering what had happened the last time they were in the office together, he rushed to make another suggestion. "Or we could ride into town—let you see the shops and maybe introduce you to Brother Trotter and a few of the townspeople."

"Brother Trotter?"

"He's the preacher where we attend church. He says he's not fancy enough to be called 'reverend,' and the pastorate is only part-time here in the country. He might even be willing to perform the ceremony today." They could go ahead and get it behind them. Quick and with no fuss, like a business deal, which wasn't far from the truth. And doing it that way might set a precedent for her future expectations.

Hannah's eyes widened. "Your family won't mind?"

Rupert drew his shoulders back. Would they? Paul and Jane had married when Rupert was fourteen, too young to care much about the big celebration. Since both Simon and Troy had married away from home, Paul's was the only wedding Rupert had attended. He'd never want such a huge production himself, and the circumstances didn't call for it.

"I don't know. I reckon we can ask Millie. She usually knows what others might say."

Hannah scraped back her chair as she stood and started collecting dishes. Her jerky movements caused the dishes to clatter against one another. Had he said something to upset her?

Rupert stacked his cup and utensils atop his plate. "Unless you'd rather do something else..."

She sighed and rotated to face him, but Jewel hurried in and waved them away. "Y'all go on now and leave my work be.

These can soak while I clean up the cake platter I found in the top o' the pantry."

"A cake?" Hannah's eyes lit up. "You have the ingredients for a cake?"

Jewel patted her hand. "I been workin' on gettin' what I need since yestidy. Yes'm, we'll have cake to celebrate. We's got to have cake for a weddin', don't we?"

Rupert steered Hannah to the hallway. "I guess that settles the question of the ceremony. We could still ride into town, if you like, just to get out of the house for a bit."

⁓

*R*upert's suggestion about visiting the preacher had taken Hannah aback. Why would he even think of that, especially when he planned to be working in the field tomorrow? Did he simply want to get the matter done with as little fuss as possible? Wouldn't that make people wonder even more about their relationship? Although it had begun as an expedient remedy to her problem, she'd thought perhaps he was coming to like her. Had she read him wrong? Could he be struggling, as she was, to figure out how to navigate new waters?

As for riding into town, though, she welcomed the opportunity to see something of the place and the countryside where she might be spending time in the future.

Over the course of two days, she'd learned she could trust him to behave properly. But what would people in the community think to see them arrive together?

"Would that be proper? I mean, since we're not married yet?" she asked.

"I don't see why not." He motioned down the hallway to where Miss Connie crossed from the bedroom to the parlor. "We can ask Ma."

His mother turned their way. "Ask me what?"

"Whether it would be proper for Hannah and me to ride into town together before we're married."

Miss Connie tilted her head. "I think it would be all right as long as you don't dawdle. After all, day after tomorrow's the wedding."

"Yes'm. I promise to return promptly." With a grin to Hannah, he kissed his ma on the cheek and headed the door. "I'll go hitch up the buggy and be right back."

Hannah hurried to grab her shawl and bonnet. A glance at her dress gave her pause. She would never choose this dress for a shopping trip to Newnan, but it was all she had besides the rose one she was saving for the wedding. She slapped at the skirt to shake out any wrinkles, then donned the bonnet and tied its ribbons.

Tossing the shawl over her shoulders, she slipped out the door to wait on the porch for Rupert. It would be good to have some time with him away from his family. She'd have his undivided attention and no chance of others interrupting their conversation. With the wedding quickly approaching, she needed to be sure he understood just what he'd find when they reached Whitfield Hall.

CHAPTER 15

*N*ever one to pay much attention to all the shops in town, it surprised Rupert to find so many stores had sprung up in the last year. He wouldn't have noticed now if not for Hannah's delight when she spotted them. As a youth, his only interests had been the mercantile and the livery. Now, painted signs proclaimed a dress shop, a tobacconist, a millinery, and a bootmaker lined up on one side. Across the street, enticing smells drifted from a new café and the familiar bakery.

Hannah clapped her hands and emitted a little squeal. "How wonderful to have a seamstress close by. Oh, and look, a millinery! The last time I visited a millinery was before Mama died. It was for my twelfth birthday, and I felt so grownup."

Her pleasure convinced Rupert to park the wagon in that block. "C'mon. We don't have time to do much shopping, but you can see what they have through the windows. Perhaps later...." He let the suggestion hang, unsure how the future would unfold. So much depended on how matters progressed at Whitfield Hall.

As he assisted Hannah to the ground, her demeanor

changed from that of enthusiastic, almost adolescent delight to the polished manner of a lady. Despite his remark about not shopping, she entered the millinery and strolled the aisles as if searching for a particular item. Out of his element, he followed. Perhaps he could whisper a discreet reminder of their lack of ready funds. Doubtful that this place would allow customers to establish a credit account as the mercantile did.

After a few minutes, an older woman approached them, her black bombazine rustling as she glided down the aisle. Her dark hair was swept from her angular face into a low chignon. White lace at her cuffs and collar did little to soften the severity of her dark dress and expression. Her gaze swept over them with ill-concealed disdain. "May I help you with something?"

Rupert's face burned. His work clothes and Hannah's plain dress didn't recommend them as potential buyers of such finery. Changing clothes hadn't occurred to him. He slid a sideways glance to Hannah, who stood ramrod straight and somehow appeared to peer down her nose, though she wasn't as tall as the other woman.

"Perhaps. I noticed my fiancé's cousin had a lovely hat that must be a new style. She might have purchased it in Mobile, but I thought I would see if you have anything similar. I would like to add one to my collection for an upcoming special occasion."

When she paused, the other woman said, "Can you describe the hat you have in mind? As you can see..."—she swept her hand in an arc to include all the merchandise—"we have a vast selection to choose from."

Hannah motioned with one finger to her head as she obliged. "Mrs. Thurman's sat at an angle above her left eyebrow..."

Rupert glanced around him at the various creations decorated with feathers and flowers, in more shades and fabrics than he'd ever seen. The two women kept talking as they wandered to another aisle, but Rupert hesitated to move and risk knocking something over. Ready to quit the place but hesitant to leave without Hannah, he shifted from one foot to the other. Why did Hannah even ask about hats? They needed to put all their funds into the farms until they could bring in a good harvest. He caught her eye and mouthed, "Let's go."

She nodded but continued speaking. "And of course, Governor Jenkins, although I expect he might be replaced soon. Well, I see that I've overstayed my time in here." She moseyed toward Rupert.

The saleswoman followed. "Did you want to order the rose tulle to pick up later?"

With a slight smile, his bride-to-be answered in a soft, cultured voice. "Not at this time, thank you. I'm just acquainting myself with what the town has to offer. Perhaps after we return from Georgia...." She let her voice trail off, and she turned to Rupert as if asking a question.

Why did she do that? He didn't play these games. All he could do was nod, which must have pleased Hannah. She turned her smile on him and led the way outside.

When she started walking to the next store, he grasped her arm. "What was that about?"

Heaven help him if Hannah turned out to be as manipulative and vain as Wilma.

Her wide-eyed expression suggested ignorance. "I'm not sure I know what you mean."

"Your performance"—he pointed to the store they'd just left —"in there."

Hannah's hand fluttered at her neckline. "Oh, I'm sorry. You've probably never been in a ladies' shop before. Mama always said a lady had to present herself well in those shops. Otherwise, the shop workers tend to get on their high horses. I'm sorry if it distressed you."

"The thing is, she could tell by our appearance we don't

have money to spend on hats and gewgaws. I didn't expect to go in there, as I told you, and I don't usually dress up to go to the mercantile." He slapped his gambler-style hat against his leg.

Hannah patted his arm as if he needed calming. "All the more reason to present ourselves well. But don't worry, I won't put you through that again. In the future, maybe your mother can come with me."

"I think that would be best." He extended his arm. "Let's skip the other stores and stop in the mercantile." Maybe he'd have a talk with Ma before the wedding. Dealing with females was like learning a foreign language.

At least Hannah resumed her normal attitude for the rest of the trip. She chatted easily with the storekeeper's wife while Rupert picked up a few items and paid his bill. Afterward, they crossed the road to Byron's law office. "We'll need the money he kept out for our trip to Georgia."

After a perfunctory knock, Rupert opened the door and ushered Hannah inside. "You got a minute to spare, Byron?"

His friend rose from the desk and stretched out his hand in greeting. "I'm always glad to take a break from this paperwork. Miss Whitfield, how are you today?"

She bobbed a brief curtsy. "Fine, thank you. Do you mind if I peek into the schoolroom?"

"Go ahead. It's through that door." Byron pointed to the back of the room, and Hannah sauntered in that direction. He pulled a key from his pocket and unlocked a desk drawer. "I have your money from the land sale. I hope you have a safe place to keep it during your travels."

Rupert accepted the envelope he held out. "I do. Did Wilma give you any trouble about the transfer?" He slid the package into his trouser pocket.

Byron chuckled. "Nah. I think she just likes to push you around. She was perfectly behaved with me. In fact, she was quite congenial. How long has she been widowed?"

"Over a year." Rupert frowned. Did Byron think to pursue his cousin? "I wouldn't fix my interest there if I were you."

"She's far above me, anyway." As Hannah started back their way, Byron lowered his voice. "How are things going with the two of you?"

With a mighty huff, Rupert ran a hand through his hair. "I wish I knew."

By the time he found out, it might be too late to do anything about it.

～

*T*he ride back to the farm started in silence. Hannah glanced at Rupert's profile for the third time, but anything she said would lead back to their conversation outside the millinery. Though he'd calmed down since then, their relationship had cooled like the early-spring evening.

While her shawl provided a little protection from the chill in the air, she had no idea how to guard her feelings from Rupert's frosty attitude. She'd stayed mostly in the background after they left the milliner's. She didn't know how else to appease him. Would he now renege on his decision to marry her? With a sigh, she kept her gaze forward.

They must have been halfway to the house when he finally spoke. "You mentioned going shopping with your ma for your twelfth birthday. How old were you when she died?"

"I'd just turned fifteen. Caleb was only one, and Rachel had already married and moved to Savannah."

"No wonder you feel responsible for your brother. You practically raised him."

"I had help from our old cook and Aunt Ginny." Memories carried her back to those years. "When the war started, Papa left Uncle Liam in charge and didn't come home until he got hit at Antietam. By then, he was a broken old man."

Rupert cleared his throat. "You wouldn't know it, but Connie isn't my mother by birth—or my other brothers' except for Troy. When my real mother died, I was about the same age as Caleb when your ma passed. Having me wore her down, I reckon." He mumbled something about her death being his fault, then drew a deep breath and went on. "Pa said she stayed sick most of the time afterward, then she died. According to Pa and the pictures I've seen, I have her looks, but I don't remember her at all."

Hannah reached across the space between them to rest her hand on his arm. "You can't blame yourself for that. Childbirth can be dangerous, and none of us knows how long we have on this earth."

The conversation lagged, but at least they'd found some common ground and avoided the touchier topics. By the time they arrived at the house, Hannah relaxed and set aside her worry that Rupert would change his mind about escorting her to Whitfield Hall. Making their marriage work wasn't going to be easy. She relied on his commitment to the decision and her own determination to carry it through.

While Rupert put away the horse and wagon, Hannah hurried into the house. Miss Connie met her at the parlor door. "We're back. Did we stay within our time limit?"

"You did, indeed. I was just on my way to check with Jewel and ask if Millie needs help with the children."

"I hope I have time to stop by my room and freshen up."

"Certainly. You can tell us all about your trip to town during the meal."

Hannah made her escape. Would Rupert feel the need to share about their argument outside the millinery? How would he characterize her "performance," as he'd called it? Hannah cringed. After two days of getting to know each other, would Miss Connie and Millie regret their hospitality?

～

wice during the meal, Ma gave Rupert a probing look which indicated he hadn't quite convinced her all was well. Like any mother, she worried about him, but there were some things he couldn't run to her to fix. How could he say anything that might contaminate her opinion of Hannah?

Did Hannah have similar thoughts? She'd plunged right into the first question about their trip with exclamations over the schoolroom—a subject near to Ma's heart. Their conversation saved him from needing to contribute his opinion.

"It is a pity so many people don't get the opportunity to attend school." Ma gave Amy another scoop of rice and gravy. "Like you, Hannah, I would've enjoyed continuing my education if things worked out, but raising a family is just as important. And I'm glad to pass along what I can to the next generation."

Everyone had eaten, and no one had said anything about the new stores. Rupert breathed a sigh of relief, not ready to discuss his feelings about the millinery incident.

As if she read his mind, Millie glanced from him to Hannah. "I'd heard there were new shops in town, but you haven't said anything about them. What did you see there?"

When Hannah didn't respond, Rupert sputtered. "Uh, yeah, one or two."

Ma intervened. "Mrs. Varner told me about those while she was here for Henry's wake. She was excited to have a new seamstress come to town. I do hope the woman gets enough business to stay on. Hopefully, we'll have a good summer and folks will rebound from the previous years' losses."

Millie pushed aside her plate and cradled her teacup. "Amen to that. After making clothes for Amy out of my old ones, I'll soon need a new dress myself. And a new bonnet. Did you see whether anyone had hats?"

Hannah shot a quick glance his way. "Yes, the millinery has a good selection. I went inside for a minute to see if they had the new style of hat like Mrs. Thurman had on yesterday."

"You mean that scrap of fabric on her head?" Millie scoffed. "While I confess it was fetching, I can't see many women choosing those in place of a full bonnet. Especially not in a farming community."

Ma's eyes shifted from Hannah to Rupert. Did she notice the tension between them?

"I have to agree with you, Millie. But you never can tell what folks will like. I've made a few ill-advised purchases in the past myself." She stacked Millie's dish with her own and nodded toward Hannah. "I trust you'll hold to your own good taste whenever you visit the new stores. Some of the workers might pressure you into buying an item you wouldn't otherwise, and a few will cater only to women like Wilma, who can afford to buy more expensive items."

When Ma rose from the table, so did the others. "Come on, Amy." Ma grasped the toddler's hand. "Let's clean you up and go finish the book we started."

As soon as they left the table, Hannah turned to Rupert with a grin. "See?" she whispered. "Your ma knows how things are."

"She only said you had to be careful, not that you should put on an act."

Millie caught their exchange and chuckled. "I guess I missed something." She raised her hands, palm out. "But don't worry, I won't ask. I reckon every couple has to adjust to one another's habits and preferences. Heaven knows Troy and I did, and we'd known each other for years."

Rupert stifled his groan. How would that work for him and Hannah, who'd never known each other existed until a few days ago?

~

he women had the house to themselves all the next day. After laundering and hanging her few items of clothing, Hannah joined Millie and Miss Connie in the parlor with their needlework.

She had missed seeing Rupert at breakfast because he'd already gone out to begin the plowing, but his oldest brother, Paul, came to the house at midday. A younger version of Mr. John, Paul shared only blue eyes as a similar feature with Rupert. He walked with a noticeable limp, which reminded her that he'd lost part of a leg in battle. His lighter hair and beard included auburn strands like his father's.

He slipped into the house while Hannah and Millie were chuckling over Miss Connie's story about her husband and grandson chasing their pigs that escaped the pen during a storm. He leaned against the parlor threshold. "Are you tellin' tales on us, Ma?"

Miss Connie sprang from her place and led him to the closest chair. "I didn't expect you to be driving the plow. Why didn't you send Hosea? That's why you hired him, isn't it, to help with the field work?"

"Because, Ma..." He sank into the chair with a sigh. "I'll soon have to be working my own fields. I'll be headin' home soon as I eat a bite. Workin' a couple of mornings will help me prepare for those sunup to sundown hours." His gaze swung from Miss Connie to Hannah.

His mother crossed to pick up her knitting and resumed her chair beside Hannah. "Oh, sorry. Paul, this is Miss Whitfield. I'm sure Rupert has told you about her." She patted the arm of Hannah's chair. "As you must have guessed, Hannah, Paul is Rupert's oldest brother. He tells me I'm overprotective, but he's still adapting to a new artificial limb—"

"Which is more than Miss Whitfield wants to know, I'm sure." He gave her a sheepish smile. "Please forgive me for not executing a proper bow, Miss. I fear Ma would push me back into the chair."

Hannah set aside her needles and yarn. "Of course, Mr. McNeil. Can I get you some tea or anything?"

"No, thank you. I'll rest here until the meal is served."

Not long afterward, when Jewel called them to the dining room, Paul escorted his mother to the table. He sat at the end that Mr. John usually occupied.

Although he cast curious glances her way throughout the meal, Miss Connie and Millie kept the conversation on local matters. Hannah breathed more easily when he rose to leave. How many more family members would she meet before she and Rupert left for Georgia?

Miss Connie walked him to the door, and Hannah could hear their conversation from the parlor where she joined Millie and the children.

"We'll have a small ceremony, probably tomorrow evening after John gets back, so plan on bringing Jane and the youngsters. Ask Etta to send a couple of dishes, too, please."

"All right, Ma. I hope Rupert doesn't live to regret his decision."

Paul's parting words echoed in Hannah's head throughout the day. Would Rupert regret his choice and blame her? She still hadn't said anything about Caleb's condition. She'd planned to mention it yesterday, but after Rupert reprimanded her outside the millinery, she'd decided to wait.

Lord, please help me do what's right. She had no one else to help her save Whitfield Hall—and didn't want anyone else.

Rupert arrived in time for supper but spoke little. His shoulders drooped with fatigue. As soon as he finished eating, he excused himself. Was he only exhausted, or was he having regrets?

Hannah overslept the next morning, after a night of nerves

and restless dreaming. When she entered the dining area, only Millie sat at the table, finishing her breakfast. Her gaze swept over Hannah.

"Are you ready for this day?"

"I don't know. Is it normal to wonder if you're doing the right thing?"

Millie winced. "My situation was very different from yours, but I believe it is common."

Jewel bustled in and set a plate of flapjacks and a cup of coffee in front of Hannah. "Here you go, Miss Hannah. You best eat up while it's hot, afore Miss Connie puts you to work."

When Jewel scurried away, Hannah faced Millie. "She's gonna put me to work? Doing what?"

"Getting everything ready for the wedding." Millie reached across the table to pat Hannah's hand. "You have to understand, she hasn't been able to put on a wedding celebration in nearly ten years, when Paul and Jane got married. Simon met and married his wife on his way home from the war last summer. Troy and I had our wedding in Louisville, Kentucky. That's where General Sherman sent the mill workers in '64. Having you and Rupert get married here gives her the chance to do a little decorating and invite a few folks over."

Hannah's breath caught, and she choked down the bite she'd taken. "How many folks is a few? And what's she planning to decorate?"

With a gesture to Hannah's plate, Millie pushed aside her own. "You go ahead and eat now, and I'll tell you. There'll be Paul and Jane with their children, Preacher Trotter, the Callahans, and the Varners." She held up fingers as she spoke. "Those are the nearest neighbors. The Callahans are quiet, the Varners not so much, but they're all good people to have around when you need them. Thankfully, Troy made it back in time so he can help with moving the furniture."

Hannah fiddled with her cup "I heard Mr. John come in

after I retired last night. Did he get everything settled with Wilma?"

"I reckon." Millie shrugged. "I wouldn't worry about her showing up for the wedding, though. She's probably on her way to Mobile by now."

That was one less concern, then. Hannah cut off a small section of the sweet pancake while trying to organize her thoughts. "Jewel mentioned making a cake."

"Yes, and Ma probably asked Jane to bring something. Knowing Velma Varner, she'll bring a dish as well. As to the decorations, I expect you and I might be sent to gather whatever flowers we can find close by. Hopefully, we won't have to fend off the bees."

Hannah forced down the last bite and picked up her cup. "Did Miss Connie also give Rupert a list of chores, or will he be in the field all day again?"

"My guess is, he'll work all day. I noticed he took some sandwiches with him for his midday meal." Millie stood and stacked their dishes. "We probably won't see him until near supper time. Come on. We might as well get our marching orders."

Hannah followed and tried to put her worries aside. She'd come too far on this journey to turn back now. Perhaps staying busy would keep her fears at bay.

∽

The sight of two wagons heading toward his barn halted Rupert's trek to the house. Although Ma had explained her plan to invite the neighbors, he didn't expect them to arrive this early. It was still full daylight, although the afternoon heat had diminished as the sun sank lower behind the western tree line. He'd have to go in the back door and get Levi to help him clean up before he faced the company. At Ma's insistence that a dunk in the creek wouldn't do, a tin tub would be waiting in his bedroom.

He altered his course to enter through the kitchen, where he found Jewel surrounded by an array of dishes. A mixture of aromas tantalized his nose and set his stomach to rumbling. Several hours had passed since his last hasty meal.

When Jewel glanced up from the stove, she yelped in surprise. "Mistah Rupert, you best get cleaned up quick. Levi's waiting on you. Here." She pointed him to a dented kettle and gave him a folded cloth to wrap around the handle. "This oughta be enough to warm up your bath water. Now get on in dere."

On the way to his room, voices floated from the parlor. He identified Brother Trotter's booming bass and Mrs. Varner's piercing soprano above the general chatter. The same crowd who'd been there only days ago for Henry's wake. The two events so different and yet coming so close together struck him. For all that mattered in life, neighbors helped one another.

How would Hannah react to this gathering? Did she avoid crowds as he did, or was she more like Ma, who enjoyed having people around her? He should've warned her Ma might insist on a big celebration.

He needed to be on hand to offer her some protection from the questions sure to assault her. Spurred by the thought, he hurried to his room.

Levi jumped from the chair when Rupert entered. "You got to hurry, Mistah Rupert. Mam says P.J. and me can't go outside till you's ready to say your 'I do.'"

Ah, the pressures of boyhood. Rupert's nephew, Paul Junior, dubbed P.J., had become fast friends with Levi. Now Rupert had double the reason to speed through his washing. He poured the hot water into the half-filled tub, shucked off his clothes, and climbed into the tepid bath. No time to soak his tired muscles, but Levi handed him the sliver of scented soap. "Miss Connie says to make sure you use this."

Ten minutes later, clean and dry, he donned his Sunday clothes and sent Levi from the room. Rupert faced his reflection in the mirror above his bureau. How different would his life look after today? No longer a confirmed bachelor, he'd assume the responsibilities of a family. Though he and Hannah didn't always see eye to eye, they tended to work things out. What about her brother? Would he resent Rupert's place in their lives, or would he welcome another male figure? Then there was her aunt—how would she feel about getting Rupert instead of Henry?

So many questions with no immediate answers. Such was the lot of a married man.

He rubbed a hand across his jaw. Should he shave? A glance out the window reminded him of the passing time. He combed his hair, then spied the bottle of cologne Troy had given him at Christmas—along with a remark about catching more flies with honey. Rupert grunted. "Huh, didn't need this stuff after all." He pulled off the top, poured a small amount into his hand, and dabbed it on his neck. Would Hannah notice?

That he wanted her to warned him this was more than a business transaction, no matter what he might tell himself.

CHAPTER 16

$\mathcal{H}$annah forced herself to stop pacing and sat in the straight chair in her room. The shaft of light from the setting sun had narrowed and moved to the foot of the bed. Should she light the lamp? She'd wait a little longer, until the light slid off the quilt. No sense wasting oil. At least Rupert had finally come to the house, according to Millie. Her future sister-in-law had knocked on Hannah's door to let her know.

Earlier, after they'd finished decorating the parlor, the women had eaten a light meal and then taken turns with baths and helping each other dress for the occasion. They "fancied up" Hannah's best dress with bits of lace and ribbons Miss Connie found in a dresser drawer in the main bedroom. The beige trim created a pleasant contrast to the rose-colored fabric.

Thanks to all the preparations they'd done, the time had gone quickly. Then the first guests had arrived. Miss Connie advised Hannah to wait in her room until Rupert came to escort her to the parlor. "Everyone will be curious about you, of course, but you need not face them alone. You and Rupert should enter together."

Millie's supportive presence had calmed her nerves. Otherwise, Hannah might have called off the entire affair. What had seemed a simple plan when she'd set out from Georgia had grown far beyond her imagination. Complications had cropped up at every corner—from Henry's death to searching for the missing letters to questions about the McNeil military associations. And of course, she couldn't back out now. Her family depended on her.

Hannah stood to pace again, and another knock called her to the door. She opened it and caught her breath to find Rupert there.

Dressed in a black suit with a blue vest that reflected the color of his eyes, he toyed with the black cravat at his neck. His hand dropped to his side as he surveyed her appearance. His Adam's apple bobbed, and he returned his attention to her face. "Uh, Ma said I should escort you to the parlor if you're ready."

She retrieved the fan Miss Connie had left, glad to have something to hold onto.

After she stepped out, Rupert placed her free hand on his arm. He must have felt her tremble, for he offered a crooked half smile as he rested his hand atop hers. "I promise the people won't bite, but they do bark loudly."

Her laughter bubbled up, and she relaxed. "I trust you to keep them at bay." She meant it. For all his serious mien, Rupert had a sense of humor that delighted and set her at ease.

In the parlor, most of the men stood in small groups while the women occupied the chairs. There must be close to twenty people in there. How would they ever accommodate everyone for supper?

"Ah, here they are." Mr. John excused himself from the gentleman beside him and joined Hannah and Rupert as they crossed the threshold. He focused on Hannah and kept his voice low. "You look lovely, Miss Whitfield. Are you still agreeable to this arrangement?"

She moistened her dry lips and nodded. "Of course."

Mr. John questioned Rupert with raised eyebrows. "You ready, son?"

"Yes, sir."

Hannah took courage from his assurance. *Lord, I'm depending on You to help us make this work.*

~

*A*fter a single moment of panic, Rupert squeezed Hannah's hand and stepped toward the minister. As if the two of them were important dignitaries, the crowd of family and friends created a pathway, then closed it again as soon as he and Hannah had passed.

Brother Trotter opened his Bible and fiddled with a paper stuck between its pages. "Dearly beloved, we are gathered here today to join this man, Henry Rupert McNeil, and this woman..." He peered at the paper. "...Hannah Victoria Whitfield, in holy matrimony."

The pastor's voice continued with the reminder that marriage was ordained by God and should not be entered into lightly. Rupert cast his bride a sideways glance. Though they'd only met a few days before, neither of them was acting on a whim. During the hours of following the plow over the last two days, he'd given the matter much thought and even appealed to God for direction. Surely, Hannah had done the same long before she'd left Georgia, probably before her aunt had penned her first letter to Henry. To ensure her brother's legacy, she'd obligated herself to a stranger for life.

Rupert faced Hannah when he spoke his vows. Did the tears she blinked back indicate regret or a deep sense of wonder similar to his?

She spoke her promises, and then the pronouncement came that they were married. Just like that.

"Go on, son. Kiss your bride."

Hannah's eyes widened as he leaned her way, then her face tilted upward. Aware of their audience, he held her hands against his chest and touched his lips to hers. The warmth drew him in, urged him to explore.

A smattering of applause penetrated his brain, his signal to stop before he got carried away. Face burning, he set one arm about Hannah's shoulders and turned her to face the crowd.

❧

*I*n the dining area, four long tables lined the walls. Two held large platters of food, while the other two were flanked by benches for extra seating. Some of the guests had already eaten and prepared to leave. The men shook Rupert's hand, and the women wished Hannah well as they ushered their children out the door.

"Why are they leaving so soon?" she asked him.

"Farm chores don't wait for weddings." Rupert spoke near her ear, sending shivers along her arm. "Not unless you're the lucky one gettin' married."

Did he think he was lucky? She searched his face for an answer and was rewarded with a smile. When his gaze dropped to her lips, her knees threatened to buckle, and his grip on her waist tightened as she swayed.

Across the room, Mr. John called to Rupert while Miss Connie motioned them to chairs decorated with ribbons. Hannah grasped his arm. "Please tell me I don't have to make a speech."

A chuckle rumbled from his throat. "Probably not since you're the bride. But Troy looks much too smug, so be prepared for some teasing. And maybe a story or two from our childhood to embarrass me."

"I'm glad no one knows any of my embarrassing stories." She touched his hand. "Don't worry, I'll stay beside you."

Rupert helped Hannah sit first, then took his chair. He picked up his fork, and Hannah nudged him. "Did they say grace already?"

"I'd say so. Everyone else is eating. We'd better get what we can before my brothers start with their tall tales."

Since many of their guests had gone home, only family members remained...and Byron Harris, seated next to Wilma Thurman. The woman in question turned a coquettish smile on Byron as he cocked his head to catch what she was saying.

Hannah lifted her napkin to whisper behind it. "It looks like your cousin and Byron are getting along well. Maybe she's decided against moving to Mobile."

Rupert grunted. "I hope she's not trying to use Byron as a means to get whatever she wants."

"What does she want?" Hannah wouldn't voice the obvious prospect—the farm. Could there be another reason?

"Darned if I know." Rupert picked up Hannah's hand and linked their fingers. "I'm sure we'll find out soon enough. Let's not let her ruin tonight's celebration."

Though Hannah nodded, she tensed every time her gaze strayed toward Wilma. The questions about his cousin's intentions vied with Hannah's concerns about what might happen in a few hours. Marrying Rupert might have solved one problem, but it had come with a whole basketful of others.

∼

*A*fter an hour of good-natured teasing, sampling the dishes, and praising Ma and Jewel for putting together a grand celebration on such short notice, Rupert excused himself to make a trip to the outhouse. He met Paul on the path. "It's gettin' late, Paul. Might be awful dark drivin' to the homestead."

Paul shook his head. "It'd be crazy to drive this late. We'll head back in the mornin'."

"Where we gonna put everybody? That's why y'all didn't stay after Henry's funeral, ain't it? Because we don't have as many bedrooms as y'all do."

"Ma said we'll make a pallet for P.J. and Levi in the parlor or in the office. They'll think it's great fun. Lucy can join Amy in her bed, and Jane and I will take the room Hannah's been using."

"Oh, I forgot about that room bein' available now." Rupert rubbed the back of his neck. "It's gonna be strange, sharing a bed after all these years of sleepin' alone."

With a smirk, Paul punched him on the shoulder. "You'll get used to it real quick-like. Did Pa give you his 'advice to the new groom' speech yet?"

Thankful the dark hid his burning face, Rupert laughed. "Yeah, he didn't know I'd eavesdropped when he gave it to you nearly ten years ago. I think he's relieved this is the last time he'll have to do that."

"Well, you better get on and hurry back to your bride before she comes huntin' you. Too bad it took losin' Henry to get you to settle down."

"Yeah." Rupert gazed into the distance, reminded of why he'd resisted marriage until now.

Paul started back to the house, then stopped. "Rupert."

A few feet away, Rupert looked over his shoulder. "Yeah?"

"You're not to blame for Mama's death, you know."

His breath clogged his chest. "How do you...what makes you say that?"

"I remember you crying about it when we were boys. I think we all blamed ourselves—you, Simon, and me. We were too young to realize sickness could be fatal, and it had nothing to do with your birth or our behavior."

Rupert nodded. "Thanks for telling me." He continued on

the path, not willing to delve too deeply into that pain. Would Paul think differently if he knew about the other times he'd suffered premature losses? A beloved horse, his closest friend... Like he was cursed or something. The last thing he wanted was to bring that ill fortune upon Hannah, who so desperately needed his help.

A person's behavior *could* affect others' lives if they weren't careful. Oddly, it was those left behind who were hurt the most.

CHAPTER 17

*R*eleasing a shaky breath, Hannah stashed her bag in a corner of Rupert's bedroom. Not ten minutes before, Millie and Miss Connie had helped relocate her things and prepare for bed. They'd removed her lovely dress and hung it on a hook. They'd taken the pins from her hair, brushed it out, and braided it, all the while offering tidbits of information on what might happen over the course of the night.

The conversation had not been comfortable, made even more uncomfortable as Hannah surveyed the room where she'd spend the first night as a married lady. With her new husband and her new name. Mrs. McNeil. Hannah McNeil. Mrs. Rupert—oh dear, should she start calling him Henry so no one would question his right to serve as Caleb's guardian? Now that the elder Henry had passed on to glory, perhaps Rupert wouldn't mind going by that name.

Having missed the last minute of Miss Connie's explanation, which must have concluded with a question, Hannah had nodded at the woman's expectant face. Her new mother-in-law beamed, kissed her on the cheek, and bid her goodnight.

Millie had hugged her. "Don't worry, Hannah. Rupert is kind and considerate. You'll be all right."

Now, Hannah paced over the rug. Why did no one say exactly what she should expect to happen? Millie and Miss Connie acted as if she should know already. Maybe they thought Aunt Ginny had explained, but she'd only said, "Read the seventh chapter of First Corinthians."

Hannah paused to see if a Bible might be available. The dusty bureau top held stacks of papers, a comb, and various bottles of cologne. A stack of books threatened to topple beside the bed, rumpled where he must have sat on it earlier. Perhaps this room would feel less intimidatingly personal if she organized things a bit. She reached for a discarded undershirt.

When the door opened behind her, she jumped like a thief caught sneaking into the house.

Rupert stared, holding the door open as if he might turn around and leave. "What are you doing?" Though softly spoken, the words made her heart pick up speed.

She dropped the discarded shirt she'd used to wipe the bureau surface. "Nothing. Just tidying up a bit."

Beneath her long cotton nightgown, her legs trembled. Though she was completely covered, facing Rupert in her nightclothes provoked a feeling of vulnerability. She crossed her arms and lowered her gaze. Her toes peeked from the hem of the gown.

"You were cleaning." He shut the door and drew closer. "What is this compulsion you have to clean?" Was that humor in his voice? Indeed, a twinkle lit his eyes.

She relaxed a bit. "I like things in order. Is that so bad?"

"Hannah." He reached out to caress her cheek. In the lamplight, his eyes glittered as his mouth hitched up on one side. His hand dropped to his side, and his shoulders drooped. "We have a long day of travel ahead of us tomorrow, and I'm tired. We'll sort things out later, but now we should get some sleep."

Ah, yes. At last, they would begin the journey to Whitfield Hall. Reminded of the reason for this marriage, she willed her heart to cease its staccato pace. She swallowed, nodded, and shuffled to the bed. How would two people even fit in that narrow space?

Behind her, the sound of something dragging on the floor preceded Rupert's declaration. "You take the bed. I'll sleep here."

She swung around to find him unrolling a bundle between the bed and the dresser. Once it lay flat, he shucked off his coat and tossed it over the lone chair. Dumbfounded, she didn't move until he slid his thumbs under his suspenders and slipped them from his shoulders. A strange choking sound escaped her throat.

He twisted toward her and grinned. "Would you mind passing me one of those pillows?"

She grabbed the nearest one and tossed it his way. He caught it, dropped it on top of the bedroll, and leaned across the dresser to extinguish the lamp.

Hannah scrambled onto the bed, pulled up the covers, and lay listening to the rustle of fabric as he settled in. Her mind wouldn't calm. Rupert confused her at every turn. What did he mean about sorting things out later? Was this the way their marriage would proceed, or should she expect changes?

He'd been attentive to her all evening, and he had worked long hours the last two days, so she couldn't complain. She gripped the light quilt until her fingers cramped and a series of snores indicated Rupert slept. Her last thought was how would they get along when they got to Whitfield Hall.

*W*ith the reins in one hand, Rupert kept an arm about Hannah, who dozed against his shoulder. The rocking motion of the small carriage had lulled her to sleep.

Her trust was a prize hard-earned the night before. She'd trembled with wide-eyed trepidation when he'd touched her face. Had she feared he would insist on his conjugal rights? Not that he was unwilling, but the poor girl probably had no idea what to expect...unless someone had paid her a visit and suggested what might happen.

That probability prompted his decision.

Her relief had been palpable, which wasn't encouraging, but Pa had warned him she might not be ready for intimacy, considering the newness of their acquaintance. Rupert's claim of fatigue and the long trip ahead served as valid reasons to postpone the consummation in consideration of his bride's feelings.

But how many nights would he have to sleep on the floor before they made this a real marriage? What would it take to win her over? Those questions, more than the hard floor, had troubled him long into the night, until exhaustion had won out.

From the dark circles under Hannah's eyes, she hadn't slept much either. He'd stifled a groan early that morning, anticipating how his family would interpret that. Placing a hand at her back, he'd braced for the indulgent smiles at breakfast and done what he could to shield Hannah from his brothers' teasing. He'd never been so glad to bid his family goodbye and get on the road.

While Hannah slept against him, Rupert plotted his course of action. They'd been denied the normal custom of courting, so he'd have to find ways to woo her in the days ahead.

Rupert's stomach growled, and he searched for a spot to pull off the road. He hated to wake her, but the horse needed a rest, and the sun overhead told him it was time to spread their first meal on the road.

"Hannah, you need to wake up." He shifted his arm and jiggled a finger on her side to find her ticklish spot. "Hannah."

She squirmed and slapped at his hand.

A ribbon of water sparkled through the trees on his right and revealed a small meadow. That might be a good place to rest. He steered the horse toward a shady area and slowed to a stop. He tickled Hannah's side again. "Hannah, sit up so I can set the brake. We'll take our midday meal here while the horse rests."

She straightened, and he brushed the side of her face where imprints from his shirt marred the soft skin. When she smiled, he couldn't resist planting a kiss on her forehead. "Let me release the mare from her traces, and I'll be back to help you down."

After he set the horse free to graze, he turned back to lift Hannah down, then grabbed the blanket and basket Jewel had packed for them. They worked together to lay out the blanket and several food packages and jars of water.

"Ah, wedding cake." He peeled back the edge of a napkin-wrapped bundle.

Hannah covered it back up. "That's for dessert. You can have it after you finish the bread and cheese. Here you go." She held out a large portion of the food she'd unwrapped.

"Yes, ma'am." He set the cake bundle aside and handed her a jar of water.

A slight breeze drifted through the trees and offset the building heat. In the distance, the excited yip of a dog punctuated the nearby droning of bees. The tranquil atmosphere, combined with the filling meal, induced drowsiness. Rupert moved the basket to a corner of the blanket. As he stretched out, he tugged Hannah down beside him. "How are you feeling, Mrs. McNeil?"

Her cheeks pinked, and her lashes swept down to hide her eyes. "I'm fine, Mr. McNeil. And you?"

He covered a yawn. "I'm thinking we have a long way to go before we reach Franklin. Otherwise, I'd stay here and take a nap with you."

"That would be nice. It's so peaceful here, almost as if there's no one else in the world. Did we pass anyone on the road?"

"Not for a while." Another yawn elongated his last word.

Hannah sat up. "I'd like to walk closer to the stream. Maybe I'll refill our jars and see if I can pick some flowers. Why don't you rest for a bit? You've been driving since sunup."

"I believe I will." With one arm over his eyes, he blocked out the sunlight. "Wake me up in a quarter hour. Don't go far."

Fatigue pulled him into a light doze.

~

The resting spot Rupert had chosen reminded Hannah of a picture in a book she'd read as a child. Even this early in the season, the grass grew lush and green between clusters of trees. It was as if a giant hand had cleared the space to provide easy grazing for the resident wildlife.

In the distance, she counted four rooftops. Were those moving figures horses or cows?

With careful steps, Hannah eased closer to the edge of the brook. She unscrewed the lid off the first jar and set the other one in the grass. After gathering her skirts, she squatted and leaned over the water, submerging the open jar to collect the cool liquid. A blue jay chattered in the tree to her right as a noisy squirrel scampered up the trunk.

She capped the jar and set it aside, then searched the grass with her hand for the second container. Instead of the smooth surface of glass, her fingers found a scaly, rough texture. Tree bark? Leather?

Her breath hitched when the object moved closer. Fear slithered like melting ice from her chest to her knees. Papa's voice in her head demanded she stay still, but she never had achieved that level of detachment. She jerked upward and flew in the opposite direction, her scream clawing past her throat as she ran. The carriage—her nearest refuge—seemed miles away.

She tossed a glance over her shoulder to gauge whether she'd gained enough distance from the creature and collided with a broad chest.

Rupert's arms gripped her shoulders, and she sagged against him. "What's wrong? What happened?"

Hannah curled into his side and pointed back the way she'd come. "S-s-snake. By the brook." She shuddered and tried to press closer, but Rupert set her away and stalked in the direction she'd indicated.

"Stay here." His firm steps continued into the foliage where he disappeared from view.

Hannah chewed her bottom lip. What would he do? He had no weapon that she could see. What if the snake attacked him? "Lord, please protect him."

She recalled the loose page from a book in the farm office on how to treat snakebite. What were the instructions? She closed her eyes in an effort to picture the words.

"Hannah." Rupert's voice broke her concentration. Her eyes popped open and found him several yards away. He held out a wiggly object that stretched from his hand to the top of his boots. "Is this the one?"

He started toward her, and she inched backward. "Please don't... Is it dead?" She extended her hand, palm out, to stop him. Did he detect the quaver in her voice?

He halted and stared at her. "It's a common garter snake.

Some call it a farmer's friend 'cause it keeps critters out of the garden. It won't hurt you."

"Please...just get rid of it. I'm going to the carriage." Her hands shook as she collected the remnants of their meal into the basket, grabbed up the blanket, and carried the items to the carriage. By the time she set them behind the seat, Rupert had returned, carrying the abandoned water bottles.

"You forgot these." He stashed them between the basket and the blanket, then caught Hannah in a loose embrace. "Did some stinkin' boy torture you with a snake when you were younger?" The depth of concern in his eyes contrasted with his half grin and teasing words. The comfort of his arms encouraged her confidence.

"My brother, Colin, but only once." She focused on the chipped button in the middle of Rupert's shirt. "When Papa learned of it, he tried to teach me to stand still in my fright, but I couldn't keep from quivering. Just one more way I disappointed him."

Rupert pulled her close, his breath stirring the tendrils of hair on her forehead. "Hannah, everyone is afraid of something. It's just that some people are better at hiding it." He released her and glanced toward the sky. "I guess we'd better get going if we're gonna make Franklin by sundown." He assisted her to the seat and then took his place, but silence stretched between them for the remainder of the day's travel.

Several times, Hannah started to speak but decided against it. What was Rupert afraid of?

~

*N*ear dusk, they reached Franklin, and Rupert followed Hannah's directions down the main street to an inn with a crude sign that read *Brown Hen*. A plain building in the middle of a row of dark shops, its well-lit porch welcomed visitors. How wise would it be to subject his new wife to whoever occupied or patronized this establishment?

Rupert parked the carriage and secured the reins. He vaulted to the ground, strode to Hannah's side, and helped her down. "Is this the only place to rent a room?"

She shrugged. "The only one I know of. Elmer did some work for them last week. There's a shed in back for the horse and carriage."

Rupert tucked her close to his side as they made their way to the door. The noise inside was tolerable, but Hannah seemed to shrink at the sight of half a dozen men sitting around as many tables. After a brief visual sweep of the room, Rupert nudged her toward the counter set under the staircase.

A woman rose from a nearby table and joined them at the counter. "You folks needin' a room or victuals?" Wrinkles creased her face, but she smiled, and her wide brown eyes seemed to warm as she noticed Hannah's wariness.

"Both, please," Rupert said. "What's the cost, including a place for our horse and carriage?"

She named the price, which was a mite more than he liked but much less than what some folks had charged during the war. He handed her the money. "Could we get the meal brought to our room? My wife is rather fatigued." Although true, the real reason had more to do with not exposing her to the men's open stares.

"You're lucky my daughter's still around. I'll have her bring it to your room." She motioned to Hannah. "If you want to lie down while your mister puts up the horse, I'll take you up now."

Rupert quickly agreed. "You go ahead, dear. I'll be back soon." He ignored the sudden flick of Hannah's eyes at his term of affection. She'd have to accustom herself to that and more.

He retraced his steps to the door and paused to glance back as Hannah climbed the stairs behind the older woman.

Uncomfortable with leaving her alone in a strange place, however close it might be to her home, he rushed through the motions of settling the horse.

All day, he'd wrestled with the way to approach their relationship. While he would be glad to make this a normal marriage, he had to think of the future. Little by little, Hannah was coming to trust him, which was gratifying but also frightening. It would be so easy to let her into his heart. He couldn't risk it. What if she decided to stay in Georgia when he returned to Alabama? Or what if they started a family and he lost her? He had to tread carefully and protect them both.

Hannah thought her fear of snakes rendered her helpless, but with diligence, she could avoid the reptiles. Rupert had put himself smack in the middle of his greatest fear—the danger of falling in love with someone he could lose.

Outside the horse shed, he lifted his gaze to the sky and sniffed the air. A cooling breeze carried the hint of rain. Movement in a lighted window on the tavern's second floor took his breath. Hannah's blond hair floated around her shoulders as she worked her fingers through the tresses. Framed by the open shutters, without her shawl to shroud her figure, her curves held him spellbound—until she spun around as if frightened. When her hand flew to her chest, he broke into a run.

~

*B*ehind Hannah, the door opened without the courtesy of a knock or call. She whirled with a reprimand on her lips. Instead of someone delivering a supper tray, a skinny man in baggy Union trousers gaped at her. He advanced into the room with slow steps, never taking his eyes from her.

"Thought it was you." His words slurred from his open grin.

"Boss will be glad to know you're—*hiccup*—back. He's all het up 'bout gettin' his hands on that treasure."

Boss? The man must work for Prescott. What did he mean about a treasure? Whitfield Hall? Surely, he didn't refer to her. She backed up and bumped into the window. Her fingers gripped the ledge. Would she have to jump to avoid him? A dresser and one chair sat on the other side of the room. Where was Rupert?

"You kin tell that thar fella"—he waved his hand toward the door—"I'll be the one to take ya home." He swayed and grabbed hold of the metal bedpost. "After I get a taste—"

Footsteps pounding on the stairs drew him around. Rupert barreled into the room, snatched the man's shirt collar, and jerked him off his feet. He glared at the intruder, who clawed at Rupert's arms. "You seem to be in the wrong room, mister." Rupert ground out the words. "D'you want to leave by way of the window or the door?"

When the intruder's attempt to answer only produced wheezing, he pointed to the door. Rupert carried him over the threshold and released him, then slammed and locked the door behind him.

Hannah wobbled to a chair and collapsed.

Rupert knelt beside her. "Are you all right? Did he hurt you?"

She shook her head. Yes. No. At last calming her breath, she confessed her fears. "He must work for Captain Prescott. He said the boss would be glad to know I was back."

"Don't worry about that. He has no claim on you or Whitfield Hall. We're married, so he'll just have to accept it." He rubbed her hands and whispered more assurances to settle her.

A light knock at the door accompanied a timid voice. "Is it all right to bring in the food now?"

Hours later, after they'd eaten and taken their rest, Hannah wakened to the comforting patter of raindrops on the tin roof.

She rolled over on the narrow bed and peered over the side. The figure bundled in blankets on the floor wiggled and scooted away from the steady ping of drops growing into a puddle near his feet. Once again, Rupert had chosen to sleep on the hard floor, this time to block the door in case anyone tried to slip in again.

Hannah sighed. If she wasn't careful, he would wiggle his way into her affections. She couldn't risk that—not yet, anyway. Maybe after he met her family. She should have told him about Caleb's circumstances already, but they'd had plenty of trouble getting to know each other. He'd find out soon enough. Then they'd see whether this marriage would last.

CHAPTER 18

WHITFIELD HALL, COWETA COUNTY, GEORGIA

*A*fternoon shadows played tricks on the eyes as Rupert followed Hannah's directions onto a tree-lined road. Rain always made driving in the country adventurous, creating dips in unexpected places, and even more so when the driver tried to shield his passenger from splashes.

Rupert tried to avoid the ruts on the approach to Whitfield Hall. Was it so bumpy it caused Hannah to bounce in her seat, or did she do that in her excitement to return home?

"There it is!" Hannah leaned against his side and pointed toward the building that emerged as they followed a curve in the road. Though his inclination was to slow down the carriage, Hannah's exuberance urged him to keep the mare to a trot until they entered the drive that circled in front of the house.

A shiny black landau stood before the steps that led to the extended porch, where a group of people had gathered.

Hannah grasped Rupert's arm, her alarm evident in her stiff posture. "Oh, no. I was hoping we'd have a day or two to settle in before he came around again."

"Who is it?"

"Oscar Prescott."

The landau jerked into motion as the driver cracked his whip above the team.

"His carriage is pulling away. Maybe he didn't see us." Rupert had already slowed the horse to a walk. He eased the carriage off the driveway and into the shadows of a spreading oak as dust rose behind the other vehicle. The horse shook her head as if to question why they'd stopped but didn't release her from the harness. Rupert held her steady while they waited for the way to clear.

When he was sure they hadn't been spotted and the other carriage had truly gone, he jiggled the reins to get the mare moving again. "I think we're in the clear now."

Hannah released her hold on his arm and sagged with the sigh she blew out. "Thank goodness, he's gone." As they drew even with the stocky buttress at the foot of the wide steps, she patted Rupert's arm. "Stop here. Thomas will take care of the horse."

Before he could stop her, Hannah clambered over the side and scurried up the steps to the people waiting there.

Rupert exited more slowly, surveying the welcome committee.

The older white woman hugging his wife had to be Aunt Ginny. The stout black man must be Thomas. He guessed the black woman was Thomas's wife, her slender form half the size of her husband's.

When Rupert reached the man midway up the steps, he offered his hand in greeting.

Thomas's eyes widened, but he returned a firm grip.

"Evening," Rupert said, "I'm told you're called Thomas."

"Yas, suh. You be Mistah McNeil?"

"That's right. Could I prevail on you to settle the horse for me? I believe the journey has aged my back muscles about twenty years."

A glimmer of respect lit the man's eyes when he smiled. "I be glad to tend to it. You g'wan in and rest up."

"Thank you, Thomas." Rupert mounted the top two steps, removed his hat, and bowed in front of Hannah's aunt. Equal in height to her niece, the woman possessed gray eyes that matched the hair peeping from a black crocheted snood. Deep lines etched her forehead and framed her mouth, now pursed as if she'd tasted something sour.

"Mrs. Murphy, I presume? Henry McNeil. It's a pleasure to meet you."

Her eyes narrowed as she scrutinized him, but she nodded. "Mr. McNeil. I believe we should further our acquaintance inside. Silvie, would you bring some tea to the parlor? Hannah, you know where you'll find Caleb. See if you can convince him to leave his room and join us."

The older woman led the way inside the house.

Rupert caught Hannah's hand before she slipped away and pulled her toward him. "Hurry back, please."

She gave him a saucy smile. "You're not afraid of Aunt Ginny, are you?"

He mock shuddered. "Terrified."

After a quick peck on his cheek, she traipsed away, and Rupert entered the parlor.

Mrs. Murphy stood beside a tufted Queen Anne chair, giving the impression she matched the furniture for stiff elegance. "We only have a few minutes before I must return to my husband. I trust Hannah told you something of our situation?"

"Yes, ma'am. I know your husband suffered a stroke some time ago, Hannah lost both her father and her brother last year, and her father's will named Henry McNeil as the trustee for Caleb."

Her gaze went to the black armband on his sleeve. "And you say you are Henry McNeil?"

"My name is Henry Rupert McNeil, and I inherited my Uncle Henry's farm on his death, which occurred a week ago this past Friday." He drew the unfinished letter from his shirt pocket. "We found this letter in my uncle's office, stashed with the letters you sent to him."

She took the paper and read the message, sinking onto the chair.

Silvie returned and set the tea service on the table near Mrs. Ginny.

Hannah followed, walking beside a boy in a wheeled chair. This was her brother?

$\sim$

*H*annah watched Rupert's gaze bounce from her to Caleb and back to her again.

He recovered from his surprise and strode to the place where Caleb positioned his chair near the tea table. Rupert extended his hand. "You must be Caleb. I'm Henry McNeil." He canted his head Hannah's way. "Did she mention she brought a husband back with her?"

Caleb shook his hand but looked solemn when he answered. "Yeah. I know she was hopin' you'd marry her. Just don't know why it took so long for y'all to get back."

"Well, we're here now." Hannah stroked his blond hair. "I don't want to hear any complaints from you. You'll get to hear about our journey soon enough."

"Hannah." Aunt Ginny waved toward the tea tray. "Pour the tea for us, dear. Silvie's going to watch Liam so we can chat awhile."

Hannah prepared the cups and passed them out, along with corn fritters, then chose the settee near Aunt Ginny's chair so

169

Rupert could sit with her. That put them across from Caleb, who studied Rupert with the unabashed directness of a six-year-old boy. What kinds of questions would her family subject them to?

Aunt Ginny set down her tea. "I suppose you noticed Captain Prescott's carriage?"

"We did." Rupert laid his hand over Hannah's. "What was the purpose of the visit?"

"He asked for an audience with Hannah. When we told him she was still gone, he left in a huff."

"So it wasn't the first time he'd been by since I left?" Hannah sat forward.

"He's been by every couple of days. Which is why, first thing tomorrow"—Aunt Ginny pointed a bony finger at them—"you two must present yourselves at the courthouse in Newnan. Introduce Mr. McNeil as your husband and the boy's guardian."

Rupert had already discussed that first requirement with Hannah. "Shouldn't we meet with the family attorney as well?" he asked. "If you have his direction, we'll visit him too."

Aunt Ginny's lips pinched. "That would be wise, as he holds a copy of my brother's will. Not that I care much for the man who took Luther Donaldson's place, but I'll write a note of introduction." She sipped her tea, then set it aside. "Now I want to hear all about your family, young man, and how they feel about Hannah bringing you to Georgia."

Rupert blew out a breath. "Well, ma'am, my folks took to Hannah right away, all the way from my parents to my little niece, Amy. My pa is John, who's a few years younger than Henry."

Hannah joined in and helped him with descriptions of his family and their willingness to come to her aid. Rupert's teasing about Hannah always trying to clean elicited agreement from Caleb and a chuckle from Aunt Ginny.

"That's my Hannah." She struggled to her feet, smiling

gratefully as Rupert rose and helped her stand. "Now I must relieve Silvie and see how Liam fares. You can visit him after supper, Hannah, if you wish."

Was her aunt moving more slowly than before, or had Hannah's perspective changed during her time away? Rupert's mother, only a few years younger than Ginny, didn't exhibit such advanced signs of aging. Caring for Uncle Liam and helping Hannah with Caleb had worn Aunt Ginny down. Perhaps having Rupert here would lighten her burden.

Sitting again, he glanced at Caleb. "Tell me what you like to do around here, Caleb."

Hannah bit her lip. She should have told Rupert about Caleb's situation before they arrived. At first, she hadn't wanted to saddle him with more information than necessary because the man already had a wagonful of responsibilities. Once they were married, she'd selfishly wanted to enjoy the luxury of their time alone without talk of family. Then there had been the scare of the man Prescott sent.

"I read." Caleb's answer carried his typical petulance. "That's about all I get to do."

Rupert stroked his chin. "Do you play checkers?"

"I would if anybody had time to play with me. Hannah used to. Uncle Liam can't, not since his stroke. Everybody else is always busy."

"I think I could find time for a game or two before supper." Rupert sent a conspiratorial smile her way. "That is, if Hannah won't mind us ignoring her for a while."

She tilted her head and pretended to think about it. "I'm sure I can find something else to do. Caleb, do you remember where the checkerboard is?"

"On the third shelf in the library." He turned the wheels on the chair to face the doorway. "I'll get it." Though he acted as if he didn't care, the way his eyes lit up gave him away.

When he was gone, Rupert turned to her. "Why didn't you tell me?"

She didn't pretend not to understand his question. She bowed her head. "I'm sorry. I should have. He's a smart boy, so he can learn to handle the business of the farm."

"I'm sure he can, but he'll have to surround himself with trustworthy workers to do the physical part. And he'll need to work extra hard to prove himself to the businessmen he deals with. When Paul came home with his injury, I saw how he struggled—"

"Shh." Alerted by the *thump, thump* of the chair wheels, Hannah stiffened. "He's coming back." And he was already grim enough without overhearing them talking about him.

~

*H*is first sight of Caleb had caught Rupert by surprise and roused both sympathy for the boy and anger at Hannah. Why hadn't she mentioned her brother was crippled? Though their marriage had doubled his responsibilities, dealing with the boy had been the least of his worries. He'd developed a decent relationship with Levi, whose only fault was his eagerness to help. But he'd never been around someone confined to a wheeled chair. How would they work around his limitations?

Caleb's condition was just another adjustment to make, not something either of them could change. With the war limiting normal life, then his uncle suffering a stroke, his pa and brother dying, and the women carrying all the burdens of home, it was unlikely anyone had encouraged the boy to test his limits. Also, Rupert wasn't sure how much time he should spend with Caleb. Slow changes would be best. He didn't want to begin something he couldn't finish.

Some inner voice scoffed at that. *Ha, yeah, like marrying Hannah?*

That was different. The choice hadn't been entirely his. And, thinking of Hannah, what other surprises might she spring on him? She had some explaining to do.

As Caleb rolled into the room, Rupert lifted the tea tray and looked around for a place to set it.

"Here, I'll take it to the kitchen." Hannah gathered the other dishes. "I'm not sure which of you I should wish good luck."

Rupert chuckled. "Probably me."

Denying himself the torturous pleasure of watching her walk away, he moved the table in front of the settee and took his place.

Caleb positioned his chair on the other side. He plopped the board on the surface and pulled the box of checkers from under his leg. "Black or red?"

"Whichever color you don't want." Rupert pressed the fold lines on the board to level it.

Caleb set the box in the middle. "I'll take black first, then we can swap and see which one is luckiest." He grabbed the black markers from the box and set his pieces in array.

From his experience playing with P.J., who was a year or so older than Caleb, Rupert gauged the boy's skill and temperament with the first game. Though Caleb sulked a little when he lost a man, he recovered and countered the next move.

Hannah rejoined them in the middle of the second game. Good. Rupert could blame her for making him lose that one.

Caleb crowed when he captured the last man. "I won. You spent too much time looking at Hannah."

"You're right. She made me lose my concentration."

With a playful huff, Hannah wagged her finger at him. "I wasn't the one who distracted you. It was either your belly or Caleb's I heard growling. Silvie's putting supper on the table, so let's put up the game for tonight."

"Aw, just one more?"

Rupert shook his head. "I'm tired after driving all day. In fact, I hope I don't fall asleep before I finish my meal. I'd hate for Hannah to have to carry me to our room." His remark elicited a laugh from Caleb and a flash of concern from Hannah, who rolled her eyes when she caught his smile.

After a simple supper of beans and cornbread, Rupert accompanied Hannah to visit her uncle so she could introduce them. A single lamp near the canopied bed gave enough light for them to see the figure there. With his first breath of the room's pervasive odor, Rupert reeled at memories from the army hospital. The acrid scent of urine and sweat spoke of the women's difficult task of caring for the invalid.

Hannah stepped close, and Rupert followed. "Uncle Liam, I've returned from my trip to Alabama and brought my husband to meet you. This is Rupert, Henry McNeil's nephew. You and Aunt Ginny met Henry McNeil a long time ago. Do you remember?"

The old man's eyes shifted from Hannah to Rupert, but he gave no other indication of understanding.

"Anyway, Papa named Henry as the trustee for Caleb after you, and he's here now. So you don't have to worry about us anymore. All you have to do is rest and heal." Her voice broke, but she went on. "I'll come again tomorrow. I love you."

From her words and the way the women were acting, they expected Mr. Murphy to pass soon. Had he been holding out for their sake?

When she took a step back, Rupert moved forward and gripped the man's flaccid hand. "It's good to meet you, sir. I want you to know I'll do my best by Hannah and Caleb and Miss Virginia."

Hannah's tears came when they got outside the room, and Rupert wrapped her in his embrace. With the pain of his uncle's death fresh in his memory, he didn't offer words.

Perhaps by sharing Hannah's sorrow, he'd earn more of her trust. A good bit of Pa's marriage talk had revolved around that word, *trust*, implying much more than physical closeness. Though their marriage had started under unusual circumstances, it could still be a good one. As long as he didn't fall in love with her, he'd be all right.

∾

A bath after days of travel was a luxury. Hannah had selfishly soaked so long that she sent Rupert to fetch more hot water before he could claim his turn. It also gave her time to dry off and don her nightgown while he was gone. The way he'd twisted his mouth said he was on to her game, but he kept quiet as he disappeared behind the screen and poured the water.

When she'd led Rupert to her suite earlier, he had tossed his baggage on the floor between the bed and dresser. Unsure of his expectations, she'd pushed aside the screen that blocked off the dressing room. "The couch in here is quite comfortable and rather long...."

She pulled a quilt from a basket next to a bedside table and tossed it over the sofa, daring a peek at his face.

Rupert gave a slow nod. "It should do for now."

Before he could say more, Thomas brought in the second round of hot water for the tub, and Hannah had used the distraction to leave Rupert to settle in. She could trust him to respect her privacy—couldn't she? By the time he finished his bath, she'd be safely tucked into bed.

Were his splashing and singing meant to punish her for manipulating things to her advantage? Rather, they elicited a smile and then a chuckle when he changed "Oh, Susanna" to "Oh, my Hannah."

She laid the hairbrush on the dresser and tiptoed to the

screen, speaking through the thin fabric. "Not so loud, please. You'll have Aunt Ginny comin' to find out if you're in pain."

"Are you insultin' my singin'?" The words held humor, but he quieted.

She returned to the bed to turn down the covers, and drops of water rained on her as Rupert grasped her by the waist.

A squeal escaped. "You're getting me wet." She shivered. "You're all wet." She peeked over her shoulder in time to catch his grin.

"Just my hair." He stepped back. "My body is dry and properly clothed, so I won't put you to the blush."

Face burning at the suggestion, Hannah spun away, putting distance between them. "Thank you. I explained to Caleb you'd be staying here, but if a nightmare wakes him, he still might barge into the room."

"I guess that's something we'll have to work on." Rupert sat on the bed and rubbed the towel over his head. "So he doesn't need help to get in and out of the chair?"

"Not anymore. He built up his arm strength when neither Aunt Ginny nor I could lift him alone anymore."

"How does he get up and down the stairs?"

"Papa enlarged the dumb waiter in the old kitchen area when Caleb got his chair." She wandered to the dresser and rearranged the comb and brush set, keeping her back to him.

"Ingenious." She listened for Rupert to retreat to the dressing room. Instead, he came up beside her and put a hand on her shoulder. She stiffened, but he snugged her head under his chin. "Will you tell me what happened to Caleb? Was he born that way?"

"An accident when he was four. He'd gone with Aunt Ginny and Uncle Liam to church. People had started leaving Atlanta, and a frightened horse got loose. From what I was told, everyone scattered, Caleb must've been knocked down and crushed. It was days before they found a doctor to examine him."

Rupert rubbed her back in soothing circles. "Poor little fellow. I can't imagine the pain he went through."

Hannah's hip bumped the dresser as she shifted, and Rupert's arm draped her shoulders. "It wasn't long after that when Uncle Liam had his first stroke." She lifted her face to his. "I hope to never experience someone I love hurting like that again."

Rupert placed a soft kiss on her temple. "I know what you mean. We'll do our best to make sure that doesn't happen."

His arm tightened around her, and she let the sensation of his protective care ease her fear for a while. She'd already asked so much of him—the shelter of his name and presence to ward off interlopers. She had no right to ask the impossible. Only God could watch over them and make everything right again.

CHAPTER 19

*R*upert sat up, stretched his stiff back, and glared at the instrument of torture Hannah called a couch. It was a step up from a bedroll on the floor, but not by much. The small room seemed to have shrunk since last night. At that time, he'd been surprised to find rows of shelves lining two walls, and all the shelves filled with clothes, shoes, and hats. A bathing station occupied one corner, complete with a hip bath and a stand with porcelain bowl and pitcher. He'd have to push aside the screen to let in enough light to determine whether it was morning.

No farm chores waited for him here, but he did have tasks to accomplish without delay—namely, paying the taxes on Whitfield Hall and letting word get around that he'd arrived to oversee its farmland.

He jerked on his trousers, then shoved the divider out of his way. Bright sunlight streamed through the window and cast a golden glow over the foot of the bed where his wife lay. Her soft breathing tempted him to tease her awake. He tiptoed across the floor and swiped a strand of Hannah's hair under her nose.

She slapped at the irritant, and he chuckled. "Time to wake up, Mrs. McNeil. We've both slept past dawn."

Hannah blinked, clutched the covers over her, then rolled on her side toward him. Her moss-green gaze met his for a heartbeat, then skittered away. "I can't believe Aunt Ginny let us sleep so long. We should hurry downstairs and hope there's still something left for breakfast." Her eyes flicked down to his chest, then up again. "Um, are you dressed?"

Rupert grinned. She must be getting used to seeing him in his long-sleeved undershirt.

"Not for going beyond this room. I need my clothes, which are over there." He grabbed his bag and, bowing to her sensibilities, returned to the dressing room. When he remembered she'd hung his shirt in the armoire last night, he turned back inside the door. And froze at what he saw.

Hannah had tossed the sheet aside and swung her feet to the floor on the side away from him. The gown did little to disguise her figure. At the dresser, she brushed her long blond hair and then began to work it into a braid. Her graceful movements transformed the mundane task into a sensual dance.

Rupert forced his gaze away and searched for his boots. He needed a distraction.

"Is there a place in town where we could get a meal?" he called into the outer room. "Either now if we missed breakfast... or at noon? I have no idea how long it will take us to get all our errands done."

"I suppose the hotel still serves meals. Those carpetbaggers have to eat somewhere, don't they?"

After Rupert pulled on his boots, he returned to the main room. "Is my shirt in here?"

Hannah pointed to the armoire "I hung it up to let the wrinkles fall out. When we get downstairs, I can iron it for you. I didn't want to ask Silvie last night. She looked so tired."

He put the shirt on and worked the buttons. "It's fine like this. My vest and coat will hide most of it."

Once they finished dressing, they emerged from the room and stopped at the sight of a group at the bottom of the staircase. Three people stood in the entryway, speaking in hushed voices. Whatever the reason for the gathering, it couldn't be good news. Rupert moved closer to Hannah and followed as she quickened her pace down the stairs.

"What's going on? Silvie, where's Aunt Ginny?"

Rupert followed her to the couple he'd met yesterday—Thomas and Silvie. A younger man with a strong resemblance to Thomas stood with them, all wearing solemn faces.

"Oh, sugar, she in dere, sayin' her goodbyes to Mistah Liam. Her and Caleb. Mistah Liam was done gone when she tried to wake him dis mornin'. You gwan in, too, 'fore we lay 'im out for de wake."

Hannah grabbed Rupert's hand and drew him with her down the hall. This morning, the man's room was bathed in light from the eastern-facing windows. The odors remained the same, but the atmosphere had changed.

Mrs. Murphy clutched the back of Caleb's chair, which was parked at Mr. Liam's bedside. She turned toward them and extended a hand their way.

Hannah released his hand to clutch her aunt's, and memories of his own uncle's death had a lump rising to Rupert's throat.

How fortunate his family had been that Henry's illness had not lingered. They'd had little time to prepare for the end, but at least he'd not suffered much.

Hannah's family had endured her uncle's slow demise for over a year, and still they would hold on longer if given the choice. The pain that came with the loss of someone close—that's what Rupert planned to avoid as much as possible.

After several minutes of saying their goodbyes, Hannah

and Caleb turned from the bed to give their aunt a final moment alone with her husband. Rupert ushered them from the room. "Is there someone we should contact? A doctor or a minister?"

With a tremulous sigh, she nodded. "I'll send Silvie's son with a note. He doesn't speak well, but he knows the way to Reverend Covington's."

"Should I drive him? I suppose we'll wait until tomorrow to make visits, but I would like to send a wire to Simon to let him know we've arrived."

"That will be fine." She touched the black funeral band on Rupert's sleeve. "I guess Uncle Liam decided he would go on to heaven and meet the other Henry. Maybe they'll send some angels to guide us until things smooth out."

～

After Rupert left with Quentin, Hannah pushed through the heaviness of loss to prepare the house. Where had they stowed the crepe to cover the mirrors from the last wake? While Caleb helped Silvie stop the clocks, Hannah trudged to the attic to unearth the material.

Panels of sunlight filtered through the wooden shutters, barely illuminating the area. She lit a candle and held it aloft, hoping to find what she needed without moving farther into the room. The trunks and discarded furniture represented a life that no longer belonged to her. The war had stolen it and left only memories. Memories, both good and bad, best left undisturbed.

She swiped a hand across the closest trunk and found the latches. The disturbed dust danced across the surface. Setting the candle on the floor, she lifted the lid and spied the black fabric on top, neatly folded. "Thank you, Lord."

Her hands trembled as she removed the coverings, closed

the lid, and picked up the candle. She didn't snuff out the light until she reached the door and returned the stub to the table.

Silvie met her downstairs. "I take care o' dat while you go eat sumpin. We's all gwan ta need strength t'day and t'morrow."

Hannah retreated to the kitchen and forced down several bites of biscuit and gravy, then returned to the parlor to help Silvie with other tasks. At the tea table, Caleb cut and folded lengths of fabric for arm bands. Hannah whispered her thanks to Silvie as they covered the mirror in the entryway. "I'm glad you found something for Caleb to do."

Thomas emerged from the back hallway. "Miss Virginia says to clear a space in de parlor." He lifted a handkerchief to his eyes.

Hannah pretended not to notice as she followed him in. "We might need to bring chairs from the other rooms too." How many visitors should they expect for the wake? The war had thrown normal customs into disarray, and they'd held no wake for her father, so she had little experience to guide her.

By the time they brought in the extra furniture, an hour had passed. Caleb had suggested using his lift to transport chairs from upstairs, then helped with placement. While Thomas moved a Queen Anne chair closer to the fireplace, Hannah kept an eye peeled for Rupert's return. How strange that she'd already grown so used to having him around and missed his comforting presence.

"Hannah, dear?" Aunt Ginny stood tall but gripped the parlor doorjamb with white knuckles. "Where's that husband of yours?"

"He drove Quentin with a note to Reverend Covington's."

"Soon as they get back, I'll need him and Quentin to help Thomas bring Liam into the parlor." To a stranger, Aunt Ginny would seem to be unmoved by her husband's death.

Caleb's eyes widened. Did their aunt's brusque tone upset him?

Hannah waited for her aunt to wander away before she moved close to Caleb's side. "Aunt Ginny believes she has to pretend nothing has changed, dear. She thinks it will make things better for everyone if she goes on as usual. It's just her way of dealing with any problem."

Only in the last year had Hannah come to that conclusion. People called Aunt Ginny a "tough old bird" because of her demeanor. Those folks hadn't witnessed the strain on her face in private moments as Hannah had. In a rare instance of vulnerability, she'd told Hannah, "Never reveal your weakness to anyone who can use it to hurt you, and that's everyone."

Maybe that was why Hannah hadn't told Rupert about Caleb. She'd had the opportunity to tell him, either in Alabama or on the trip to Whitfield Hall. She'd kept the news to herself not because she didn't trust Rupert, but because she viewed Caleb's disability as a family weakness.

An hour later, Rupert returned, giving her a kiss on the temple as if it were the most normal thing in the world.

"What did Reverend Covington say?"

"He'll pass the word and come by later this afternoon to confer with your aunt."

"That's good. Aunt Ginny wants you and Quentin to help Thomas move Uncle Liam's body to the parlor."

"All right. I'll get Quentin and do that now. By the way, you remember that Ma said I should wire my brother, Simon, when we arrived? I went to do so while we were in town and found a wire from him. Is there a spare bedroom he can use? He's in Decatur and might be here as early as tomorrow."

～

inding the message from Simon shouldn't have surprised Rupert. Simon had always been a step ahead of everyone else in the family. So Rupert's reply had noted the passing of Liam Murphy and included an invitation to Whitfield Hall at his earliest availability. If Simon could fit it into his schedule, having his brother on hand for advice would be a boon to Rupert.

Hannah's eyes widened. "Tomorrow? How could he get here so quickly?"

"He got my letter just before he left Gainesville to meet with a client in Decatur. He included the client's direction, so my message went there. I reckon he'll come here when he finishes his business since Decatur is closer to us than Gainesville."

When Hannah didn't say any more but stared at him with a strange, faraway look, he took her aside. He'd seen soldiers react in a similar manner when they were hit or during their first battle. He led her to a chair near the front window. "Hannah, I want you to sit here while I go help Thomas. Do not move from this spot, all right?" At her nod, he kissed her forehead. "I'll be back in a few minutes."

Quentin met him in the hallway. "Pap says—"

"I know. You and I have to provide our muscles." Despite the somber atmosphere, Quentin returned Rupert's smile. At least he'd made strides toward winning over one more person here.

Once they carried Liam's body to the parlor, Rupert joined Hannah, still sitting where he'd left her. Her sorrow resonated with his own at Henry's passing, and he wrapped his arms around her. The action must've broken through her grief, for her sobs welled up.

He held her, offering his handkerchief. She accepted it and dabbed at her face. "Uncle Liam held out until he knew we'd be taken care of, didn't he? Until you arrived to take over the job he'd tried to do."

"It looks that way." He nodded toward the parlor doorway where Silvie escorted the first visitors to Aunt Ginny. "Judging from the respect your people have for him, I believe he was a man who took his responsibilities seriously."

"He was a good man. Always treated everyone well." She blew out a breath. "Thank you for being here."

At the risk of shocking her aunt, who sat across the room and would frown upon a public display of affection, Rupert leaned in and placed a kiss at the corner of Hannah's mouth. "I'll come up with a way you can express your appreciation later."

A rosy blush tinted her cheeks, but her eyes sparkled at his teasing. "You presume much, Mr. McNeil."

He coughed to cover his chuckle, which would be unseemly under the circumstances. But he'd chased away the lost countenance she'd had earlier. They were growing into a friendship as Hannah seemed to trust him more and he learned to read her moods. But so many changes pressed upon them, would circumstances drive them apart or bring them together?

∾

The next day, Hannah fought off a headache as she sat through another round of visits from neighbors. Though she appreciated everyone's kindness, the duty was wearing her down.

Aunt Ginny had decreed a change to their routine. "Silvie has enough to do, with preparing and carting refreshments to the parlor. Until the wake is over, we'll take the noon meal in the kitchen, two of us at a time."

Caleb groused to Hannah as she passed him on his way to the kitchen. "I don't like having to spend all day in the parlor and listen to the adults."

"You could take a book to read," Hannah said.

His frown deepened. "But I can't play with any games or toys. Aunt Ginny says I have to sit quietly."

Hannah rubbed her forehead and shared her concerns with Rupert as they ate their meal. "I'm worried Aunt Ginny might collapse under the strain of holding in her emotions. And Caleb grows more irritable with each passing hour."

Rupert swallowed his last bite of cornbread. "I don't know what to suggest for your aunt, but maybe I could help with Caleb. Let me take him outside for a while. He's too young to handle long hours of such a duty. He needs some time away from this depressive atmosphere."

Hannah stacked their dishes and took them to the sink as she considered his suggestion. "I suppose he didn't get outside much while I was gone. Just watch that he doesn't take a chill."

Rupert followed with his empty cup. "I'll take care of him. We won't go far, and we'll be back before your aunt misses us."

"I hope so. She might not think it's a good idea for him to be out of the house at this time."

"Hannah..." Rupert settled his hands on her shoulders. "She wanted me to come—well, she wanted Uncle Henry, but she got me instead. Now, I'm Caleb's guardian, and I take my responsibilities seriously. Why don't you go back to the parlor and send Caleb to me?"

His kindness stirred feelings she'd never experienced. She found herself seeking opportunities to be with him, thrilled when he sent a smile her way or put his arm around her. Unsure of how to deal with those emotions, she nodded and hurried from the kitchen.

An hour later, she gathered the most recent guests' used plates and cups to return to the kitchen and check on her husband and brother. A glance out the back window revealed them beside the barn. Rupert stood several yards away from Caleb's chair and tossed him a ball. Caleb stretched out one arm and caught it, then he threw it back. The ball went back and forth a dozen times, Rupert increasing the distance from Caleb with each toss. Though he'd only known her brother for a day, Rupert had already connected with him and was teaching him a new skill. And getting his mind off his loss.

A knock sounded at the front door, and Hannah scurried to answer it, knowing Silvie had her hands full with the guests already there.

The stranger on her porch removed his hat, and though she'd never met him before, she knew who it had to be.

"If this is Whitfield Hall," he said, "then you must be my new sister-in-law. I'm Simon McNeil."

"Rupert didn't tell me you were twins." With his features so much like Rupert's, people must confuse the two.

He laughed. "We're not, but we've been mistaken for each other enough that we could pretend, if we wanted."

"I'm so glad to meet you, Simon." She stepped back. "Unfortunately, we've had a loss in the family. Please, come inside. Would you like to hang your hat?" She indicated the hat rack stand in the corner. "Let me introduce you to my aunt, and I'll send someone to fetch Ru—Henry. He's outside with my brother."

She met Silvie coming from the kitchen. "Silvie, please ask Quentin to let Mr. McNeil know his brother has arrived."

"Yes'm." The older woman did a double-take, then hurried to do her bidding.

In the parlor, Hannah introduced Simon, who bowed to each lady and took Aunt Ginny's hand. "My condolences on your loss, Mrs. Murphy. I hope my presence doesn't bring an additional burden to your time of grieving. As I'm sure you know, my brother requested that I come to offer him some guidance on the estate."

"Of course, Mr. McNeil. We are pleased you could make the trip. You're welcome to stay as long as you see fit."

Hannah stepped away from the women toward a pair of chairs flanking a window. "May I offer you some tea while we wait for Rupert?"

"I would welcome a cup, with a bit of honey, if you have any." He didn't sit but gazed out the window until Hannah returned with two cups. She passed one to him, and both claimed their seats.

"I know I should ask about your trip," Hannah said, "but what I really want to hear about is your wife. Millie said her name is Daviana. Did I get it right?"

Simon's smile broadened. "That's right. She made the trip with me, but she's resting at the hotel in town. Our nephew is with us, and we didn't want to impose on your family without ample notice."

"Oh, please bring them. We have plenty of room. How old is your nephew? He might prove good company for Caleb."

"Albert just turned eight. Perhaps I'll bring them over after your uncle is laid to rest."

A soft knock sounded on the window behind them. Hannah and Simon turned that way at the same time. What was Rupert doing out there without his hat and coat? He gestured for Simon to come to him.

Simon grinned. "It seems my brother needs me to meet him outside. What has he been doing, running the grounds?"

"Tossing a ball with my brother. I hope Caleb doesn't look as ragged as Rupert does."

Simon rose, still holding his teacup. He glanced toward Aunt Ginny and her visitors on the other side of the room. "I suppose I should give your aunt some excuse..."

Hannah took his cup and set it with hers on a sideboard. "I'll tell her you're going to retrieve your baggage, then I'll follow so I can check on my brother."

How wonderful it was to have a family ready to come to one's rescue on such short notice. Going to Alabama had been the right thing to do. *Thank You, Lord. And please pass on my thanks to Mr. Henry.*

CHAPTER 20

*R*upert paced away from the window when Simon
stood.

Simon stepped onto the porch and held the door for
Hannah to follow. His wife's brisk walk indicated either displeasure or concern about something.

Simon lagged behind while Hannah raked her gaze over
Rupert. Her mouth pinched, but she kept her voice low. "I
thought you were with Caleb. Where is he? He isn't hurt, is he?"

He greeted her with a cheerful voice. "Hello, Hannah. Caleb
is fine. Quentin stayed with him. I ran from the field when I
heard Simon had come." Then he held out a hand to his
brother. "Good to see you, Simon. I trust your business went
well?"

Amusement danced in Simon's eyes. "Yes, I merely had to
deliver some important papers and get a client's signature. I see
you're keeping in shape. Where did you run from?"

Grinning, Rupert gestured behind him with his thumb.
"Caleb called it the south cotton field."

"And you left my brother out there?" Hannah's face went

from fiery to pale. She gathered her skirts and turned toward the barn. "We've got to get him."

With a quick move, Rupert hooked her arm. "Hold on now. Quentin is a responsible young man. He'll bring him back directly."

"But the south field!" She glanced in that direction, then rounded on Rupert. "How did you get so far? I saw the two of you tossing a ball not long ago."

Heat rushed into Rupert's face. "I, uh, pushed his chair. The path there is remarkably smooth."

Hannah's mouth twisted to one side. "May I ask *why* you took him so far?" Without waiting for an answer, she addressed Simon. "My brother is confined to a wheeled chair, you see, and he's only six years old."

An expression of mild alarm replaced Simon's amusement. He grasped Rupert's shoulder. "Perhaps we should take a wagon and bring him back in it."

Considering his wife's attitude, Rupert nodded. "Sure, we can do that."

"I would appreciate that." Hannah started toward the house, then turned back to Rupert. "When you get back, I recommend you and Caleb clean yourselves up and take your places in the parlor."

She ascended the steps and marched inside.

Simon gave a slow whistle. "I think you've got some making up to do there, bud."

Rupert led the way to the barn. "Yeah, it probably wasn't a good idea. But the boy has been cooped up in the house for who knows how long. It's not the family's fault, since the women can't lift him and the uncle who just passed was bedridden. As far as I can tell, the only other occupants are Quentin and his parents, who stay busy keepin' up the house."

While they hitched up the wagon, Rupert relayed the story of Caleb's injury. "I reckon it might be hard for Hannah to loosen the leading strings, so to speak, and let him test his limits."

"You might be walking a fine line there." Simon climbed aboard as Rupert took up the horse's reins. "Now, concerning the person who's been plaguing Hannah about taking her property, I did a little research. Not to disparage your wife's home or family," Simon said, "but I wonder why this Captain Prescott is so determined to take over Whitfield Hall. Between here and Atlanta, there are several large homes that escaped the Union torches and might be available for purchase."

"Perhaps the draw is not the land so much as its current mistress, and I don't mean Mrs. Murphy."

"Maybe, but your marriage should have put her beyond reach. From what I heard in town, though, he's set on taking the property." Simon gripped the bench as the wagon hit a rut. "And gossip indicates he has conflicting interests elsewhere."

"What gossip?"

"According to my client in Decatur, Prescott used to frequent a popular men's club when he was in the area. He would brag about having a fiancé up north, which turned out to be false, but he also liked to visit a certain madam in Decatur."

Rupert pressed his lips together to keep from uttering the words that popped into his mind. What was the real reason Prescott wanted Whitfield Hall?

"We could ask around town," Rupert said, "but I have no idea which citizens might be Prescott's allies." He stopped the wagon a few yards from Caleb and Quentin.

Simon caught Rupert's arm before he disembarked to help them board. "You might ask your wife some direct questions too. Is there a reason Prescott would overlook other properties and focus on Whitfield Hall?"

Rupert scoffed. "Surely, Hannah would've told me if she knew that answer." But a nagging voice questioned his statement. She hadn't bothered to tell him about Caleb's condition. Was she hiding something else?

~

*R*elieved that daylight was fading and thus ending the long hours of sitting with her aunt through this second day, Hannah packed away her needlework and rose from her chair. She greeted the neighbor who'd come to sit through the evening, then followed Aunt Ginny into the hallway in time to see the office door open across the hall.

Rupert preceded Simon to the threshold and shook hands with him. "I know you're ready to get back to Davi. Tell her I appreciate her letting you spend the afternoon here."

Aunt Ginny spread out her hands. "Oh, won't you stay for supper, Mr. McNeil?"

"Not tonight, ma'am." Simon stuffed a notebook in his pocket and plucked his hat off the hat rack. "My wife is at the hotel, and I promised to dine with her and our nephew. Rupert will explain what we discussed, and I'll be back tomorrow." He settled his hat and turned to the door. "Goodnight, Mrs. Murphy, Hannah."

As soon as the front door shut behind Simon, Caleb maneuvered his chair beside Rupert. "I'm hungry. Ain't it time for supper?"

Had her brother been in the meeting with Simon all this time? She'd thought maybe he'd gone to his room when the men returned. Silvie had only said they were back, and she'd given Caleb and Quentin a glass of buttermilk to tide them over till supper.

Aunt Ginny either didn't take note of Caleb's improper language or decided to overlook it. "Supper should be ready by the time we all freshen up a bit. Get cleaned up, Caleb, then meet us in the dining room. Maybe Henry will share with us what he and his brother discussed." Her gaze swept over Rupert's disheveled appearance. "It must have presented quite a struggle."

Aunt Ginny followed Caleb down the hallway. Hannah smirked as Rupert offered no excuse for his dishevelment. She turned toward the stairway, but Rupert caught up to her on the second step.

"Now I know where your cleaning obsession comes from. Your aunt trained you well."

She continued to climb. "You and Simon talked for quite a while this afternoon."

"Yeah, we went over your pa's will and some of the Georgia laws about property. After your uncle's funeral, I need to check the county records concerning taxes and find out how to get Caleb's name on the deed. Simon suggested having your uncle's will read as soon as possible so we can see whether it affects anything related to the property."

They reached the top and continued to the bedroom door. Rupert paused with his hand on the doorknob. "Uh, if you want to go first, I can wait out here."

Hannah turned her face away to hide her blush. "Thank you. I only need to wash my face and hands, then you can have the space to yourself." She entered the suite and hurried through her ablutions. In minutes, she let him in. "The dressing room is all yours."

Rupert grinned as he held up a crock. "Thomas brought more water. Your aunt must think I rolled in the dirt."

Hannah laughed as he headed to the smaller room. She perched on the stool set beneath the covered mirror. "I'll wait here for you." Using only her damp fingers, she smoothed her hair as best she could. Would it be so awful if she uncovered just a corner of her mirror to check her appearance? The late Henry McNeil had instructed his family to ignore such traditions.

In the dressing room behind her, Rupert sang and splashed water. A grin teased her lips. Maybe it was a good idea to leave the mirror covered in case he wandered about unclothed. What was he doing? She slapped her cheeks to chastise herself for her curiosity. Marriage certainly wasn't turning out the way she'd expected.

When Rupert's hands gripped her shoulders, she startled and rose from the stool. "Are you ready to go downstairs?"

Serious blue eyes roamed her face. "I'm sorry we abandoned you and your family at this time. Sitting through a wake can wear on a body."

His apology almost made up for his absence. She dropped her gaze and shrugged. "Your discussion was important. We're depending on you to do what's necessary for the family's future."

"I also need to apologize for causing you alarm concerning Caleb—"

"No." Her head jerked up. She touched his lips with her fingers. "I'm sorry I got upset. You're right that he needed to be outside, to enjoy being a boy. I should have—"

"You've done everything you could for him, which I learned first-hand." Rupert squeezed her shoulders and then nudged her toward the door. "Caleb knows you and your aunt have had your hands full here. He's pretty perceptive for his age."

Rupert gestured for her to precede him to the stairway. "He asked about people calling me by different names. He found it confusing. I explained that legal papers are usually issued in a person's first name, even if it's not the name the person goes by. Hopefully, he'll give the same explanation if anyone asks him about that."

"Ah, good thinking." And fortunate he'd used Caleb's question as a teaching opportunity. Someone might try to trip up Caleb about Rupert's legitimacy as her brother's trustee. She should have considered that as a possibility. She wouldn't put anything past Captain Oscar Prescott.

~

*A*fter tossing for an hour on his lonely couch, Rupert gave up trying to sleep. The fault wasn't his narrow bed, however, but the questions that kept running in circles through his mind.

He pulled on his trousers and eased past the partition into the larger room. A full moon shining through the window provided enough light to make his way to the cup and pitcher on the dresser. He poured some water and gulped it down. When the metal cup scraped across the porcelain pitcher, he cringed and shot a glance toward Hannah's sleeping form. She didn't stir as he made his way to the window and stared across the sloping lawn.

He ran through his conversation with Simon when they'd taken the wagon to bring Caleb back to the house. Why would Prescott overlook other houses in the area? From what Rupert had seen and Simon had said, Whitfield Hall wasn't the largest holding, nor was it the only one with back taxes to be paid. Perhaps he'd thought it would be easier to seize, with only women and uneducated slaves to watch over the young heir.

Since the captain hadn't come around today to press his case, maybe he'd heard of Hannah's marriage and given up. Still, Rupert wouldn't let down his guard against potential trouble. And he meant to question his wife in case she had knowledge she hadn't yet shared.

CHAPTER 21

S ince Rupert had taken over the household's legal and financial responsibilities, Hannah put those worries out of her mind. Her primary duty for the next couple of days centered on helping Aunt Ginny during the wake and funeral.

She brought a basket of ferns, marigolds, and a couple of purple tulips she and Silvie had picked into the parlor. Creating an arrangement for Uncle Liam's grave would occupy her during the long hours. Unfortunately, while her hands stayed busy, her mind wandered to her husband and their growing relationship. She'd never anticipated the intimate details of marriage because she hadn't had the time or opportunity to think about it. All her energies had focused on her family's needs.

Rupert's attention roused mixed feelings and pointed out her lack of experience with men. Before Hannah's visit to Alabama, Aunt Ginny had assured her an older husband would be happy to guide Hannah through the intricacies of marriage. Having a husband close to her own age created a problem, for Rupert seemed to have no clear idea of how to be a husband any more than she did of being a wife. Sometimes he appeared to study her as if she was a rare creature he'd never encountered before. Though he showed her deference and shared his thoughts on matters that affected them all, he seemed to hold back some part of himself. Honesty forced her to admit she might be doing the same. Did they both fear making a misstep?

Silvie stepped into the parlor. "Captain Prescott be here, ma'am."

Hannah stood from the settee, where she'd hoped Rupert might join her.

Aunt Ginny paused in her conversation with a widow whose name Hannah never could get right.

It would be unseemly to turn Captain Prescott away from a house of mourning. Had he not heard about her marriage, or did he come to find out if the rumors were true?

At Hannah's hesitant nod, Aunt Ginny told Silvie to show him in.

Hannah gathered her stems and scissors, preparing to move to the chair next to her aunt, but the odious man must have waited at the parlor door. He took quick strides to bow before her aunt and then stood before Hannah.

Parted in the middle, his dark hair lay flat against his head, with a faint indentation left by the hat he now held at his side. His pale blue eyes seemed incongruent with his angular face, now set in stern lines. "I'd hoped to have a private audience with you today, Miss Whitfield. Would you step across the hall or outside where we may speak?"

"I'm sorry, but I can't do that for several reasons." She picked up the flowers again. 'Twas rude of her, perhaps, but it kept her confidence from flagging in the face of Captain Prescott's boldness. "One, my aunt needs me here with her. Two, it would be unseemly for me to meet privately with a man who isn't my husband, and three, my husband wouldn't allow it." She twined two stems together, then looked up. "By the way, my name is Mrs. McNeil."

His face darkened with ire while she spoke, and he sneered down at her. He must believe it gave him an advantage to loom over her. "I heard rumors you'd married, but that name isn't familiar. Where is this fellow?" He looked around as if she'd hidden Rupert behind a lamp. "Is he from the area? I haven't seen any new faces around town."

Hannah snipped leaves from a marigold. "My husband and I arrived several days ago. I believe we just missed your last visit, or so my aunt told me. As for Henry, you can imagine he has many estate issues to attend to with my uncle's passing. Why, we've hardly had any time to ourselves since we arrived."

Her unwelcome visitor raised one eyebrow as he studied her. "My dear Miss Whitfield, I believe you are lying about your married status."

She gasped, outraged. "How dare—"

"I believe this marriage is all a ruse to deny me my opportunity to obtain Whitfield Hall. Why you would do so, however, completely escapes me. As you know, I was prepared to overlook your Confederate connections and marry you so your family could remain here. But my patience is at an end. I will consult with the county officials tomorrow about paying the back taxes so I may take possession as soon as possible."

Trembling with anger, Hannah pointed to the door. "You would be wise to show yourself out now, Captain, before I have someone throw you out."

He sneered. "On the contrary, it's you who'll be thrown out in a few days. Best start packing your wardrobe"—he made of show of looking around—"but leave the furniture." He strode from the room without a word to the others.

Hannah closed her eyes and took deep breaths to calm herself, waiting to hear the door's closing to announce Prescott's departure.

Rupert had paid the back taxes on the land first thing that morning. After proclaiming his status as Caleb's guardian, the threat should be over. What did Prescott think he could do to take it from them? She shouldn't let him upset her, but the coldness with which he predicted an outcome suitable for himself raised her ire.

She tried to focus on her handiwork again, vaguely aware of the widow taking her leave as Silvie led Simon and his wife into the parlor.

She dropped her materials into a basket and rose to greet them. Simon introduced his wife to Aunt Ginny first. Daviana topped Hannah's height by a couple of inches, with her dark hair, close to the same shade as Simon's, parted in the middle and pulled into a simple chignon. A plaid shawl adorned her dress of dark blue, set off by a white lacy collar.

Simon turned her to Hannah. "And this is Hannah. She deserves our thanks for bringing Rupert a little closer to our home. Hannah, this is my wife, Daviana. I'm not sure which of you is more excited to meet the other."

Hannah clasped Daviana's hand, willing the anger at Prescott from her mind. "I'm so pleased you could come. I hope the journey didn't overtax you." She cast a quick glance at the slight bulge at Daviana's waist. "If you'll take a seat, I'll bring you a cup of tea. Simon, will you join us?"

He held up his hands. "No, I should go out and supervise the boys. We spotted Caleb and Quentin in the yard as we arrived, and Albert begged to join them. I didn't see Rupert, though. Is he in the office?"

"No, he left the house right after he returned from town. Said he wanted to view the fields before he hires laborers." She leaned toward Daviana and whispered, "I think he just needed to be outside."

Simon grinned. "He's like our pa, ready to start planting soon as the calendar says it's spring. I'll see if I can round him up."

He sauntered toward the door, and Hannah directed

Daviana to a chair near Aunt Ginny while she poured tea into cups. "Do you take your tea with honey, Davi?"

"Yes, please." She sat and leaned toward Aunt Ginny. "If you don't mind my asking, who was the officer who left as we arrived? He was quite rude."

Aunt Ginny's eyes snapped to Hannah. "That was Captain Prescott, the man who wants Whitfield Hall for himself. Whatever did you say to him, Hannah?"

"When he accused me of lying about my marriage to Rupert, I told him to leave." She handed Davi the cup she'd prepared and took her own seat. "But I'd rather not waste time speaking of the captain. I want to hear all about Davi and Simon."

No need to bother the others with Prescott's delusional prediction. He had no claim on her or Whitfield Hall, not as long as Rupert was around.

~

*S*imon, Daviana, and Albert provided a welcome distraction from the sorrowful atmosphere. Rupert had worried that having overnight guests might disturb Hannah's aunt, but even she seemed to enjoy Simon's stories during supper.

Caleb and Albert got along right from the start. The moment Albert had returned from his tour of Caleb's room, he'd rushed to the parlor to tell Daviana about the converted dumbwaiter.

"It's like a lift in the mines I heard about in Tennessee, and it goes from this floor up to the next one, right into Caleb's bedroom."

"Please contain yourself for a minute, Albert." Daviana claimed his attention with a hand to his shoulder. "Say hello to Caleb's sister, Hannah."

"Hello." His eyes lit up. "Since Mr. Rupert is Uncle Simon's brother, does that make him my uncle and Caleb my cousin? Then I could call you Aunt Hannah too?"

Rupert ruffled the boy's hair. "That may be a bit of a stretch, but we can always use another nephew."

From Hannah's smile, Albert had won her over. "Certainly, if you wish to. Nice to meet you, Albert."

Caleb wore a broad grin throughout the meal. Because of his injury, Hannah had confided, he'd never had a friend his own age. "Soon as we finish eating, we're gonna take the checkerboard to my room. Is that all right?"

His hopeful gaze touched on each adult, ending with his aunt Ginny. Her shoulders drooped with fatigue, but the lines in her face softened as she answered. "One hour only. We all need our sleep before the funeral tomorrow."

The boys hurried to finish their meal and set off for their game. The adults followed more slowly, each going to their designated rooms.

Rupert closed the bedroom door behind him as Hannah removed her shoes and set them beside the dresser. She must be deep in thought, since she didn't rush him into the sitting room. Either that or she was too tired to care—or perhaps she'd grown accustomed to his presence.

Like iron to a magnet, she drew his gaze and his interest. Curiosity and compassion melded with desire to urge his feet forward. She pulled pins from her hair and worked her fingers into a braid. Standing behind her, he gently joined her work. After a startled, "Oh," she succumbed to the offered gift and dropped her hands, humming her pleasure.

Once her braid was free, he moved on to her neck and shoulders.

Her words came out slow and breathy. "Rupert, what are you doing?"

He leaned close and whispered in her ear. "Massaging the

tension from your body so you can sleep." His lips traveled to her neck as his hands drifted to her waist. "Do you have any more questions, Mrs. McNeil?"

"Mmm." She sniffed. "What's that smell?"

He raised his head, inhaled, and stiffened. "Smoke."

Rupert rushed to check the rest of the house. He met Simon in the hallway. "You smell it too?"

"Yeah. It's outside. I saw a glow in the field from my window. Davi had a bad experience with fire years ago, so I told her I'd send Albert to stay with her."

Hannah emerged from their room. "What can I do?"

"Check on your aunt and the boys in Caleb's room, and send Albert to stay with Davi." Rupert hurried toward the stairs after Simon. He turned back as she knocked on Caleb's door. "Where's the water pump?"

"One in the kitchen, one outside the barn."

Downstairs, the neighbor—Mr. Jenkins?—who'd volunteered for this night of the wake stopped Simon outside the parlor door. "Thought you folks had retired. What's all the ruckus about?"

Drat. The custom of having neighbors stay overnight in the house meant more people to watch out for.

"There's a fire. We'll let you know if there's any danger of it spreading. Which direction is your place?"

The older man raked a hand over his balding head. "East of here, a couple miles."

"The window in Simon's room faces northwest, I believe. Your place shouldn't be in danger." Rupert turned to Simon. "Let's grab some pails from the kitchen."

They found three pails and a wooden bucket and then raced outside.

Thomas and Quentin came around the barn. "It be jes' de hay shed," Thomas shouted.

"Thank You, Lord." Simon's expression of gratitude echoed

Rupert's thoughts.

Hannah dragged a couple of shovels from the barn. When did she slip past him? "I thought you might need these to dig a trench or toss dirt on the fire."

He plucked them from her hands and passed one to Simon as they followed her. "You should've stayed inside..."

She was running to the pump, paying him no heed.

No point in arguing. He tramped closer to the fire and started digging, but his gaze tracked Hannah's movements and kept up with the others' locations.

Though the night turned cool, the fire's heat and exertion had Rupert huffing and wiping sweat from his brow as he dug a trench, then tossed buckets full of water on the flames. Time passed in a blur as the group worked together to keep the blaze from spreading to the other outbuildings.

At last, the fire fizzled out.

Thomas and Quentin bid them goodnight, and the others dragged into the house near midnight.

Rupert clapped Simon's shoulder as they climbed the stairs. "Sorry to give you this kind of welcome."

Simon swiped his brow. "Well, at least we'll have an exciting story to share about our visit. Davi says my law practice pays the bills, but our farming keeps life interesting. Let's try to get a few hours of sleep now."

He trudged to the guest room while Rupert and Hannah returned to their room.

Hannah kicked off her shoes. "I'm sorry we lost the hay shed, but at least the damage was limited to one building." She sounded half asleep as she padded to the bed. "It was probably close to empty, anyway."

"So what could have caused the fire? Hay fueled it, but I can think of no reason for it to burst into flames." Rupert didn't like to speculate without cause, but Hannah had reported Prescott's visit and rude remarks. It would be easy enough for someone to sneak on the property and set up a fire trail that would eat its way to the shed.

"Good question. I'm just thankful the grass in that area was sparse so the blaze didn't spread."

He sat on the stool by the dresser to remove his boots. "Tomorrow, after the funeral, I'll ride around the property and examine the site."

"What do you *think* caused the fire?" Her voice drifted on another yawn. She lay back on the bed.

Rupert hedged. "I couldn't say. It was too dark to identify anything." If Prescott caused the fire—as he strongly suspected —then the man was sending a message. Rupert needed to meet with Prescott so he could figure out what the captain really wanted. After Liam's funeral in the morning, maybe Simon could assist.

He rose and crossed to the window, peering into the night for questionable movements. Unable to detect any threat, he turned back, his gaze drawn to the fully dressed woman sleeping on top of the covers. Three steps took him to her side.

A glimmer of moonlight revealed her pale neck and hair that splayed across the pillow like a wild halo. This woman had upended his life and dragged him far from his roots, pitching him into a potential struggle for which he felt ill-prepared. Yet a wave of emotion caught him unaware. Gratitude. Admiration. Fondness.

Not love. He wouldn't allow it. Love was too dangerous.

With careful movements, he sat, then stretched out beside her. His heavier weight dipped the mattress and brought her closer. Hannah's soft snores vibrated against his chest. She might rail at him in the morning, but tonight she'd sleep beside him, where she belonged.

CHAPTER 22

a gentle rain had fallen around dawn, giving way to overcast skies as the family assembled for Uncle Liam's final farewell. For the first time in over a year, Hannah stood in the family graveyard, a stretch of land separated from the house by a line of dogwood trees about to bloom. Fatigue and sorrow pulled her thoughts toward darkness, but Reverend Covington's voice broke through the gloom.

"The apostle Paul admonished us 'concerning those who are asleep, that ye sorrow not, even as others who have no hope.' We who know Christ have the promise of being reunited with our loved ones after death." He read another Scripture, then prayed for the comfort of those left behind.

Rupert's presence beside Hannah bolstered her spirit. He had positioned himself between her and Aunt Ginny. The hint of his cologne reminded Hannah of waking to find him next to her.

Her sharp inhale must have wakened him, for his eyes had flickered, then opened wide. Her initial alarm had evaporated as his gaze changed from surprised to teasing.

Rupert had slanted her a smile. "Good morning, Mrs.

McNeil. I trust you slept well?" He'd brushed a strand of hair from her face, and her heartbeat sped up.

A smudge of soot near his temple made her sit up to appraise Rupert's filthy clothes. "I can't believe we slept in this condition. We've got to get cleaned up."

Rupert had chuckled and propped himself up on one elbow. "I think you look rather fetching in all your sooty glory." His gaze had swept her from head to toe. When she'd snatched down her skirt to cover her ankles, he'd swung his legs over the bed's edge. "All right, I'm going. But be prepared to discuss new sleeping arrangements this evening."

What could that mean?

The pastor's "amen" brought Hannah back to the present. She lifted her fan to cool her flushed face. She ought not to be thinking about such things at her beloved uncle's funeral.

Neighbors and friends shifted to leave. Across the furrow where the coffin rested, Silvie and Quentin flanked Thomas as his rich baritone floated on the air. "'Swing low, sweet chariot, comin' for to carry me home.'"

He continued the song, and the visitors dispersed, many stopping to offer condolences to the family. Hannah introduced Rupert to those he hadn't met during the wake.

When Oscar Prescott sauntered into view, his hands stuffed in his pockets, Hannah's heart thumped.

Aunt Ginny frowned at his mumbled greeting, then motioned to Rupert. "And may I present Mr. Henry McNeil, Hannah's husband."

Hannah pressed closer to Rupert. "This is the man who expressed an interest in acquiring Whitfield Hall."

When the captain made no move to shake hands, Rupert nodded. "Sorry to disappoint you, Prescott, but it's not for sale. I might consider leasing part of the property, depending on how you plan to use it. Perhaps we can schedule a meeting to discuss your interest. Say, next week?"

Prescott narrowed his eyes and grumbled, "I'll let you know." He shot a malevolent scowl at Hannah, then stalked away.

Only when he was out of sight did Rupert take the handles of Caleb's chair and push it toward the house. He gave Hannah a lopsided grin. "I'd say that went well."

She walked alongside him, her arm linked with Aunt Ginny's on her other side. Hannah pressed her lips together. Did he think Captain Prescott could be pacified with a small section of the property? She didn't see that as a viable option at all. Prescott would be too close for her peace of mind.

What was Rupert up to? Maybe they could discuss it in private later.

He maneuvered Caleb's chair around a gopher hole. "With Captain Prescott showing up today, I'm glad Simon left earlier to gather information in town so we can plan our next move. When he returns, we'll review it. I think he's eager to get back to his own farm."

Was Rupert thinking of his place in Alabama? Did he feel the pull to return? If so, she could hardly travel with him now, not so soon after Uncle Liam's passing. Something akin to panic quickened her breath.

Caleb pointed to the remains of the hay shed as it came into view. "Weren't you going to search around the shed today and see if you could figure out how the fire started?"

Rupert's uncertain gaze met hers. Did he feel he should stay close while neighbors would be in and out of the house? "Maybe later, Caleb—"

"Oh, go ahead and do your investigation." Aunt Ginny patted Hannah's hand where it rested on her arm. "Hannah and I will take care of things at the house and hear what you find when you're through."

Hannah agreed—they'd all rest easier when they had more answers.

~

*I*n less than half an hour, Rupert and Caleb had collected all the evidence they could find from the hay shed. They returned to the house, asked the women to join them, and spread the items on the desk in the room across from the parlor. Hannah called it the library, but Rupert envisioned it as a place for family gatherings. Shelves of books covered two walls, true, but the room was cozy with several chairs, settees, and lamps set about. A piano sat in a corner opposite the fireplace, the desk on the other side of the instrument.

Aunt Ginny—as he'd started calling her—studied the cigar stubs and pieces of a broken kerosene lamp. "It's definitely arson, but why? If Prescott is after Whitfield Hall, wouldn't he want all the buildings in good condition?"

Hannah tilted her head. "The hay shed was almost empty, and it would be easy to replace. Still, it does seem odd."

Rupert sifted through the items and picked up a cigar butt. "Do you know anyone else around here who smokes these? My guess is, they're too expensive for most folks. Farmers and mill workers seem to prefer snuff or chewin' tobacco."

Aunt Ginny slapped the table edge. "Prescott does. I asked him not to smoke in the house when he first visited. He *wanted* us to find them. It's a warning."

"That's what I think too." Rupert dusted off his hands. "I'm of a mind to see if I can reason with the man, but it will depend on what Simon's learned."

Caleb wheeled his chair from the window. "Maybe that's him coming down the road. He rides a gray horse, don't he?"

"*Doesn't* he," Rupert corrected, then caught the women's amused smiles. "Hey, my ma was a schoolteacher, remember?" He crossed to the window in time to see Simon dismount and hand the horse's reins to Thomas.

As soon as the front door opened, Rupert called out, "We're in the library, Simon. Come and see what we've found."

With saddlebags over one shoulder, Simon joined them. He dropped the baggage on the floor and strode to the desk. "Did all this come from the building that burned down last night?"

"Yep. What do you think?"

"I think the person who set the fire was far from subtle." He picked up the same cigar stub Rupert had. "One of my clients in Gainesville keeps a box of these cigars on his desk, but he's never offered me one. They must be expensive."

Rupert shook his head. "The culprit must think we'll throw up our hands and quit. What did you learn in town?"

Simon's mouth twisted to the side. "I hope you have some money saved up." He pulled papers from the saddlebags and handed them to Rupert. "Another round of taxes due in July, plus a small lien against the property matures in another month."

He'd hoped paying the back taxes would hold them until next year. Hannah's careful notes had indicated as much, but she'd admitted she'd been guessing at the numbers. The small payments she'd been able to make had helped to safeguard the property, but the lien was news. He flipped through the sheets as Simon recounted his experience.

"I introduced myself as Mr. McNeil in case the local clerks tried to refuse me access to the files. Except for Mrs. Murphy's attorney, that is, who knew I was acting on your behalf. You'll find a copy of Mr. Whitfield's will there, which names Henry R. McNeil as the trustee upon the death of Mr. Liam Murphy. A codicil added shortly before his demise."

Simon's gaze went to Aunt Ginny. "Mrs. Murphy, I hope you don't mind that I requested your husband's will be read tomorrow morning. All things considered, I thought the earlier that's done, the better for all of you."

Aunt Ginny's head bobbed. "Just as you say, Mr. McNeil. We must arm ourselves with every weapon available."

"Then you'll be staying until that's done, Simon?" Hannah glanced from him to Rupert. "I'm sure you have work waiting for you at home, but we'd love for y'all to stay as long as you can."

"I can only promise you a couple more days," Simon said. "After that, we'll see how Davi's feeling. Traveling in her condition isn't easy. I hope y'all might consider visiting us before long, perhaps about the time the baby comes. I'm sure Davi would welcome some help."

"Oh, I'd love to be there then. It's been a while since I've taken care of a little one." Hannah's cheeks bloomed in a genuine smile.

The sight lit a spark of pleasure in Rupert's heart. If only he could ensure she retained such joy.

Aunt Ginny rose from her chair. "You are family now, young man. You and your wife will always be welcome here. The children too. Now, if you'll excuse me, I think I'll lie down until mealtime."

Though the woman's step didn't falter, her shoulders sagged.

When she was out of hearing, Hannah sighed. "These last few months have worn her down. Not that she'll admit it."

Rupert stuffed the papers in a desk drawer and sank into a chair. The burden of responsibility sat heavily on his shoulders. Back in Alabama, he had only Malachi, Jewel, and Levi to worry about. Adding Whitfield Hall more than doubled the people relying on him.

Simon reached into his inside coat pocket. "I forgot about this." He held out a paper to Rupert. "A wire from someone at home."

Rupert extended his hand. "Probably Byron. He's watching

out for my interests in Alabama." But what would prompt Byron to send him a telegram so soon?

CHAPTER 23

$\mathcal{H}$annah held her breath as Rupert opened the message. *Please, Lord, no more problems. We have enough already.*

When his brow cleared, she exhaled.

He read the message aloud. "'All is well. The surveyor arrived.'" He folded the paper and stuck it in his pocket, then glanced at Hannah. "So I guess our new neighbor isn't wastin' any time getting her house started."

"New neighbor?" Simon picked up his saddlebag. "Who would that be?"

Rupert turned to Simon. "Didn't I tell you? Wilma bought two acres that back up to Callahan's farm."

"Why? Doesn't she have enough houses?" Simon's voice carried the same note of hostility toward his cousin Rupert's had on occasion. Did the woman go through life making enemies?

"She sold the one in Jacksonville and used part of the proceeds to purchase the land and hire an architect to build the new one."

"You'd best watch her, brother. Before you know it, she'll be runnin' your life."

Simon's reaction confirmed Hannah's fears about Wilma.

Rupert shot back, "I'm not seven years old. I've learned not to let her push me around. Besides, I don't expect her to live there all the time. She likes the Mobile shore too much."

Simon relented with raised hands. "Hey, sorry. I just remember how she treated you when we were kids. I haven't seen her in seven or eight years, so maybe she's easier to deal with now."

Hannah shook her head but kept quiet. Although the message in the telegram didn't bring bad news, something about it bothered Rupert. Did it say more than he'd shared, or did he find it strange that Bryon sent a wire so soon?

She waited until they retired for the night to mention it. "You seemed troubled about the telegram Byron sent. Did you hope Wilma would wait until all the planting was finished?"

"Yes, but that's not what bothered me. I left off the last line to avoid Simon asking questions I couldn't answer." He crossed to the window, and Hannah followed. The dark glass reflected their image in the lamplight.

"Do you mind telling me what it said?"

He shifted to trail a hand from her shoulder to her hand. "Of course not. We're in this together, but Simon...well, he's a big brother. Bryon said he's coming here with a proposition for me. At least, that's the way I read it." He pulled the paper from his pocket and handed it to her.

She unfolded it. *All well. Surveyor here. See you in two days.*

"Two days? But why?"

"My guess is Wilma has talked him into bringing a proposition of some kind. More land, maybe? She's had time to learn about why we married and is using the information to bargain for more. She must have promised Byron a bonus to speed up the process."

Hannah leaned into Rupert's side. "I'm sorry you have to be here when you must want to be there to keep her in check."

He bent his head and gazed at her, then grinned. "I'm not sorry. I'd much rather be with you. Let Byron take care of Wilma."

His eyes darkened, then he captured her lips with his. Hannah clutched his shoulders as her knees threatened to give way. Sweet and tentative, the kiss symbolized their relationship and offered hope for the future.

As he'd said, they were in this together. Whatever came of Byron's visit, they would face it as a unit. Hopefully, that unit would remain intact. Hannah already couldn't imagine her life without Rupert in it.

~

*T*he next day's reading of Uncle Liam's will revealed other close connections at Whitfield Hall. When Mr. Grantham arrived, Daviana discreetly took Albert into the library to work on his arithmetic. Hannah and Rupert took the settee with Caleb in his chair beside them and Simon beside Aunt Ginny next to the tea table. On the other side of the fireplace, Thomas, Silvie, and Quentin perched on the edge of the brown horsehair sofa.

The attorney held up a sheaf of papers. "I will leave this copy here for members of the family to share. It's rather brief, since Mr. Murphy converted all his assets into cash when he moved here." Mr. Grantham quickly covered the required legal wording. "Here's the part that directly affects all of you. It reads, 'The proceeds from the sale of the house in Atlanta are to be divided between my half brother, Thomas, and my wife, Virginia.'"

Silvie gasped, and Hannah nearly did as well. She glanced at the others. Silvie had clasped Quentin's hand, both wide-eyed at the news. Aunt Ginny's mouth quirked in a slight smile as she nodded at Thomas, who wiped his eyes with a wadded handkerchief.

All these years, she'd never heard anyone mention the relationship between Thomas and Uncle Liam. If she'd ever wondered why he and his family stayed at Whitfield Hall when they could have left, she'd simply attributed it to loyalty and reluctance to start over somewhere else. Thomas's loyalty was rooted in love, without a smidgen of jealousy or ill will. Now, at last, his loyalty was rewarded and his status as brother made known.

Hannah's heart swelled to know these faithful helpers, now acknowledged as family, would have the means to support themselves. Any amount of money was a boon these days, but especially a blessing to those who'd never held any.

The lawyer peered over his glasses at Rupert. "Mr. Murphy sold the house in 1861 when he and Mrs. Murphy moved here to help with her niece and nephew. He had the foresight to deposit half the money in a bank in Pennsylvania, where it didn't suffer the devaluation of Confederate currency. Since Caleb is Mrs. Murphy's nearest male relative, and you are named as his trustee, Mr. McNeil, that legacy falls under your control."

Beside her, Rupert stiffened, and Hannah slipped her hand over his. Poor man. In less than a month, he'd gone from essentially no responsibilities to having two properties and a new family thrust upon him.

Mr. Grantham presented Rupert with an envelope. "You'll find all the information you need in here. I'll keep a copy at my office also. I understand your preference to be represented by your brother"—he waved toward Simon—"but if you should need me, I'll be glad to assist."

"Thank you, sir. I'll remember that." Rupert stood and escorted the gentleman to the door. When he returned to the parlor, he gave the envelope to Simon, then offered Thomas a handshake. "I don't know the extent of the money available to you, but if you have questions about setting up accounts or such, Simon and I are glad to help you however we can."

"Thank you, sir." Thomas wrapped an arm around his wife. "Me and Silvie will take some time to talk it over and let you know."

"Fine. Take as long as you need."

As Thomas led his family away, Rupert assisted Aunt Ginny to her feet. "I trust none of this came as a surprise to you."

She retained his hand and raised her eyebrows. "Certainly not. Liam and I talked over everything of importance." She glanced from Rupert to Hannah. "I would advise you two to do the same. As for the portion Liam left to me, you use it as needed to keep up this place for my nephew. I won't interfere unless you give me cause to distrust you."

Holding her gaze, Rupert laid his other hand atop hers. "I promise you, as I did your husband, I will do my best to care for all of you and to secure Caleb's inheritance."

Aunt Ginny gave him a curt nod, then tapped Caleb on the shoulder. "Come to the library with me. It's time we got back to your arithmetic lessons so you're ready to take the reins one day."

"Aw, Aunt Ginny, I was hopin' me and Albert could go out and play catch."

Hannah finger-combed Caleb's hair into place. "Studies first, young man. Perhaps this afternoon, you and Albert can toss around that ball. Maybe Rupert and Simon will join y'all."

Simon flashed a bright smile. "I'm always ready for a game outside, as long as it's not a race. Nobody can beat Rupert."

Caleb laughed at the comical face Simon made, and Hannah smirked. "So I've been told, but one day, he's gonna have to prove it."

≈

"*I* take that as a challenge, Mrs. McNeil." Rupert bowed in her direction. "I guess I'll have to come up with a way to show you. Caleb's smart. Maybe he can help me figure that out. What d'ya say, Caleb?"

Aunt Ginny angled the boy's chair toward the door. "After his studies."

"All right, I'm going." Caleb pushed his wheels and headed for the library. "Albert's probably half done with his work."

Rupert and Simon remained in the office to work out a schedule for paying the remaining taxes and loan while the ladies joined forces in the library to oversee lessons for both boys.

When they stopped for the midday meal, Rupert stood and stretched to work out the kinks in his back. "Don't tell Caleb and Albert," he said, "but I dislike paperwork as much as they do."

Simon slapped his shoulder as they followed the others to the dining room. "I confess, I'm looking forward to spending some recreational time outside myself. We'll have to come up with something more than a game of catch. Reckon we can improvise and play baseball with just the four of us?"

"Make that five." Rupert gestured toward Quentin, who set a tray of dishes on the sideboard. "We can rotate positions. One batter, one pitcher, and three in the field to catch."

Simon grinned and raised his eyebrows. "You want to invite Hannah to join us? I doubt Mrs. Murphy would participate, and Davi's condition exempts her, but Hannah might—"

"No." Rupert elbowed Simon as the women took their seats. "I'm sure she has things to do. She'd only be a distraction." He shouldn't let Simon goad him.

"Cousins Wilma and Martha played without distracting us." Simon sat beside Daviana while Rupert rounded the table.

Hannah raised her head. "What's that about Wilma?"

Rupert glared at Simon. "She and her sister Martha used to play ball with us and our brothers at family outings."

Displaying an innocent smile, Simon said, "I wondered if you would want to join us for a game in the field."

Hannah glanced from Simon to Rupert. "Thank you, but no. I'd rather visit with Davi."

Spending time in the Georgia sunshine—setting aside all thoughts of heavy responsibilities—restored Rupert's spirits.

One moment during the game stood out—though no one mentioned it then or later. The ball had sailed toward Caleb but over his head. He stretched his arm to haul it in, and for half a second, he'd stood, the other hand touching the wheel of his chair. Cheers went up when he caught the fly, but the others focused on the catch. Indeed, when Rupert glanced around to verify what he'd seen, they acted as if nothing unusual had occurred. He'd keep it to himself for now, but he planned to watch the boy. Caleb might be capable of more than any of them imagined.

To that end, Rupert repeated his suggestion to Hannah as they climbed the stairs to their room that evening. "Simon agreed with me that Caleb needs to stretch himself in as many ways as possible. We pulled a piece of wood that escaped the fire today to use as a bat. Thomas offered to whittle a better one and sand it for future use."

Hannah preceded him into the room and reached up to pull pins from her hair. Like the simple beauty of an eagle soaring through the sky or the strength of a horse in full gallop, the commonplace action captured Rupert.

Unaware of his reaction, she leaned to the side and let her hair fall over one shoulder as she brushed through the blond curtain. "Thomas is good at all kinds of woodworking."

Rupert twisted away to pick up the thread of his story. "Uh, yeah. So we invited Quentin to join us, and each of us took a turn at batting and pitching, even running—or, in Caleb's case, wheeling—from home plate to first base, which was the only base. The exercise is good for both Caleb and Quentin. It's too bad there aren't more fellows around to make up an actual game."

"With spring planting around the corner, everyone will be busy in their fields. But later in the year, we might ask if others would like to join you." Hannah laid her hairbrush on the dresser.

"Yeah." The reminder of time slipping away pricked his bubble of joy. He padded across the room and, on a whim, stopped Hannah from braiding her hair. "Leave it loose."

She turned and tilted her head in silent question. He tugged her closer and drew a handful of the silky blond strands to his nose. "Tomorrow morning, I'm going to see Prescott. To see if I can figure out why he's so set on this property. Can you think of any reason, besides your own beautiful self, why that would be?"

Her eyes widened. "I've been thinking on that question myself, I can't figure it out. Although..." Her brow furrowed. "Something the man in Franklin said before you burst into the room came to mind."

Rupert's hand tightened on her waist. "Not a good memory. What'd he say?"

"Something about the boss—who I took to be Prescott—being impatient to claim his treasure. I thought he referred to Whitfield Hall and the land. Could he have meant Prescott thinks we have some hidden wealth?"

Hannah's troubled gaze met Rupert's straight-on. "Do you?" he asked, though he guessed what her answer would be.

"No. If we did, I would have used it long ago."

"I figured." He dropped a quick kiss on her lips. "But if Prescott *thinks* you do, that could be the problem. I'll see what I can weasel out of him."

~

*A*fter breakfast the next day, Hannah waved to Rupert and Simon on their way to town—Simon to scout for farm workers while Rupert confronted Prescott. Aunt Ginny offered to oversee the boys at their lessons so Hannah and Daviana could take a stroll around the vegetable garden. Overcast skies kept the temperature low enough to merit donning their shawls, but the dew had dispersed so they didn't worry about the damp seeping into shoes or hems.

Daviana pointed to the bushes at the corner of the house as they descended the front steps. "Your azaleas are beginning to bloom." Delicate pink flowers graced the otherwise-plain shrubbery.

Hannah walked closer to peer at the bushes. "It's too bad they don't last longer. With all the dogwoods and azaleas showing off their beauty, Georgia must be the loveliest place on earth during early spring."

"You won't get an argument from me on that. When those fade, other blooms come out. God is a master gardener who gives each plant its own time to shine."

During their slow amble over the grounds, Hannah learned about Davi's life in North Georgia and shared about her own family history. As it had for so many others, the war had changed the course of what their lives might have been. Hannah forced a smile as they reached the far perimeter of the vegetable garden and stopped to gaze over it. "I'm sorry we rambled to such a sad topic, but it's heartening to have someone nearer my age, who understands, someone with similar experiences."

Daviana squeezed her hand. "From what I gather of your situation, you and Rupert married for similar reasons as Simon and I did. Are y'all adjusting to each other all right? Not that I lay claim to any wisdom, but I can listen if you need someone to talk to."

Hannah fingered a vine that had crept over the garden fence. "As you say, we're still adjusting. Sometimes I feel Rupert wants a closer relationship, but then he pulls back. Perhaps I'm at fault. I wasn't close to my father or older brother, and I never had a suitor, so my experience with men is limited."

"I'm afraid my knowledge isn't much better." Daviana sighed and gazed into the distance. "The war interfered in so many ways, took our youth and forced us to grow up fast." She turned back to Hannah. "Simon and Rupert approach life differently. Where Simon is learning not to rush into action, I think maybe Rupert needs a nudge to overcome his cautious nature at times. You may need to provide that."

Hannah glanced at Daviana. "Millie indicated much the same. I didn't want to overstep my position as a wife, but you're right. If I keep waiting for Rupert to decide the direction of our marriage, and if he's waiting for me, we'll never accomplish anything. Pray that I have the courage to do what's best for all of us."

While she and Davi planted the seeds of friendship around the vegetable garden, she prayed for Rupert and Simon on their errands in town. If they could find enough workers to get Whitfield Hall operating again, that would give Rupert some relief. But a lot depended on his discussion with Oscar Prescott. Was there a way to make peace with that man, or would he continually be a thorn in their side?

CHAPTER 24

*T*he smell of spirits and stale cigar smoke in the tavern set Rupert's stomach to clenching. Pa hadn't allowed such vices, and Rupert followed rules, regardless of pressure from his peers. Only in the army had he been exposed to alcohol, so the odors brought memories of carnage and men trying to forget the crimes they'd committed in the name of states' rights or whatever they claimed as a just cause.

He swallowed his disgust and surveyed the room. A dozen tables filled the space, with chairs scattered haphazardly around them. In the far corner, an old woman in a long apron maneuvered a broom around the furniture. Except for her off-key humming and the rhythmic scrape of bristles on the floor, quiet pervaded the room. The only customer sat with his upper body sprawled across a table, snoring. Rupert had expected Prescott to have an office in town where they could have a civil conversation, but everyone had directed him to the tavern. Rupert hid his distaste.

He sidled up to the counter and nodded to the barkeep. "Looking for Prescott."

The man grunted as he passed a dingy rag across the

wooden surface and pointed to a door on the far side of the common area.

Hoping the private room might offer a cleaner atmosphere, Rupert crossed to the door, gripped the handle, and stepped inside. On the far side of the small room, Prescott and another man jerked their attention from the papers spread over the tabletop.

"McNeil." The name came from the man sitting beside Prescott. Rupert studied him for a moment, unsure if it was the same person he'd encountered in Franklin.

Prescott shuffled the papers, folding them into a square.

Rupert hooked his thumbs in his waistband and ambled closer to the table. "You ready to hear my proposal, Prescott?" He ignored the empty chairs as well as the lackey who casually closed the ledger in front of him.

A frown pulled Prescott's brows low. "I'm not in much of a mood to haggle, but go ahead. Let's hear what you got to offer."

Rupert schooled his expression and kept his voice even. "I reckon I could sacrifice fifty acres on the south side for the right price. As you must know, most of the property has lain fallow for a couple of years, so it should yield a good crop for whatever you plant."

Prescott laughed, and his companion joined in. "It seems no one has properly explained to you what I want, McNeil. Running a farm is of little interest to me. It's the house I want, the house and its close surroundings. My fiancée will be joining me from New York in a month or so, and I need it for her."

Rupert clucked his tongue. "You and I both know that's a lie, a story you cooked up to impress your army friends." He paused to see if Prescott would deny the accusation. "Besides, you spent weeks trying to convince Hannah to marry you." Rupert curled his right hand into a fist. "If there was a fiancée in the north, which woman were you being untruthful to?" He waited only a heartbeat for an answer. "Never mind. I've heard you don't place much value on faithfulness, and it's a moot point, anyway. The house is not for sale."

He turned to leave, but Prescott called after him. "I believe there's a matter of a lien coming due on the property. I'm prepared to pay that and a decent price to take it off your hands."

Rupert faced him again with a sneer. "How kind of you, but it's not for sale. You see, I'm named as trustee for my young brother-in-law, and that's his legacy. With proper care, Whitfield Hall will soon be thriving again, a treasure to be passed down to his future children. It was never meant to be yours." Would mention of treasure cause his opponent to reveal his true intent?

Prescott scowled at his companion, then he pushed his chair back and pulled a loose paper from the ledger. He held it aloft. "I'm informed you have another property in Alabama. You could move your little wife and her family there and enlarge it with the money I'll pay for Whitfield Hall. You wouldn't have to worry about their safety, and you'd save yourself running back and forth."

Holding on to his temper, Rupert took a step toward his adversary. He wasn't surprised Prescott knew about his holdings—anyone with spies and a turkey's brain could ferret out such. It was the mention of his family's safety that stirred Rupert's ire. "I don't know how they do things where you're from, Prescott, but here in the South, we hold a few things in high esteem—among them our elders, our women, and the legacy we leave our children. McNeil farm is my legacy. Whitfield Hall is Caleb's, and it's been entrusted to me to preserve until he's able to assume the reins himself. I will not have that taken away from him and wasted on someone who has no concept of its value."

Prescott chuckled. "I have a better idea of its value than young Whitfield does. As for him taking over the reins, I don't know how you expect a cripple to run such a large operation. We should've burned it to the ground when we had the chance."

"That sounds like a confession, Prescott."

Prescott scoffed. "Ridiculous. Why would I burn down something I planned to buy? I was talking about when the Union army arrived here last year."

Rupert fake-smiled. "Seein' as this discussion is going nowhere, I'll be takin' my leave."

Prescott fluttered the paper he held. "You might want to take this with you. It seems your Alabama overseer is expecting you to return soon."

His anger flaring, Rupert stalked to the table and snatched the paper from Prescott's grasp. "I believe there's a law against procurin' mail that's not your own." He stuffed the paper in his vest pocket, refusing to open it in front of a hostile audience.

Prescott lifted his hands in a show of innocence. "I have no idea how it got delivered here."

Rupert strode to the door but turned back before he opened it. "Be warned, Prescott. If harm comes to any person or property connected to Whitfield Hall, you will be blamed, and I will come after you."

～

The sun was still climbing in the sky when the men returned to Whitfield Hall. Hannah and Davi had joined Aunt Ginny in the parlor while Caleb and Albert took a break from their studies.

"The weather's too nice to keep them inside longer," Aunt Ginny had said. "They deserved a respite, and I needed a cup of tea."

No sooner had the women picked up their teacups than

Rupert and Simon entered the house, their boots ringing on the hallway floorboards until they reached the carpeted parlor.

Hannah tried to determine from Rupert's demeanor whether the brothers were at odds after Rupert shared the full contents of Byron's wire with Simon. "You saw how he reacted when he learned about Wilma buying part of the property," her husband had said. "If Byron's coming here with a proposal for more, I want to be prepared. Simon might have some thoughts on how to counter it. Once he fusses and warns me again about Wilma," Rupert had assured her, "he'll help me figure out the best plan of action."

When both of them approached with smiles, she nodded to Davi, but Aunt Ginny spoke first. "I trust you have good news to share with us. You found some workers?"

"We did." Rupert drew a chair close to Hannah's and angled it so he could see everyone. "Found a family of three brothers. Said they came to town looking for work, so Simon took 'em to the café to discuss the arrangement while I talked to Prescott."

Hannah placed her free hand on Rupert's arm. "And how did he react to your peace offering?"

Rupert grimaced. "About as graciously as a donkey who dislikes pulling a wagon."

"I believe that's his usual manner," Aunt Ginny said. "He must have never been taught the difference between using honey and vinegar to get what you want."

Davi chuckled at that, then asked, "Isn't there a sheriff or some official you can appeal to for help if he keeps harassing y'all?"

"The new governor appointed everyone last year, same time as Prescott arrived," Hannah said, "but we never had much dealings with folks in town, anyway. We don't know who, if anyone, might be in cahoots with Prescott and who we can trust."

"What about these workers you've hired?" Aunt Ginny

peered at Rupert and lowered her cup to her lap. "Can we trust them?"

Rupert crossed one leg over the other and rested his ankle on the other knee. "I believe so. They're new to the area. They drove into town right after Simon and I did. Said they're from a farming area south of Macon. Decided to move after their folks passed."

Daviana grinned at her husband. "It sounds as though the Lord put y'all in their path at the right time. He provided for them and for you."

Simon nodded. "He did, for sure. I'd barely whispered a prayer for divine direction when Rupert noticed them."

Hannah whispered a prayer of gratitude. "Davi and I prayed too. Isn't it amazing how that worked out?" And if God answered those prayers, surely, He would help them figure out how to deal with their peskier problems—namely, Oscar Prescott and Wilma Thurman.

$\sim$

*D*ivine direction? Rupert studied Simon. Had his scapegrace brother settled into the role of saint after his years away? As if it was yesterday, Rupert heard Aunt June's declaration of Simon's character. *"He's well named,"* she'd said. *"Like the apostle Simon Peter, his impulsiveness might land him in enough trouble that he'll do a complete turnaround one day."* She hadn't lived to witness it, but it seemed she'd been right.

Perhaps Simon's disregard for society's rules had influenced Rupert's carefulness. He tended to stay beneath everyone's notice so he didn't cause trouble. He'd earned his reputation as the obedient child and later the young man always willing to help.

What did Simon's change mean? Last year, Rupert had thought his brother's peaceful demeanor was due to Daviana, that he'd settled down and modified his behavior to please her. These last few days with him, though...it seemed he credited his change to a spiritual experience.

"When your workers arrive," Simon said to Rupert, "perhaps we should ride the perimeter of the property. We can discuss a plan I have in mind and see if there's been any more mischief."

"Yeah, I'd planned to do so. Should've done it before now." For someone who was known to proceed with caution and help others with problems, Rupert wasn't doing a very good job of managing his own affairs.

Daviana patted his hand. "From what I've heard, you've had your plate full since you arrived. And that on top of losing Uncle Henry. I'm sorry we couldn't make it to the funeral, but you probably had a houseful of people."

Thankful for Davi's sympathy, he picked up Hannah's hand. "Yeah, that's true. People came from miles around. Then a blond female showed up, bushwhacked me, and dragged me to Georgia." He grinned and planted a kiss on her knuckles while the others laughed. "She rescued me from life as a lonely bachelor." A status he'd never go back to willingly. Even as strained as their beginning had been, he and Hannah got along rather well. And he intended to convince her to make it a real marriage in every sense, preferably sooner rather than later.

~

*A*mid the chuckles at Rupert's teasing, the clatter of footsteps brought Hannah's attention to the parlor doorway.

Albert pushed Caleb's chair into view, both boys' eyes wide in pale faces.

"...shooting at us!" Caleb pointed toward the back of the

house. His breath came in short puffs, and his knuckles showed white where he gripped his chair.

Albert recovered his breath and shouted over Caleb's jumbled words. "Hurry, Uncle Simon, before they get away!"

Someone was shooting in the field?

The boys' alarm fed Hannah's. She rushed to calm her brother while the men followed Albert to the back door.

Caleb gripped the arms of his chair, his jaw clenched in an obvious attempt to keep from bursting into tears.

Aunt Ginny and Daviana joined Hannah as she knelt beside him.

"Caleb, it's okay. You're fine." Despite her words of assurance, she ran her hands over his head, shoulders, and arms, searching for damage. Thankful to find no injury, she peered into his eyes. "Can you tell us what happened?"

"Albert and me left the hay shed to toss the ball and was headin' in when a bullet went between us. We froze at first, then we heard another shot. Albert told me to hold on, and he pushed my chair back to the house as quick as he could. I didn't see who was shootin', but I think Albert did."

Rocked by his answer, Hannah grabbed the chair to steady herself.

Daviana helped her to stand, then slipped an arm around her waist.

Silvie had entered and was urging Aunt Ginny back to her seat when the rasp of the front door opening announced the men's return. Hannah's gaze sought Rupert as he and Simon entered, but he went straight to Caleb.

Squatting beside the chair, he repeated Hannah's earlier actions, searching for injury. When he stood, his eyes blazed like blue fire. "It's a low-down skunk who shoots at children. I've sent Thomas for the sheriff."

Silvie left Aunt Ginny's side and approached Rupert.

"Quentin seen sumpin, too, Mistah McNeil. He come in the kitchen shook up."

"I'll go talk to him—"

"No, Rupert." Simon stretched out an arm to stop his progress. "Best wait until the sheriff arrives, or he could accuse you of planting ideas in Quentin's head."

Rupert ran a hand over his mouth as if to prevent words from escaping. "All right. Silvie, would you let him know he'll need to describe whatever he saw?"

The cook nodded slowly. "Yassir, I do dat. Don't spect it to do much good, but I tell 'im."

After she left, Simon quirked an eyebrow at Rupert. "Will Quentin refuse to cooperate?"

Hannah exchanged glances with Rupert. "Oh, he'll cooperate," she said. "The trouble isn't with Quentin, but with the authorities. Because he has trouble speaking, they think he's weak-minded."

Simon flattened his mouth. "They'll consider him an unreliable witness."

"And there's his skin color. Most folks count that as two strikes against him." Rupert plowed his fist into his open palm. "And we don't know whether the lawman's someone who will side with Prescott."

❦

The sheriff arrived quickly, surprising Rupert. Either he was exceptionally diligent, or else he'd been expecting the summons. Perhaps Rupert should have contacted him to investigate the fire earlier in the week, but it was the day of Liam's funeral and Caleb had been keen to inspect the site right away. Having the sheriff here now provided an opportunity to mention his suspicions.

Maybe a decade older than Rupert, the man had a

leathered face and dark hair with threads of silver. Thomas guided him to Rupert, then retreated to tend the horses.

The sheriff shook Rupert's hand. "Gordon Wesley. Thomas tells me you folks had a little scare." He eyed each person as everyone gathered on the front porch.

"Henry McNeil. Thank you for coming so quickly, Sheriff Wesley." Rupert introduced him to Simon and Albert. "I believe you know Quentin, who's lived here most of his life."

With a nod, the sheriff pulled a pencil and paper from his pocket. "Who wants to tell me what happened?"

Albert stepped forward. "Me and Caleb was out in the field, playing catch, but we got hungry and was comin' to the house when we heard a gunshot. I swear, I felt it go right next to my head. When we heard another, we took off runnin'. Well, I was runnin' and pushin' Caleb's chair."

The sheriff stopped writing. "Where's Caleb? Did he get hit?"

"No, sir. He's all right, he was scared somethin' awful."

Rupert figured Albert had been just as afraid.

Sheriff Wesley glanced at Rupert and Simon. "I'll need to speak with him too."

Simon gave a brisk nod. "Of course. We'll take you inside to interview him when you're done here."

"Fine. Now, young Albert, did you see who was doin' the shootin' at y'all?"

"Yes, sir, but not too good. There was two men went runnin' that way." He pointed in the direction of town. "I could tell they had rifles and no hats."

"All right. Was Quentin with you and Caleb?"

"No, sir."

"What about it, Quentin?" The sheriff turned to the young man. "You see anything?"

Quentin nodded and started to speak in his halting way,

using gestures to supplement his words. As they all watched, Silvie interpreted.

Rupert rubbed his jaw. "Two men with rifles, just as Albert said. Did you know these men, Quentin?"

He shook his head, holding up one finger, then circled fingers around his eyes.

"Are you saying one wore glasses?" After a nod, Rupert asked, "What kind of clothes?"

Quentin's brow puckered as he looked around. He pointed to Simon's dark-blue trousers, then drew the shape of a chevron on his arm.

"He wore a uniform?"

Quentin held up two fingers.

"Both of them wore uniforms?"

Vigorous nodding.

Rupert's gaze sought Simon's. "It seems our culprits are connected to the United States Army."

"Not necessarily," the sheriff drawled. "It's no secret Captain Prescott has a hankerin' for this here house, which could lead to some disgruntled feelings betwixt you and him. However, that don't mean he's crazy enough to shoot at a couple of young'uns. And a chevron would be the wrong insignia for a captain. We get men passin' through all the time, some still in their old uniforms, both blue and gray."

Rupert stepped toward the lawman. "Yeah, but how many of them have a reason to do their target practice on children? And more to the point, on the boy who happens to be the sole heir to this property?"

With a pointed look at Rupert, Sheriff Wesley put away his pencil and paper. "You just let me do my job, Mr. McNeil, and don't go lookin' for trouble. Now, let's go discover what young Mr. Whitfield has to say."

Albert took the lead into the house, and the sheriff followed.

Simon pulled Rupert back to fall behind them. "You have a right to be upset, but try to hold your tongue until we know more. Let's see if any of our workers know anything about men in town who wear Union jackets." When Rupert nodded, Simon smirked. "It's interesting to play the part of the calm brother for once. I hope you control your anger better than I used to. It won't do your family any good to have you hauled off to jail."

Rupert blew out a breath. "Good to know you have my back, brother."

～

*H*annah tried to eat the meal Silvie had served, but her mind kept drifting to where the men met with the sheriff. She silently blessed Simon for bringing Daviana and Albert. What might have been the outcome of today's events if the boy hadn't pushed Caleb to safety?

She glanced at her brother's plate, still half full like her own. As much as he tried to act older, he had years of tough growing ahead of him.

Aunt Ginny had pleaded a headache and retreated to her room, leaving Hannah and Davi to wait for the men to bring a report from the sheriff.

After several minutes, Albert rushed into the room. "Sheriff wants to see you, Caleb. Should I push you to the parlor?"

Rupert entered and clapped Albert on the shoulder. "I'll take him, Albert. You go ahead and eat your meal." He backed Caleb's chair from the table and reversed it toward the hall.

Her husband's abrupt manner didn't bode well. Hannah caught a glimpse of Daviana's furrowed brow as Albert took the seat beside his aunt and tucked into his meal. Hannah couldn't contain a small smile. While the disturbing events sapped her appetite and Davi's, now that it was over, Albert had bounced back to normal. He would probably tell the story to all his friends when he returned home.

When the boy paused to sip his water, Davi asked, "Did Quentin tell the sheriff what he saw?"

Albert nodded as he swallowed. "Yes'm. He said the men had on Union Army uniforms and one of 'em wore glasses."

"Hmm." She drummed her fingers on the table. "He must've been closer to them than you were. Did you know Quentin was there?"

"No, ma'am." He paused with his spoon halfway to his mouth. "Wait. I think Caleb waved at somebody right after I turned to throw a pitch. I forgot about that when I talked to the sheriff. Should I go tell him now?"

Hannah's gaze went to Daviana, who shrugged. "Perhaps Caleb will mention it to him. When you've finished eating, we'll find out if the sheriff is still here."

The door to the kitchen opened, and Silvie poked her head into the room. "Mistah McNeil and his brother eat yet?"

"No, Silvie. Would you put back some dishes for them? What about Quentin and Aunt Ginny? Did they eat anything?"

"Yes'm. I seen to it. Y'all done here?"

Hannah glanced at Daviana, who'd already set aside her plate. "Davi and I are, but Albert—"

"I'm done." The boy pushed back his plate and stood. "I gotta go see if the sheriff's left yet."

Daviana caught his hand. "Wait for us, please. And don't say anything until we talk to Simon." She moved to the end of the table so Silvie could collect the plates.

Eyes narrowed in concentration, Albert looked from Davi to Hannah. "What if Caleb wasn't wavin' at Quentin but at somebody else?"

Hannah rose and waved her hand to dismiss his concern. "Not likely. Caleb has rarely left the house since his accident.

That's why he was so glad to meet you, to have someone his age he could talk to."

As they made their way to the parlor, however, the idea plagued her. She'd been away for over a week, leaving Aunt Ginny to watch over Caleb and tend to Uncle Liam. Papa had installed a wooden ramp at the back door, but she'd never known Caleb to try it on his own. Could he have slipped out while everyone was occupied and made an acquaintance? That would mean someone came onto the property, and their reason for doing so probably wasn't to befriend a lonely boy.

CHAPTER 25

*A*s if the day plotted to drag Rupert in three different directions, the new workers arrived as he and Simon returned from a ride around the property. Against Rupert's protective instincts, they'd agreed on a plan to lure Prescott into making his move so they could trap him. The sheriff's earlier assurances that he'd watch for any suspicious activity only slightly assuaged Rupert's concerns.

When he and Simon rode into the yard, the workers' wagon pulled in behind them. Sending Simon to find his supper, Rupert delayed his own meal long enough to show the newcomers to the former slave cabins so they could settle in. By the time he returned to the house, his hunger drove him straight to the kitchen, where Silvie was scouring a big pot.

"I sure hope you have some victuals left, Silvie. My stomach's shrunk two sizes."

She chuckled and handed him a plate of peas and fried potatoes with a wedge of cornbread.

He'd gobbled about half of the food when Hannah wandered into the room. "Hey, honey." He mumbled the greeting, then swallowed when her eyes widened. Where had that word come from? It had slipped out without forethought. Maybe having Simon and Davi in the house had affected his thinking. At least "honey" was close to Hannah's name, so maybe she'd think that was what he'd said.

Hannah motioned to his plate. "I wanted to be sure you found your meal. Everyone else has eaten, and we're playing games in the parlor if you want to join us when you're done."

She bounced her linked fingers against her waist as Rupert shoveled in another bite. Why would she be nervous?

"Sure. Sounds like fun." Heaven knew they could all use the distraction.

When she didn't leave, he brushed cornbread crumbs from his fingers and rose to join her. Rupert led her into the hallway and stopped. "Now, Hannah, what's botherin' you?"

"I've been thinking about the person Caleb waved at. Do you suppose he knows more than he lets on?"

Her question surprised him. "Do you suspect him of lying? Why would he do that?"

"Maybe the man threatened him."

"Doesn't seem likely if he only saw him once. Caleb implied the man only strayed onto the property to catch a rabbit."

"But what if he came back again? Or what if he was really planning to catch Caleb or—"

"Hannah." Rupert gripped her arms and peered into her face. "Stop imagining things. You'll work yourself into a state of panic. We have to think about this logically. And for now, we have to trust that Caleb has told us the truth."

"I'm just so afraid...."

"Shh. I know." He pulled her into his arms to offer comfort. She fit so well that it was as if her body melded with his. "It's normal to fear for those we love. I promise to do all I can to keep you and Caleb safe. Aunt Ginny too." He pulled back enough to smile. "Although she's much more formidable than I will ever be."

Hannah returned his smile, though the expression was dimmed by worry. It would take more than a dose of humor to lighten her concern—or to expunge his feelings for this woman. Did he dare try to act on those feelings and make theirs a forever marriage? He dredged up his usual argument, but it rang hollow in his mind. Could a few months or years of basking in her presence outweigh the risk of losing her?

He set the questions aside as they reached the parlor. Someone had brought out a pack of cards, and Simon shuffled them as he explained the concept of *vingt-et-un*. Rupert sent him a questioning gaze, to which Simon replied, "We've too many for checkers or chess. This way, we're all in the game together."

Rupert seated Hannah in a vacant chair and whispered near her ear. "I think it's a sneaky way to hone the boys' arithmetic." Her trill of laughter was his reward.

~

*H*annah returned to the parlor after fetching a shawl for Aunt Ginny and peeking into the library to check on Caleb and Albert. After an hour of games with the family, the boys had decided to set up their own tournament of checkers there.

"I guess they find our games boring," Davi said.

"Or they suspected us of reinforcing their education." Aunt Ginny wrapped the shawl around her shoulders. "Children these days are cleverer than when I was a girl."

Rupert moved to join Hannah on the settee. "It's better that they aren't privy to our conversation now. What Simon and I propose will work only if Prescott believes I've left for Alabama."

"Why would he think that?" Hannah asked. What was Rupert planning?

"Somehow, he got a copy of the wire Byron sent and misinterpreted it to say Byron expects me to arrive there on Sunday. In fact, Prescott suggested I move y'all to my farm in Alabama."

Aunt Ginny scoffed. "And let him take over Whitfield Hall? I think not."

"I believe he's taken advantage of our lack of workers, until now, to put men in place to watch us. Therefore, we will appear to give him an opportunity to seize the house."

Simon cleared his throat. "Davi and I planned to leave tomorrow, anyway, but we'll stop in Decatur and wait for word that the ploy has worked, in case we need to return."

Hannah followed their explanation with anxiety. "But you're truly not leaving?"

Rupert patted her hand. "Just going far enough that he thinks I'm gone. Then I'll turn north and approach the house from that direction. If he thinks there's some treasure hidden in or around the house, he'll take the opportunity to search while I'm away."

"But couldn't he have done that before you ever came?" Davi asked.

"He thought Hannah would wear down and marry him, then he'd have all the time he needed to search. I don't know why he's so certain there's some kind of treasure here, but I see this as the only way he'll be convinced there isn't."

"I don't like it," Aunt Ginny grumbled, "but I reckon you're right."

Rupert stroked Hannah's hand and linked their fingers together. "I don't like it, either, but I'm ready to move us past this time of wondering when he'll strike next."

*L*ater that night, Simon questioned Rupert as they lingered on the front porch. The women and boys had gone to bed, but Simon must have sensed Rupert's restlessness and followed him outside. Rupert leaned against the rail, and Simon sat in a rocking chair and made a few comments about the weather before he got to the main topic.

"I'm sure the way your marriage came about wasn't your choice, bud—"

"My *choice*...." Rupert began, then softened his voice when his brother winced. "My choice would've been not to marry at all."

Simon stopped his rocker. "When did you become so adamant about that? Did some girl back home break your heart?"

Rupert's anger dwindled like a spring shower chased away by the sun. "It wasn't some girl, Simon. It started with our mother, who died when we were still in nappies. She died because of me."

Simon straightened. "What are you talking about? Pa said I was the one who'd run off and had everyone searching for me that day. I blamed myself for a long time, but that wasn't right. It was her time to go, not a punishment. I don't claim to know why God took her, but I've accepted that nothing I did as a child could've caused her death. And the same goes for you."

"It was my birth that was so difficult, though, the one that weakened her. She hadn't recovered from it when she got sick. If not for me, you'd still have her."

"You can't know that." Simon started rocking again. "The Lord numbered her days long before you were born, brother."

"So you say, but years later, within two weeks' time, my favorite horse died and Ma—Connie, that is—lost the baby after Troy—"

"You remembered that? I didn't, not until Pa told me about it last year. It's strange how we all remember different things."

Rupert shrugged. "I was almost five. Those are my earliest memories. Then when I was in the army, my best friend died while I was in the hospital recovering from a wound. Everyone I get close to dies young."

Simon stood and grasped Rupert's shoulders. "So you are more powerful than God? Or you think God is punishing you by taking people you love? Do you not love Ma and Pa? They're still here. And though Henry passed before we would've liked, he'd had a long life and was ready to go." He dropped his hands. "We all have to die sometime."

Rupert stared and let the words wash over him. He focused on the revelation that Simon had blamed himself for their mother's death. What was it Paul had told him before he and Hannah left home? *"I think we all blamed ourselves—you, Simon, and me. We were too young to realize sickness could be fatal, and it had nothing to do with our behavior."*

"Maybe so." Rupert could acknowledge that much.

"Life doesn't end when we pass from this world," Simon said, "and neither does love. Remember how Ma made us memorize First Corinthians thirteen? Love 'beareth all things, believeth all things, hopeth all things, endureth all things.' It never stops. All those people who passed on? They still love you as you love them, and they want what's best for you."

"But is what's best for me also what's best for Hannah?"

Simon tilted his head toward the door. "Why don't you ask her? I think you'll find that Hannah's like most women. They value their loved ones above themselves."

Rupert's gaze went to the star-studded sky, recalling a moment under the stars with Hannah soon after they'd met. She'd risked herself to make the journey to Alabama without knowing what she'd find there. Then she'd carried through with marriage to him, someone she hardly knew. Yeah, she would risk everything for those she loved, and loving her was worth the risk of losing her.

At their wedding, he'd vowed to love, honor, and protect, but he'd tried to hold out on the love part. Lifting a silent prayer for forgiveness, he pledged to commit himself to honoring God in all things...and loving his wife in the way God had laid out in His Word.

～

*H*annah awoke the next morning with a headache after a night filled with frightening dreams. Even after Rupert had crept into the room and laid down beside her, as he'd done every night since the fire, worry had plagued her rest. She'd finally relaxed when he pulled her close, the weight of his arm a comforting barrier against the unseen forces of her imagination.

He and Simon had stayed up later than the rest of the household, and then he'd been gone this morning when she woke.

Hannah massaged her temples. Perhaps a cup of coffee would ease the pain.

She hurried to dress and get downstairs before Simon and his family left. She would miss them, and keeping Caleb content in their absence might prove difficult. His mood had turned sullen at Albert's impending departure until she promised they would try to make a trip to Gainesville in a few weeks when Davi's baby was due. Hopefully, he wouldn't repeat his surliness this morning.

She found the parlor empty and followed the aromas of coffee and bread to the dining room. "Good morning, everyone."

"Ah, here she is. Good morning, sweetheart." Rupert left his chair and drew her into the room.

Hannah's face heated as he led her to the seat beside his, and Silvie set a filled plate and a cup of coffee in front of her. A glance around the table showed most of the others had finished their breakfasts and lingered to finish their tea or coffee. "Sorry to be late. I didn't sleep well."

Rupert stirred some milk into his cup. "You'll have to accustom yourself to farmers' hours again. Wintertime gives us a break, but it's over now."

Hannah swirled honey onto a pancake. "Are the cabins in decent condition for the workers? I haven't checked them since last fall."

"Probably not as clean as *you'd* like," Rupert said with a teasing note, "but they're habitable, thanks to Quentin and Thomas. That's where Quentin was yesterday when he saw our two unwelcome visitors."

"We should ask him if he'd seen them at any other time." Hannah added a small piece of ham to a forkful of the sweetened bread and scooped the combination into her mouth. The contrasting flavors always tasted better together. Uncle Liam used to tease Aunt Ginny that it was like their marriage, in which his sweetness balanced out her saltiness. Would he make such a comparison of Hannah and Rupert? Did they complement each other?

On the other side of the table, Caleb pushed back his plate. "I told Albert he could borrow some of my books. Is it all right if we go and get them now?"

Aunt Ginny nodded, and the boys scrambled to leave.

Daviana caught Albert's arm as he reached her chair. "Choose only one or two, Albert. You'll still have schoolwork and chores at the farm."

"Yes'm, I know." He slipped from her grasp with ease and joined Caleb.

Aunt Ginny watched the youngsters until they were out of hearing. "I told them they could write letters to each other and discuss the books. Perhaps that will alleviate their loneliness while also working on their comprehension and penmanship."

Simon raised his cup in salute. "Excellent strategy, ma'am. I wonder if we could employ such tactics for other subjects."

Daviana chuckled. "If it accomplishes any of those objectives, I will be pleased. But Albert's penmanship may be a lost cause."

Once breakfast was finished, the men carried Simon's family's luggage outside, and Albert stowed the books under a seat. He ran back to get the basket of sweet rolls Caleb passed him.

Caleb didn't follow them out front.

Hannah pointed to the ramp at the porch's edge. "He says it's too steep."

Rupert studied the angle and nodded. "We'll figure out a way to fix it."

Hannah gave Daviana a pillow. "I hope this helps keep your feet from swelling on the journey."

"It will certainly be put to use." Daviana embraced her. "I know it will be a while before we can come back this way, so I'll be looking forward to having you visit us as soon and often as possible."

"And you'll always be welcome here. Be sure to write."

When the carriage rolled forward, Hannah took a step back and found herself in Rupert's arms. He lifted one hand to return Albert's wave but kept the other at her waist. She twisted around to search his face. "Are you leaving now?"

"In a minute." He nudged her back toward the house. "Sweetheart..." His eyes met hers, then moved to her forehead, followed the outline of her jaw, and finally lingered on her lips.

Hannah's breath caught. She felt his gaze as surely as a physical touch.

Rupert jerked his gaze away. His Adam's apple bobbed. "Hannah, if anything should happen to me—"

She covered his lips with her fingers. "Don't say it. You'll come back, and we'll be here."

CHAPTER 26

*T*wo hours after Hannah's husband rode away from Whitfield Hall, the weather turned ugly. The morning's gentle breeze gained momentum as rain cascaded like waterfalls from the eaves of the house. Lightning brought a constant roll of thunder, and the wind snapped smaller branches and tossed them across the yard.

Hannah sought safety in the library and sat at the piano. Her fingers moved into place to begin a placid sonata she'd learned as a child. The instrument needed tuning, and the high E had a tendency to stick, but she continued playing. The periodic crash of a closer strike did nothing to enhance her rusty performance.

Would the weather ruin their plan to lure Prescott here? Was Rupert getting soaked, or would he find a place to stay out of the rain? The waiting grated on her nerves. Her prayers rose in disjointed phrases for her family's protection, Rupert included. What if all this was for naught?

Caleb rolled in and coaxed her to join him in a game of checkers. "Or we could try chess if you want to teach me."

"You're off the mark there, brother." She left the piano

bench and dragged a chair to the desk. "I never played enough to figure out how to strategize beyond one or two moves. You'll have to ask Rupert when he gets back."

Saying his name brought a bittersweet longing. She kept her eyes on the board as she placed the game pieces in the proper squares.

Caleb made his first move. "Why couldn't his friend back in Alabama handle the problem there? Didn't you say Rupert had left him in charge?"

"Sometimes it takes the person with the greatest authority to make sure things are done right."

The creaking of a floorboard near the room's entrance alerted Hannah a moment too late. "An excellent deduction, my dear." Oscar Prescott stood in the doorway, water glistening on his greatcoat and a pistol trained on her.

Hannah's heart thudded in her ears, and her pawn tumbled to the chessboard. Prescott had made his move just as Rupert and Simon predicted. *Dear Lord, preserve us all.*

Prescott waved his free hand in a circle. "That's why I've decided to do this job myself instead of trusting it to my bumbling subordinates. Do not bother to raise your voice, either of you. My men have already moved through the house to locate the others and bring them here. As for your field hands, I suspect the weather will keep them from venturing out of their cabins."

Aunt Ginny's outraged voice floated down the hallway. "How dare you enter my home and hold a weapon on me! You'll regret the day you dared to step into Whitfield Hall in such a way." When she entered the library and saw her niece and nephew, she rounded on the captain. "Oscar Prescott, what is the meaning of this? Surely, you cannot hope to come out of this escapade without a mark on your reputation."

Prescott had the temerity to laugh. "Oh, can't I? You will find, Mrs. Murphy, I have much more influence than you think.

Your erstwhile savior has abandoned you, it seems, so I take that as an invitation to move in and replace him." Evil gleamed in the man's eyes.

Several miles west of Newnan, Georgia

*R*upert glanced behind him as he made the turn north. The road was clear of traffic, and he heaved a sigh. For a while, he'd imagined that someone was following him—or at least watching him. Not since he'd marched with the army had that sensation troubled him. Clearly, he wasn't cut out for playacting or sneaking around.

The path he now traveled was little more than a track such as one makes between farmhouses. The rain had moved on but left him drenched and the road filled with mud that slowed his progress.

Not that he had to hurry. It would be foolish to rush back and possibly arrive before Prescott made his move. He had to fight against the feeling that he'd left Hannah in danger. Yesterday, they'd gone over the facts again and again, searching for another way. Unless they could live with Prescott plaguing them with mischief and threats, they had to let him think he'd won. And if there was a physical treasure on the property, Prescott could take it and leave, as far as Rupert was concerned.

An hour later, the afternoon sun had dried his clothes and started hardening the mud into clods. Crazy spring weather meant a person never knew what to expect. In the distance, the tin roof of a small building shimmered in the slanting rays. Maybe he could give the horse a rest and take time to eat the sandwich he'd brought.

Rupert patted the horse's neck as they neared another

puddle. "We're both bound to wear some red clay after going through this stuff. Just a while longer, then we can head home."

The word took him aback. Did he really think of Whitfield Hall as home? When had that happened?

The snuffle of another horse behind him prompted Rupert to twist in his saddle and glimpse an object hurtling his way a second before it made contact with his head.

~

*H*annah bolstered her courage and stood to face her adversary. "You're crazy if you think you can just come in here and take over, Captain Prescott. Taxes are up to date on our home. The whole community has met my husband and knows—"

"Oh, do stop your recitation, Miss Whitfield, or Mrs. McNeil —whatever you call yourself. Do you really think my goal was to own this aging pile of rock and lumber? Or to be tied to a woman as prudish as you?"

A commotion down the hallway commanded everyone's attention.

Hannah took the opportunity to move closer to Caleb's chair, ready to shield him if Prescott grew desperate. The chance for escape dwindled as two more of Prescott's men forced Thomas and Silvie into the room. Hannah didn't recognize the men, both of whom were wearing ragged Union uniforms.

"Where's the third one, the boy?" Prescott asked.

The taller man rested his rifle on one shoulder and wiped his glasses on his shirt. The movement drew Hannah's gaze to the chevron on his sleeve. She exchanged a look with Caleb, who nodded. Here, then, was the man who'd claimed to be trapping rabbits but must have been spying on them. Anger edged out her fear.

"We couldn't find him, Captain. His pa here says he's down at the far cabins."

When Prescott scowled, the man who'd brought in Aunt Ginny scoffed. "Don't worry about him. He's an idjit, can't talk no more'n a two-year-old. Even if he seen us, nobody'd understand him."

Prescott stuck his revolver in its holster. "I hope you're right, but we need to move faster. I want to find the gold and move on before the storm lets up enough for anyone to come by."

"Gold?" Hannah startled at the word. "You think we have gold hidden here?"

Prescott's eyes glittered with avarice. "Oh, I know there's gold here. You see, my dear, departed half brother told me about it."

"Who?" Hannah crossed her arms. Didn't matter. "I think he mixed up Whitfield Hall with some other place. There's no gold here. If there were, don't you think we would have put it to use long ago?"

"I didn't say you knew about it—only that it's here. Horace found it when his unit searched one of the houses in Atlanta. He always did have the devil's own luck with such." Prescott's grin faded. "But his sergeant got suspicious, so he had to hide it. He told me, just before he died, that he'd stashed it in a house called Whitfield, a few miles south of Atlanta."

Aunt Ginny gripped Hannah's hand. "If you know where it's hidden, go ahead and get it. Then be on your way and leave us alone."

"I don't know the precise location. Horace planned to come back for it himself but died of smallpox."

"Then how do you propose to find it?"

"By searching every inch of this house." He turned to the one he called Lewis. "Let's tie them up so we can get on with the search."

Desperate to have Prescott gone as soon as possible,

Hannah pushed past Caleb's chair. "Since you're determined to proceed, it will go more quickly if we help you search."

He chuckled. "Oh, sure, so you can keep us from finding it." He motioned to the other men, who scrambled to do his bidding.

The tall one pushed Hannah into a chair and bound her to it with a stout rope. Her heart hammered in her chest as the rough cord bit into her skin.

"Tie that one extra tight," Prescott said. "I've a feeling she might cause trouble. Lester and Ben, you can start with the kitchen and dining room. Lewis will help me in the parlor and the office."

Hannah prodded Prescott. "Are you sure you can trust those two not to keep whatever they find? Think about it. How would your brother have gained access to the house? The only Union men who came in here last year were two officers, a lieutenant and a captain, as I recall, and I never heard anyone addressed as Prescott."

Aunt Ginny's nod confirmed Hannah's words.

Prescott sneered at her. "Of course not. As I said, Horace was my half brother, the son of my mother and stepfather. He was the lieutenant who inspected the house, so you see, he had access and opportunity."

Hannah slumped in her seat, her best chance of reasoning with Prescott gone. She couldn't hold out hope of Rupert returning or any of the workers coming to their rescue as long as the storm persisted. Where had Quentin got off to? Sometimes he wandered off for hours, but he always came home. Maybe they should have told the others about the plan.

She gazed at her companions, likewise frightened and despondent. What would Prescott do to them if he couldn't find the gold? Surely, if it was here, she or Aunt Ginny would have found it by now. Would Rupert return only to find the house destroyed and the occupants dead?

Another thought occurred. What if Prescott had someone follow Rupert and attack him?

Dear God, help us. Only You can make this come out right.

～

*R*upert groaned and blinked against the darkness. A drumming inside his head worked its way to his eyes and ears. Where was he? What had happened?

"Easy now," a quavery voice said. "You took quite a knock on that noggin, mister." A skinny black woman carried a candle as she neared and set it in a holder. "I did what I could fer ye, but ain't much to do for a whack on the head."

She crossed the room, pulled a curtain aside, and fastened it with a clothespin. Pale moonlight combined with the candle glow to reveal a rickety table with several bowls, one chair, and a pile of blankets that must be a bed.

Rupert reached for the source of his pounding headache. His fingers found a sticky lump above his right ear. "What happened? What is this place?"

She laughed and shook her gray head. "Why it's my home. Your friend said you fell off'n your horse and hit a rock. He took off when I come up wid Old Duke." She pointed to a huge dog lying by the door. "Said he had to git home 'fore dark but he be sendin' help. Looked mighty 'spicious to me, but I had him drag you in here 'fore he git. He ain't never come back."

She handed him a dented canteen. "Drink dis. It help wid de headache."

Rupert sniffed. "What is it?"

"Water wid a bit o' willow bark. All I kin offer."

He swallowed the drink and thanked her. His memory was foggy. "Where did you say this place was?"

"Half-day's walk from Franklin to de south. Newnan's a mite farther east."

Franklin. Newnan. Hannah. The urgency of his mission pushed him to sit up. Dizziness pulled him back down. He had to think, figure out what to do.

Answers from the woman revealed he'd been there since sunset, and a man, whose description Rupert couldn't place, had abandoned him with the unkept promise to get help.

So Prescott must have had him followed, then attacked. Thank God for the old woman and her ancient wolfhound who'd come along and prevented further damage.

Rupert slowly rose to his feet. "I appreciate your care, ma'am, but I need to get my horse and leave."

"Horse? I didn't see a horse. It must've run off when you fell. You oughta rest a while longer. Dangerous to walk in the dark when you don't know where you are."

She was right, of course. He might get lost.

But his family needed him. Hannah depended on him. He swayed and reached for the cottage wall. Weakness drove him to his knees. He groped for the bed and leaned over the edge. He'd rest for just a minute.

~

Nine hours after Prescott had laid siege to Whitfield Hall, Hannah faced the grim possibility that the man's obsession with finding the elusive gold would drive him insane. Every time he came back to the library to ask her and Aunt Ginny about the architecture or to rant about his lack of success—his speech grew less coherent and his appearance more disheveled.

Hannah hated to imagine what havoc he'd left behind. Her compulsion for order rebelled at the current state of the library. Books lay in haphazard stacks, drawers hung open, pictures had been removed from the walls, and cushions were tossed aside. Among the scattered papers atop the desk, the tip of a letter opener caught her eye. Too far away to reach. Prescott had even pried a few bricks from the fireplace. If the rest of the house had suffered the same fate as this room, it would take days to restore order.

Thanks to the intervention of his lackeys, Prescott had allowed Silvie to prepare an evening meal and let each person take a trip to the outhouse, accompanied by a guard.

After hours of inactivity, Hannah flexed the muscles in her hands and arms to fight off numbness, and her neck ached from the strain of holding her head upright. Slumped in his wheelchair, Caleb leaned against her shoulder and slept. Across the room, Aunt Ginny, Thomas, and Silvie huddled on the floor and leaned against the sofa to which they were lashed. How could they possibly rest in such positions?

One guard stretched across the library doorway, his rifle in his arms while he blinked to fight off sleep. Prescott and the others must have bedded down in the parlor. In the quiet, she could make out the continued patter of rain outside beneath the snuffling snores across the hallway.

Her own rest had ended abruptly with a dream similar to those she'd had after Papa's death. Perhaps the sight of a rifle pointed at her or the noise of stomping feet in the rooms over her head had brought it back. Did the dream only correspond to her level of anxiety, or was it a bit of memory?

For weeks last year, the images had plagued her. Soldiers riding up to the house. Papa running out to rage and shoot at them, the blast that took him down, and then soldiers digging his grave. It ended with Byron Harris glancing her way before he ordered the young soldier to put his coat back on.

What did it mean? Was there a clue in that memory? In trying to wipe it out, had she missed some important detail? She closed her eyes and let her mind take her back to that day.

She'd been on the hill overlooking the family graveyard, mourning Papa's rash behavior, following each shovelful of red clay dumped over him. An officer stood at the foot of the grave, overseeing the work. Byron paused to wipe his brow, looked her way, then pointed to the coatless soldier. She rose to leave while the lieutenant buttoned his jacket, then squatted next to the gaping hole.

Wait.

Did he drop something in there?

He had risen and pushed loose dirt into the pit with his feet, then walked away.

Hannah's eyes popped open. Had that really happened? Did the lieutenant—Prescott's half brother—hide the gold in her father's grave?

She'd have to tell him so and bring this nightmare to an end. But not until morning. Which gave her a few hours to come up with a plan. Once he had the gold, what would he do with her and her family? He'd killed during the war, but could he be so far gone as to murder them all?

Hannah eased away from Caleb and scooted back toward the desk. If she could shift enough to grab that letter opener....

Caleb's chair, lashed to hers, crept backward, and his head whipped her way. His eyes widened. "Wha—?"

Vigorous shaking of her head warned him. She nodded toward the guard, whose head listed to the side, and they both waited to see if he stirred. When he didn't move, she mouthed her intended target to Caleb. He saw what she meant to do, and together, they snagged the letter opener and slid it up her sleeve. It wasn't much of a weapon, but it was all they had.

Somehow, she slept again despite the ache in her neck and shoulders. A rough hand on her arm jostled her awake.

"Git up, gal." The guard's fetid breath assaulted her nose as he fumbled with the ropes binding her to the chair. "Boss wants you."

The ropes fell away, and he jerked Hannah to her feet. Her right hand went to the thin metal beneath her sleeve as she crossed her arms. She caught sight of Aunt Ginny's wide-eyed alarm and mouthed one word—pray—before the guard propelled her across the hallway.

Prescott was buttoning his jacket, but his attention focused on her arrival. "Now, Miss Hannah—"

"I know where the gold is." Though barely above a whisper, the words burst from her lips. Seeing Prescott duplicate the action of the man in her dream confirmed her conviction.

The stunned silence gave way as Prescott advanced and grabbed her shoulders in a punishing grip. "Why, you little tart! You knew all along—"

"No. I only remembered because of a dream last night."

He dropped his hands and stepped back as if she'd struck him. Recovering, he swept one hand to the side in a formal gesture. "Please, lead the way."

Hannah pivoted toward the door, then stopped. "Promise you won't hurt my family."

An evil smirk twisted Prescott's mouth. "Now, why would I hurt anyone? As long as I get what I want, I can be quite agreeable."

"You can take the gold. Just leave us be."

"Oh, I'm planning to leave as soon as the gold is in my hands. But you're coming with me, just in case McNeil happens to return from his journey early. Once the boys and I are in the clear, he's welcome to you. If he's still willing to have you and able to find you."

Hannah's heart picked up speed. Where did Prescott plan to take her?

CHAPTER 27

Newnan, Georgia

upert wavered between anger and chagrin as the farmer's horse plodded into town. So much for the best laid plans of the McNeil men. Prescott may have outwitted him this time, but Rupert would have that man's hide if Hannah or her family had suffered harm.

As soon as Rupert had awakened at dawn, a dark foreboding drove him to return to Whitfield Hall by the surest route, which meant retracing his steps. He'd set out on foot and reached the familiar road between Franklin and Newnan when the farmer came by. Under normal circumstances, Rupert could have outpaced the worn-out horse pulling the cart, but he still battled the effects of his knock on the head.

He thanked the farmer for the ride and strode to the telegraph office. He'd composed his message in his head, so it didn't take a minute to write it out. From there he went to the sheriff's office to demand he arrest Prescott for assault and then provide Rupert with a horse so he could ride to Whitfield Hall and check on his family.

Sheriff Wesley turned from speaking to a solemn group of men, including his new workers. "McNeil. Glad to see you. We're about to send out a search party for your wife now."

Shock rocked Rupert. "My wife? What happened to her?"

The older brother he'd hired stepped forward, wringing his hat in his hands. "I'm so sorry, Mr. McNeil. None of us went up to the main house yesterday on account of the storm. Early this morning, Quentin came to my cabin and practically dragged us to the house. I gather he'd been away from the farm, huntin' or fishin' yesterday."

The sheriff picked up the story. "They found Caleb in the yard, his chair's wheels pushed into the mud. Inside the house, Mrs. Murphy and Silvie had been gagged and tied together, back-to-back. Thomas was bound hands and feet. He had a nasty gash on his head, so Jason here went for the doctor, and Marty came to let me know Prescott had taken your wife."

Rupert staggered against the wall behind him. He'd seen cruelty in the war but never expected to have it hit so close. "I don't understand. I thought Prescott was searching for some treasure. Did he take Hannah as retribution for not finding anything?"

The sheriff shook his head. "He found the gold and took Mrs. McNeil as insurance against us shootin' him on sight when we find him, I reckon."

"What gold? If there'd been gold in the house, Hannah would've used it..." instead of running to Alabama to beg Henry for help. Rupert's heart clenched.

"According to Mrs. Murphy, Prescott's brother hid some stolen gold there last year. It was buried with George Whitfield. Prescott and his men dug it up."

Rupert fought back the bile and anger that rose. To think of Prescott subjecting Hannah and Caleb to such a scene. When they ran that reprobate to ground... Rupert shut down the images of what he might do. First, he had to find them and rescue Hannah.

"Do we know where they went, which direction?"

The sheriff pointed to a map on the wall. "Caleb said they went east as they left Whitfield Hall, but they could easily turn north. South would bring 'em too close to town, and if they'd gone west, they would've had to pass you."

"East or north." Rupert rubbed his jaw, then turned to the door. "Can you lend me a horse? One of Prescott's men jumped me last night and stole my horse. And I need to check the telegraph office to see if my brother has sent a response yet."

The men filed out the door and headed for their mounts. Someone shouting his name brought Rupert's head around to find Byron Harris looping his horse's reins over a post.

Rupert groaned. He couldn't deal with whatever Byron wanted now, but maybe Rupert could use his help. "Bad timing, Byron. Prescott's taken Hannah."

"Might be good timing, then. I have information about Prescott's associations."

∾

Several hours later
Decatur, Georgia

The tiny bedroom, though tastefully decorated with pink and beige pillows, comforter, and curtains, failed to ease Hannah's agitated frame of mind. It was warm and stuffy, with a cloying sweetness in the air. She ignored the lone chair in front of the dresser, preferring to gaze out the window at the street below. The rattle of passing carriages seemed to increase as the traffic continued despite the fading daylight and drizzle.

The farther Prescott and his gang had traveled from Coweta

County, the more Hannah's prayers had centered on those at home. Prayers, questions, and regrets. Keeping her mind on her family helped to keep it off her own predicament. She'd reviewed every moment since Prescott had arrived. What could she have done differently? When he'd insisted on Caleb going with them to the gravesite, her plan to strike Prescott there had been thwarted. She wouldn't risk her brother's safety, and the guards had hemmed her in every moment.

They hadn't traveled far, but she couldn't determine the ultimate direction after several turns. Her first glimpse of Madame Monique's had dashed her hopes. Prescott had put her in the last place Rupert would think to look, so only God could save her.

Surely by now, someone had found Caleb and the others and sent for a doctor to tend to Thomas's head wound and the rope burns on all their wrists. The physical hurts would mend quickly, unlike the injuries to one's heart and mind. Perhaps those would heal in time, and eventually, they would go on without her.

Had Quentin come back? How would Rupert react when he returned to find the house in chaos? Knowing Rupert, he'd try to find her, but his chances of success were slim. And if he didn't find her and finally gave up the search, would he leave or stay and take care of Caleb? She should have been a better wife, not so bossy and—to use Prescott's word—prudish. Rupert had proved his trustworthiness and his deference to her, but she'd held back. He wasn't like her father or his cronies. Though he might have felt coerced into the marriage, he'd shown his determination to make the best of their situation. Had she ever expressed her gratitude to him? Or even hinted that she'd come to care for him?

Now all was lost. He wouldn't want her back, not after he discovered where Prescott had dumped her. She had no illusions about what their plans might entail, especially considering her current location. Madame Monique's Boutique and Salon, purported to sell exclusive women's clothing, provided a less virtuous service for its all-male clientele. Was she doomed to be its newest acquisition? A crude voice from the past taunted her. *"Girls are plenty useful at times, just not as daughters."*

When they'd arrived, Prescott used a back entrance to deliver her into the madam's custody. That had been Hannah's first chance to fight back, while Prescott divided his men to watch the road and he focused on moving the gold. She'd pulled the letter opener from her sleeve as the guard led her from the carriage and jabbed him in the arm. Running from him, she'd collided with Prescott, who laughed and dragged her by her hair into the shop.

The woman in charge stripped off Hannah's travel-stained dress and ordered her to bathe. Then she'd provided a luxurious green gown that covered her neck to toe and fingertips but clung to her curves. A young mulatto woman had arranged her hair, then escorted her through an open sitting area similar to a hotel lobby she'd visited as a child. Their rambling route wove through chairs occupied by several men who openly gazed at them. By the time the hairdresser left her in the tiny room upstairs, Hannah was shaking with trepidation.

In the hour since, she'd calmed down, but dread sat like a leaden weight in her belly. Noise from the street below drifted through the closed window. Could she escape that way? She brushed aside the curtain and raised the window. The sash stopped halfway up. She pushed harder, but it wouldn't budge. A nail on each side prevented it. Apparently, Madame Monique didn't want any customers slipping out in secret.

A knock sent her whirling around.

The door opened. "Ah, Collette, you are a quick one, aren't you?" The woman chuckled as she breezed into the room, leaving the door slightly ajar. She took quick steps to each corner, evidently searching for anything out of place.

"Here only a few hours, one walk through our lounge, and already someone is asking for you." She came close to Hannah and hissed, "Do nothing to displease him, or you'll be punished."

Stunned, Hannah could only stare as the woman returned to the door and swept out her hand in invitation. "Come in, Mr. Morgan. Here is Collette, as you requested. You two have fun."

The door closed behind her, and Hannah froze as the man appraised her with open interest. He chuckled. "Oh, we'll get along fine."

He removed his greatcoat and shook droplets of rain from his hair. Not as tall as Rupert, her "guest" had dark eyes and moved with the subtle grace of a man accustomed to refinement. Hannah's acknowledgement of his manner did nothing to ease her fear.

He draped the coat over one of the bedposts, then turned and smiled. "First off, let's dispense with the formalities. You may call me Seth, and I'll call you Hannah."

Hannah's gaze jerked to his. How did he know her name? Was he an associate of Prescott's? What else did that devil have planned?

~

*D*usk approached as Rupert left the borrowed horse tethered to the rail in front of the tobacco shop in Decatur and ducked into the alley beside it.

The wire from Simon had come in mere minutes after Rupert left the sheriff's office in Newnan. Together with Bryon's information, it provided a good guess as to where Prescott had taken Hannah. Byron had followed Rupert to Whitfield Hall and stayed to watch over the family while Rupert continued to Decatur to assist in Hannah's rescue.

Up the outside stairs, he noted the nameplate attached to

the wall. *Henry's Salvage Company.* This was the place. He knocked on the door and pushed it open. "Simon?"

"Over here."

Rupert blinked in the darkness and charted a path around chairs, tables, and boxes until he reached his brother near a window. Pale light from the oil lamps outside the buildings along the street below allowed them to follow movement within the immediate vicinity.

Simon motioned to the chair next to him. "You made good time. How's the family back at Whitfield Hall faring?"

"A little better now that we have an idea where Hannah might be. Hopeful that we'll be able to bring this to an end and bring her home. I can't tell you how grateful I am."

Simon peered into Rupert's face in the dim light. "Do you realize what a miracle it took for this to come together? Seth and Aunt Lydia were here visiting his relatives. I'd just arrived at Miss Gay's house when she received your wire, and she's close friends with the owner of this building, which just happens to be empty until he moves his equipment in next week."

"And Byron arriving in Newnan with more information about Prescott. It is rather remarkable, isn't it? Even my getting knocked on the head is worth it if we find Hannah and get rid of Prescott." Although it stung that Seth was the one to go to Hannah's rescue instead of him. But he or Simon stood a bigger chance of being recognized, as Prescott or any of his men might be in that bordello. Not to mention, Hannah's face the instant she saw Rupert would've surely given everything away.

Simon squeezed his shoulder. "God orders our steps. I think He wanted to demonstrate how much He loves you and Hannah."

Rupert swallowed hard and nodded. "Miss Gay said the local sheriff has been watching that establishment and looking for a chance to close it down. He's ready to move in as soon as he gets the word." He tapped on the windowsill as he gazed at the building across the way. If only he could see beyond those walls. "What's going on in there?"

Simon handed him the field glasses. "Seth presented himself a couple of hours ago as a visiting gentleman, looking for 'a surprise for his wife.' From what we're told, the women are paraded through the lobby, dressed in specially designed costumes which may be purchased at outrageous prices. But the real items on display are the women."

All the windows on the front must have curtains. Rupert couldn't even make out moving shadows against the lamplight. "Are we sure Hannah's inside?"

"Sheriff Blanton verified that Prescott parked a closed carriage near the rear entrance and delivered a woman matching Hannah's description about the same time I arrived. His deputy on the roof said it looked as if she hit a guard and tried to run, but Prescott caught her."

Rupert gave a low growl.

Simon gripped Rupert's shoulder. "If Seth doesn't find her soon, the sheriff has a woman ready to pose as a maid to search the rooms."

"I want to be there when Seth brings Hannah out." If he could shield her from curious onlookers, perhaps that would make up somewhat for not being on hand when Prescott made his play and for sending Seth in instead of himself. Could Hannah forgive him for leaving her and her family vulnerable to the villain?

CHAPTER 28

"*H*ow do you know my name?" Hannah's knees threatened to give out, and she grasped the nearby bedpost.

Seth leaned against the dresser. "Your husband, Rupert, is my nephew by marriage. My wife is Lydia, Millie's stepmother. I believe you've met Millie and Troy as well as Simon and Daviana." Seth's steady gaze convinced her as much as his list of family names. "When Rupert learned about your abduction, he sent wires to a number of people. I happened to be in town, so Simon decided I'd be the least likely to be recognized by the men who took you."

Hannah sank onto the mattress. "Rupert did that? So he's at Whitfield Hall now?"

Seth pulled out his pocket watch and studied it. "I believe he's on his way, if he's not here already." He put the watch away. "And we should prepare for the next stage in this plan. Slip that coat on over your dress."

Her face warmed at his implication, and she grabbed the covering and put it on. "You were in the lobby when I walked through earlier, weren't you?"

"I was hoping to see you so I could ask for you by appearance, since I wasn't supposed to know you. Of all the ladies who passed through, you were the only one who fit Simon's description."

That made sense, but... "How are we going to get out of here?"

"We're going to walk right out the front door. The sheriff and several deputies are posted around the building, waiting for us. If we're stopped before we reach them, I will loudly claim you as my missing niece who was kidnapped while I was away."

Hannah's heart slowed from a gallop to a canter. "Can it be so simple?"

Seth's smile wavered. "Simple, yes. Easy? That remains to be seen." He motioned to the coat as she fastened it. "There's a razor-sharp stiletto in the pocket, in case we're separated. Stay close."

He opened the door but shielded Hannah from the view of anyone who might pass by. After a moment, he motioned for her to join him. His arm circling her back bolstered her courage as he urged her toward the front staircase. When she stumbled on the second step down, Seth tightened his hold and practically carried her to the bottom.

When they were half a dozen yards from the main door, a voice yelled out, "Stop them!"

Seth thrust her forward. Her hand brushed the door a second before she was jerked and spun away. The scent of cigar smoke assaulted her as a familiar blue jacket filled her vision.

Prescott's growl ended in a grunt as Seth plowed a fist into his gut. Then the room erupted in shouts and people pushing to get out while others rushed inside.

Caught in the middle of the commotion, Hannah lost her bearings. She dodged a fist and fought through a knot of men, only to be swept into a group headed toward the rear.

Someone caught her arm in an iron grip and jerked her into the alley. She sucked in the humid air and broke free, dashing for the intersection. The rattle of a carriage sounded like freedom until it blocked her way and pounding footsteps closed in behind her. Prescott trapped her against the carriage.

She cried out, her gaze going to the melee half a block away, searching for someone to help as he yanked open the door and shoved her inside. How would Rupert find her now?

~

A sudden flare of light and yelling voices across the street snapped Rupert to attention. His chair crashed to the floor as he whirled around and headed for the door.

Simon had been stretching his legs in the back of the room. "What's happening?"

"Looks like a fight." Rupert clattered down the steps, Simon at his heels.

People clogged the wide-open threshold of the boutique as men scuffled and women tried to push past them. Shouts and threats filled the air.

Rupert dove for the melee, but Simon held him back. "Let the lawmen do their job. The quicker they can thin out the crowd, the sooner you'll find Hannah."

Rupert bucked against the restraint. Every moment away from Hannah grated. How long before the authorities identified the culprits and carted them off? Would Hannah welcome his presence, or would she blame him for this catastrophe?

A muffled sound at the end of the block drew his gaze to a couple climbing into a closed carriage. When the woman looked over her shoulder as if seeking escape, alarm sizzled through Rupert, for in the spill of light from a gas lamp, Hannah's gaze widened. The man cut off her cry by pushing her into the conveyance. The crack of a whip got the horse moving.

Rupert yelled for his brother's help but didn't stop to confirm it. He leaped into action, pumping his legs into a sprint.

The pedestrians and other vehicles in the driver's path inhibited his mobility, but as soon as he reached the edge of town, the horse would pick up speed, and Rupert would lose his advantage. He focused on the rear of the vehicle and the strange rods protruding from it. Recognition slammed into him. That was the carriage from Whitfield Hall, the one to which he'd fastened the rods to hold Caleb's chair.

Rupert's feet flew over the brick street. He drew even with the back wheel. How long could he hold on if he grabbed those rods? It would slow the carriage but not stop it before they snapped under his weight. Better to latch onto the door.

The steady chuffing of his breath filled his ears. His lungs burned, and his legs felt heavy as he closed in on his goal. *Please, God, give me the speed and strength I need.*

The wheel hit a rock, the carriage jolted, and Rupert leaped for the door, thrusting his arms through the curtained window. The added weight jostled the carriage. It careened and started to slow. Hands batted at Rupert's forearms, and the carriage lurched. Grunts and curses testified to a scuffle inside.

That was all the encouragement Rupert needed. He bounced until the carriage wheels ground to a halt at the edge of the road. He jerked the door open, and Hannah tumbled into his arms.

He staggered to stay upright, but his arms tightened around her and pulled her away. "Let's go."

They turned to run, but Hannah stumbled. Rupert steadied her as a roar from inside the coach preceded the appearance of Prescott, who held a bloody hand to his belly. He yelled, presumably for the driver. "Lewis, where are you? Stop them!"

The carriage lurched as the driver leaped from his seat and darted across the road to stand a few feet in front of Rupert. Lewis grinned as he pointed the pistol at Rupert. "How 'bout I just shoot 'em?" He shifted the gun toward Hannah and then pointed it at Prescott. "You, too, boss. Then I'll take your share of the gold."

Beside them, Prescott gaped at Lewis. "After all I've done for you?"

Lewis barked a laugh. "What you did for me? You mean when you put the blame for your blunders on me and got me demoted? Sergeant Rooper told me, but I knew it was you all along. I've just been waiting for my chance for revenge. And now it's here."

Taking advantage of their arguing, Rupert released Hannah and lunged for Lewis. The gun went off and flew from the driver's grip as they both hit the ground. Lewis grabbed Rupert's arms but let go when Rupert drove a knee into Lewis's groin, then plowed a fist into his face.

Rupert staggered to his feet as Hannah rushed into his arms and Prescott sank to the road.

$\sim$

*T*he sight of Rupert leaping toward that gun had sent ice into Hannah's veins. No, this could not happen. Not now.

The blast rang out as the two men hit the ground. She'd stood frozen in place while they scuffled, barely noticing Prescott as he sagged against the carriage.

Rupert shoved upright, and she ran to meet him. He'd come for her and somehow found her. Joy and relief brought tears to her eyes.

He broke the embrace and peered into her face. "Are you hurt? I should've asked before—"

"No, I'm all right." She brushed his cheek with one hand. "Just so glad to see you."

She tensed and clutched Rupert's side at the sounds of thrashing near the trees. Had Lewis recovered and crept back? Rupert looked over her shoulder as a curse rent the air and Simon's voice followed.

"Not today, Lewis. And probably not for several years, after you both serve your sentences in the state prison." Simon edged closer, his gun trained on the driver, while Seth and two deputies moved in from each side.

Hannah drooped with relief as Rupert tightened his arms around her. In minutes, the deputies secured and loaded both Prescott and Lewis onto horses tethered to their own mounts. One deputy walked his horse to Simon. "The sheriff will let y'all know when their trial will be so you can come back and testify."

Rupert kept an arm around Hannah and stepped closer to shake the deputies' hands. "Thank you for your quick action."

Prescott whined from his saddle. "I need to get to a doctor right now. That she-devil stabbed me." His voice faded as the deputies set a brisk pace toward town.

Turning from his examination of the carriage, Seth guffawed. "I see you made good use of that stiletto, Hannah."

Warmth flooded her face as she recalled slashing Prescott's hands and midsection. The sudden release of anxiety set her head to spinning. She closed her eyes, then opened them at the sensation of floating to find Rupert carrying her.

Rupert strode toward the carriage. "If one of you fellows wouldn't mind driving, I'd like to take Hannah someplace where she can recover from this ordeal."

He placed her on the seat, climbed in after her, and shut the door. The carriage rocked as someone commandeered the driver's seat.

"Where to, Seth? Your relatives' or Miss Gay's house?" Simon asked.

The carriage squeaked as they moved forward. "Miss Gay's, I think," Seth said. "My aunt will not let us rest without a full account of what happened."

"And you think Daviana will?" The rest of Simon's reply faded as they picked up speed over cobblestones.

Rupert shifted in his seat and caressed Hannah's face. "I'm afraid we're doomed to repeat the story several times in the near future. Do you think you can endure the telling?" His blue eyes shimmered with concern. "I'm so sorry I left you vulnerable to such an attack. I thought—"

"Shh." Her fingers trembled against his lips. "You did your best to prevent it. You can't be everywhere at once."

He held her fingers in place and kissed them. "I thank God that He is, and I no longer have to try to manage two households."

A frisson of panic zipped up her spine. "What does that mean?"

"I'm leasing the Alabama farm to Byron, who is now married to my cousin, Wilma. I'll explain about that later. Right now, I'm going to enjoy having you in my arms."

"And I'm happy to be here, but what about my family? Did you see them before you came to Decatur?" Worrisome thoughts leeched some of the joy from their reunion.

Rupert squeezed her fingers. "Only long enough to introduce Byron to them. They assured me their injuries were minor, and their primary concern was for me to find you."

"Thank you for coming." She tipped her head to his shoulder. "I'd quite given up hope of ever seeing you again, sure you'd never want me after I'd been in that place."

"My dear Hannah..." He raised her fingers to his lips. "I want you more every day, and I plan to prove that to you for the rest of our lives."

Hannah sighed as he shifted and pulled her close for a lingering kiss. That plan suited her just fine.

~

*A*s thankful as Rupert was for the hospitality of Simon's client, he refused the offer of another night in Miss Gay's house. Hannah's family needed to see that she'd emerged from her nightmarish experience and to be assured that Prescott wouldn't bother them again.

Seth brought Aunt Lydia to meet Hannah after breakfast, then they all said their goodbyes to Simon and Daviana, and each couple headed to their respective homes with promises to visit soon.

Hannah leaned against his side as Rupert drove the carriage toward Whitfield Hall. "Tell me about this agreement with Byron and Wilma."

"I'm not clear on how it all came about, but they decided to get married a few days after we left the farm." He picked up her hand with his free one and twined their fingers. "Byron said something about Wilma being sick and he's going to take care of her. I didn't ask many questions because I was focused on finding my wife. He's at Whitfield Hall, so you can get all the details when we arrive."

Resting her head against his shoulder, she asked, "How do you feel about turning your farm over to them? It's *your* legacy from Henry, not Wilma's. I hate to see you lose it to her."

"I'm not losing it. Byron brought all the legal papers with him, which he will explain to both of us. He said he left off the numbers, such as how much he'll pay and how many years the lease will last, so we can fill those in during our discussion."

"Still…" Hannah's voice held a sorrowful note. "I feel like you're giving up your inheritance while you help Caleb hold onto his."

Rupert slowed the horse and shifted to face her. "Byron reminded me of the story of Boaz in the Bible. Do you recall it?"

She tilted her head and studied him. "Of course. Boaz married Ruth to redeem her family property. It's not quite the same."

"No, but then I realized what was really important wasn't the *land* but the people involved. Boaz redeemed the land so the family line could continue. Our true legacy is the people who follow us. That's what we're building, whether at Whitfield Hall or in Alabama—family. When I returned to town and discovered Prescott had abducted you, my first course of action was to let my family know. If nothing else, I knew they'd be praying for us. You and I are together today because of your papa's will and Uncle Henry's recommendation. Our family made provisions for us, and we'll do the same for our children."

"It's really quite remarkable the way everything turned out." Hannah shook her head. "Looking back, I can't believe I had the audacity to travel to Alabama and expect a man to marry me on such short notice."

Rupert guffawed and nudged her with his elbow. "I can. You presented quite a fetching sight as you marched up the road from the creek to the house that day."

She twisted to face him, her eyes twinkling. "You *were* at the creek then. And you followed me? How sneaky of you."

"So says the woman who spent the night in my barn unannounced."

"It wasn't my finest moment, was it?" She faced forward again, chuckling.

"No." Rupert led the horse to the roadside and waited for her to meet his gaze. "Your finest moment was when you swooned into my arms. From that time on, I knew you were meant for me."

"Really?" She raised her eyebrows. "You didn't seem to even like me at first."

He brushed aside a curl that danced at her temple. "As every hunter and fisherman knows, you appreciate the catch more when you have to fight for it. If I'd fallen at your feet, you might've thrown me back in the river."

"No." She drew out the word, holding back her smile, then poked a finger in his chest. "Not the river. Just the creek, and wait until I tell your mother that her sweet son spied on me before we'd met."

He laughed and leaned over for a quick kiss. "Minx. I think she'll agree that I got exactly what I deserved—a smart woman to keep me in line."

EPILOGUE

December 1866
Coweta County, Georgia

*H*annah stood at the top of the curving staircase and surveyed the scene below. Greenery and bows decorated the handrail and every piece of furniture in the entryway. Excited childish voices drifted from the library and blended with the more modulated adult ones coming from the parlor.

She descended slowly, basking in the happy sounds of a house full of family and friends. How fortunate Whitfield Hall could accommodate so many people, and that the weather hadn't complicated travel for those more distant. The aromas of baking meats and sweets filled the air and whetted Hannah's appetite.

Rupert stepped into the hallway and rushed to meet her. "Sweetheart, you should've waited for me to come fetch you."

She chuckled and straightened his cravat. "I'm perfectly capable of getting myself dressed and downstairs. *You* should've wakened me from my nap sooner."

"Now that you're here, we can proceed." He tucked her hand on his arm and led her to the parlor threshold. Chattering voices hushed and faces turned their way. When Rev. Covington moved into her vision, Hannah's eyebrows rose along with her suspicions. Yesterday, she'd intercepted several secretive smiles and glances among family members.

"Rupert, what's going on?"

He escorted her to the center of the room and faced her. "Hannah, we married back in March because of legal issues. I hadn't planned to marry, and you were persuaded to take me as a substitute for my uncle. Now, while we have most of our family here as witnesses, I want to propose properly and repeat our vows to each other. Every bride should get her special moment. So...will you marry me again, this time because you choose to do so?"

Stunned, she took a moment to respond. When Rev. Covington gave a soft cough, she realized everyone waited for her answer.

"Yes, Rupert, I choose you for however long the Lord gives us together." She chuckled and placed their joined hands at her thickened waist. "We have a legacy to pass to the next generation."

In the far corner of the room, one of the babies—either Little John or Simon's six-month-old Nathaniel—set up a wail, and the other joined in.

Rupert nudged Hannah forward. "We'd better speed this up, Reverend. The next generation is getting restless." He lowered his voice and spoke into Hannah's ear. "And we're just getting started."

-The End-

Did you enjoy this book? We hope so!
Would you take a quick minute to leave a review where you purchased the book?
It doesn't have to be long. Just a sentence or two telling what you liked about the story!

Receive a FREE ebook and get updates when new Wild Heart books release: https://wildheartbooks.org/newsletter

AUTHOR'S NOTE

This book features Rupert, the third McNeil brother in this series. Coming between the energetic and often rowdy second son, Simon, and the "baby," Troy, Rupert learned to stay out of trouble and often faded into the background. He found his place as the quiet rule-follower and the person always ready to offer help. Besides his careful decision making and steady dependability, he's known for his amazing speed in running, which proved valuable in *Managing Millie*, when he helped rescue Millie from her captors, and comes into play here.

It was a full circle moment for me to bring Mary Gay of Decatur, Georgia, back into the picture. I first learned about this remarkable woman during my research for *Rescuing Rose*, the first book in this series. Since I had indicated in *Loving Lydia* that Seth Morgan had relatives in Decatur, it made sense that he could visit them and participate in Hannah's rescue.

The setting for Whitfield Hall is Coweta County, Georgia, not far from the town of Newnan. (Yes, the name is NEWNAN, not Newman.) The only significant battle in the area was Brown's Mill on July 30, 1864. Historians believe the Union loss in this battle convinced General Sherman to abandon his strategy of dismantling the railroads and instead to focus on taking Atlanta. At the end of the war, Union troops swept through the area again, as indicated by Byron Harris's account of his encounter at Whitfield Hall.

Many writers shy away from the Civil War (a.k.a., The War Between the States, a.k.a., The War of Northern Aggression) because it's viewed as divisive. I was surprised to find out there were pockets of Unionists all over the South, and less than two percent of the people owned slaves. It's easy to paint everyone with the same brush, but that doesn't give a true picture. Although I grew up in the volatile 1960s, the attitude of respecting everyone was part of my legacy, which I believe came from numerous generations before me. We are more alike than different. That's the way I paint the world.

Through all the books in this series, there are glimpses of my part of the world. My hometown, Columbus, Georgia, is separated from Alabama only by the Chattahoochee River, so both states are very familiar to me. However, the areas in my books are slightly north of me, so I had to keep going to maps and looking up names online.

Every time I do a search for information related to a particular subject, I find something new or slightly different, and sometimes I can't locate what I read earlier (argh!). The internet is marvelous for writers, but it can be overwhelming. In fiction writing, so much of the story boils down to the writer's imagination and personal experience. Any errors that pertain to facts about the area, the government, or the lifestyles represented here are all mine, and I'm willing to be educated via email at susan@susanpsloan.ccsend.com.

You can also follow me on the social media accounts given below and on Amazon, BookBub, and GoodReads under Susan Pope Sloan.

https://www.facebook.com/susanpopesloan
https://www.instagram.com/susanpsloan

https://twitter.com/spsloan

Finally, here are some resources I used that you might find helpful. This is not an exhaustive list by any means. There is so much to explore and learn! For a writer, research is never-ending.

Douglas R. Egerton. *The Wars of Reconstruction*. New York: Bloomsbury, 2013.

Battle of Brown's Mill | Coweta County, GA Website

Battle of Brown's Mill, 1864, Civil War, Summary, Importance (americanhistorycentral.com)

Mary Gay House - Georgia Historical Society (georgiahistory.com)

ACKNOWLEDGMENTS

As always, a big thanks to my editors, critique partners in ACFW and Word Weavers Columbus, my launch team and social media friends, and to my family. More names are behind a book than the one on the cover.

To all the people who sponsor, direct, and work on writers' conferences and book fairs everywhere: thank you for providing writers a place to learn, grow, and connect with industry leaders, fellow writers, and readers. You lift us up.

ABOUT THE AUTHOR

Born into a family of storytellers, **Susan Pope Sloan** published her first articles in high school and continued writing sporadically for decades. Retirement provided the time to focus on writing and indulge her avid interest in history. Her Civil War series begins (and ultimately ends) in her home state of Georgia with references to lesser-known events of that period. She and husband Ricky live near Columbus where she participates in Word Weavers, ACFW, and Toastmasters.

If you love historical romance, check out the other Wild Heart books!

A Heart's Gift by Lena Nelson Dooley

Is a marriage of convenience the answer?

Franklin Vine has worked hard to build the ranch he inherited into one of the most successful in the majestic Colorado mountains. If only he had an heir to one day inherit the legacy he's building. But he was burned once in the worst way, and he doesn't plan to open his heart to another woman. Even if that means he'll eventually have to divide up his spread among the most loyal of his hired hands.

When Lorinda Sullivan is finally out from under the control of men who made all the decisions in her life, she promises herself she'll never allow a man to make choices for her again. But without a home in the midst of a hard Rocky Mountain winter, she has to do something to provide for her infant son.

A marriage of convenience seems like the perfect arrangement, yet the stakes quickly become much higher than either of them ever planned. When hearts become entangled, the increasing danger may change their lives forever.

∾

Lassoed by the Lawman by Renae Brumbaugh Green

Juliana Duke's dreams don't include ranching.

But as the only child of Oscar and Maria Duke and heiress of the vast Duke Ranch, her job is to marry a rancher and produce a male heir. When Lt. Cody Steves rides onto the scene, her resolve to place duty over daydreams is shaken. Now that her heart's been lassoed by the handsome lawman, will she be able to love another?

Cody Steves wants marriage and family, but he loves being a Texas Ranger. At any time, he could ride into a job and not come out alive. How could any decent man marry, knowing he could leave a widow and orphans behind? But the beautiful Juliana Duke captures him in a way no other has.

When he learns of a secret plot to take over the Duke Ranch, Cody must risk everything to save Juliana. Little does he know, the outcome will be nothing like he's planned.

~

Streams of Courage by Sandra Merville Hart
    In a world turned upside down by war and betrayal...will his role as a spy bring them closer...or tear their future apart?
    The war that Julia Dodd prayed to avoid is now reality, and with it, her world has been turned on its head. Her fellow citizens, who stood with her in their support of the union, have

crossed firmly to the side of the south. And her mother, lost in her grief over the loss of her husband and children, can think of nothing but protecting Julia's brother's inheritance. She insists that her daughter seek a wealthier husband than Ashburn Mitchell.

Ash knows what his fellow citizens think of him when he refuses to fight for the Confederacy. Shouldering the accusation of being a coward and refusing to hide behind his limp, Ash remains in Vicksburg to support his family as a saddler while his two best friends join the fight. Struggling to increase his business so he can marry the woman he loves, Ash becomes a spy in support of the Union. He can't fight for the South but won't raise a musket against them.

As tragedy instigates Ash to risk greater danger to speed the end of the war, Julia can only pray it won't cost them everything. She's already lost her father and two siblings. Must she lose the man she loves too?

Printed in Great Britain
by Amazon

60274665R00167